The Cat's Eyes

Lindsay Woodward

ISBN: 978-1-9995855-8-7

For Sylvester, Buster, Jaspur,
Winston and, of course, our lovely Sparkle.
How I love you all. This book isn't inspired by you.

ONE

I accelerated into the first space I came across in the hotel car park. My car wasn't lined up straight, and I knew this would irritate me later, but for now I was more concerned with how late I was. It was now four minutes past eight.

I grabbed my bag from the passenger seat and leapt out of the car, when I realised I was wearing my tatty flat driving shoes. I leaned in to grab my patent stilettos from the passenger footwell.

I slotted my feet quickly into my shoes and I tottered over to the hotel entrance. I had mastered walking in my four inch heels, but running was a whole other thing.

I smiled at the receptionist as I scuttled by and I headed straight for the function room towards the back of the building. It was where we always had this networking meeting, the first Friday of every month.

'Hi Terry,' I said as I entered the room, greeting the rather dowdy looking man who always took our payment upon arrival.

'Morning, Isobel,' he said.

I fumbled around in my bag, searching for my purse.

'You're not normally the last,' he said, which only

flummoxed me even more.

'No. Bloody roadworks. Took me forty minutes to get here. Can you believe it?'

'That's the Ipswich traffic for you.'

'Well, this morning was definitely worse than normal.'

I found my purse and pulled out a ten pound note, which I handed to Terry.

'Thank you,' he said, ticking me off his list.

I took a breath as I stuffed my purse back into my bag. I definitely needed coffee. Determined to make a beeline over there, I located the drinks station towards the rear of the well-lit room, when I stopped.

Now I considered myself to be a confident and composed woman. I was someone who could always handle situations well and deal with problems head on. Very little ever phased me. Whether it was presenting to a room of a hundred people or asking a man out on a date, I was always ready for anything.

That was until I'd met Jake Masters.

My breath extinguished as I looked over to where he was making his coffee.

I don't know what it was about this man that made me lose touch with my self-control. He electrified me. In his proximity I felt charged with the most sensational buzz, but it also left me weirdly dazed.

I had first joined this networking group nine months before, and I had been instantly attracted to him. His absolutely gorgeous face, dark blond hair, tall, fit physique and devastating smile left me transfixed.

Then there was the fact that he wore a tie to every meeting and never looked anything but flawless in his tailored suits. He was the only person who regularly dressed as sharply as I did, and I absolutely loved him for it. He was my dream man, fully in the flesh before me, but I just wasn't able to be myself in his company. It was like nothing I'd never experienced.

Taking a deep breath, I headed over to the drinks station

where only he was standing. The rest of our fellow networkers were in huddles around the main table in the middle. They'd all got their coffee. Maybe there was a perk to being late.

'Morning,' I said.

He placed the teaspoon he'd just finished with into the "used" bowl and looked over to see who had greeted him.

'Izzy!' he said with genuine delight - that super smile spread across his face.

'How are you? Glad it's Friday?' I said exactly the same thing to him every single meeting. I would even practise alternative lines, but every month the same old boring drivel would blurt out.

He shrugged and his smile quavered. It was just for a moment, but long enough to tell me there was something wrong. He was never anything but a beaming ray of sunshine. For him to lose that smile for even a second was the equivalent of a sheer disaster in anyone else's world. I had to ask.

'Is everything all right?' I said, my heart pumping with excitement.

'Yeah,' he said. 'Coffee?'

I paused. Was Jake Masters offering to make me a coffee? I tried to calm the jubilation that sang through me. He'd only done that once before, at the start of my very first meeting, when he'd greeted me with an extremely warm welcome. I'd re-enacted that moment in my mind for days. I knew I'd be doing the same this time.

'Thank you.'

He turned to select a mug for me and my brain instantly went back to wondering what was so wrong that it could dent the smile on this gorgeous man's face.

'You normally love Fridays,' I said, having no clue if this was really true or not. But most people liked Fridays, so I felt safe. 'I hope nothing's wrong?'

Other than seeing Jake once a month for the past nine meetings, we'd also met for a coffee for a "let's explore how we can help each other in business" discussion. I hadn't deluded myself that this was a date or anything, don't worry. I had met most people from across our group at some point. We were encouraged to have these one to ones so we could support each other better. Although, obviously, I'd made an extra special effort with my hair and make-up for the meeting with Jake. Not that it had mattered. I was sure the only impression I'd made on him was that I was a slightly strange woman who didn't say much. Words just didn't form very well around him. That electric buzz he gave me never failed to short circuit my brain. It was devastating.

But now I had an opening and I couldn't let this opportunity go.

'You don't want to hear about my grumbles,' Jake replied.

How wrong can one man be.

'Milk?' he asked.

'Yes. And one sugar please.'

'Surely you're sweet enough?' he gibed, that irresistible smile returning.

I chuckled before I felt this uncontrollable urge to justify my need for sugar. 'I don't have it in tea, but I find coffee too bitter otherwise. But that's about it really. I'm not really a big chocolate fan or anything. You definitely couldn't say I had a sweet tooth. That wouldn't describe me at all.' I had to stop talking! Suddenly words were flowing, but it was all such crap. 'You're not a sugar man?'

'No. I like savoury. Give me a bag of crisps over a chocolate bar any day.'

I chuckled again. That wasn't even funny. He ripped open a little sachet of sugar, popped it in the mug, gave it a quick stir and handed the coffee to me.

'Thank you,' I said as I carefully took the mug, making sure to brush my fingers against his as I did. I was pathetic, I know. But a girl has to take any chance she can get.

'So you've... you've got something to grumble about?' I nudged as he popped the teaspoon he'd been holding into the little bowl again.

'It's nothing really. I'm just not looking forward to this weekend.'

'Really?' I asked, trying so hard to feign casual interest. 'How come?'

Just as he opened his mouth to answer, Leonard, our chairman, also spoke up, announcing across the room, 'Breakfast is served, if you want to help yourself.'

'I'm going all out this morning,' Jake said, beaming from ear to ear. 'You coming?'

I smiled back, trying to hide my deep frustration. So close. 'Right behind you.'

I followed Jake to the large boardroom style set of tables that occupied the centre of the very functional but not unpleasant space. He placed his coffee down, bagsying his seat.

'I'll sit next to you today,' I said, as if I didn't try this trick every single month. He was a hard man to sit next to. I wasn't the only one who seemed to crave his attention. But today I'd won. Who would have thought that traffic problems would lead to such fortune?

I placed my coffee down on the adjacent place setting and dropped my bag on the floor next to the chair.

We queued up for the breakfast buffet, but before I had a chance to probe him again about why he wasn't looking forward to the weekend, someone else jumped in, asking for Jake's opinion on some boring aspect of business. I pretended to participate in the conversation, but I was far from interested. I was too curious about what terrible thing lay ahead.

When we'd piled our plates high, we headed back to our seats and the meeting shortly commenced.

Leonard, a tall, middle aged man with salt and pepper hair, stood up. I'd always thought this was highly unnecessary. He could easily do the same job sitting down. I guess he felt it gave him more authority.

'Good morning ladies and gentlemen,' he said to the

twenty-two of us that sat facing one another. 'Welcome to another meeting of Ipswich Connected business networking. And what a fine morning it is. I think summer is well on its way now.'

'It's July. I think that is summer,' someone said.

'Right you are,' Leonard nodded. 'Joining us for the first time today is Leslie Beaumont from LB Make-Up Design. Hello, Leslie. Welcome.'

We all said our mini hellos to the young lady that was sitting near Leonard on the other side of the table to me. She looked petrified. I'd never understood why people were so nervous in these settings. It was business. You put your business head on and you got on with it. What was there to be nervous about? Even with the most amazing man in the world next to me, I could still talk business. What other excuse was there?

'Shall we get started with the one minute round?' Leonard said. 'For the benefit of Leslie, we each go round the room and we have one minute to talk about our business. Don't worry if you're slightly over, we don't time it,' he added with a wink. Leonard was one of those people who thought they oozed charm, but it actually came across as creepy. 'Jake, my man, shall we start with you?'

'All right. But only because I've finished my sausages,' Jake said with a grin. Then he stood up with effortless grace.

'Good morning everyone,' he said, making good eye contact with his peers. 'I'm Jake Masters and I help to make peoples' dreams come true. No, literally. As Leonard pointed out, we are heading into the summer when things inevitably get a bit quieter for many of us. I always say, if you're given the gift of time, use it wisely. Why not take a step back and re-evaluate your plans? What are your goals for this year? Now we're halfway through, are you on track to achieving them? This is the perfect time to make some tweaks. Why just achieve your goals when you can smash them out of the park? That's what I do. If you want to exceed your expectations this year, let's chat.' Jake paused for effect, knowing that every person in the room was gripped to every word he said. He always delivered his one minute pitches with such passion and charisma, it made it impossible not to listen. I was totally in awe of him. 'I can't wait to hear from you. And I promise, working with me will be anything but boring.' He sat down and took a gulp of his coffee.

'Thank you, Jake. Brilliant as always. Isobel, would you like to go next?' Leonard asked.

'Of course,' I said. I stood up and took a moment to make eye contact with the group myself.

'I couldn't agree with Jake more. Don't hold back in those quiet times. Make the most of that gift of time to do the jobs you never normally get to do. One thing could be to evaluate how you use time in itself. You're in business because you're good at what you do. But we can't all be good at everything. And we don't all like everything either. So what could you outsource? As a Virtual Assistant, that's literally what I'm here for. I work with busy professionals, handling the tasks that you don't have time for - or simply don't like - leaving you to focus on what you do best. If you could outsource one task, what would it be? I'd love to talk to you about it. Give me a call if you'd like to discuss anything further. Why struggle along when I'm here to take that boring task off your hands? Imagine how good it will feel to never have to do the boring stuff ever again. I look forward to hearing from you.'

I sat down and turned to Jake. He was looking directly at me. It was probably just a friendly glance, but I pretended in my mind that he'd just realised how perfect I was and he was planning on asking me out. There was no harm in pretending.

I know. I'm pathetic.

I didn't listen to the rest of the pitches, except for Leslie. I was interested in Leslie as she was new. For everyone else, they just said the same thing they said every month. We all did, I suppose. We all knew each other's businesses inside and out. But that was the point of the group.

After that, Leonard announced this week's speaker. It was Terry talking about the dangers of getting the wrong level of insurance. I'm sure it would have been fairly interesting, but before he'd finished his first sentence, I was off daydreaming.

Okay, by now I probably don't even need to say it. You know who I was daydreaming about. Although I should make it clear that I wasn't obsessed with Jake. I did have other things in my life. But when the man of your dreams is sitting next to you, it's hard not to fantasise.

I knew he was single. I'd found this out during an exceptionally cringeworthy moment. Someone had asked him a couple of months before if he was married or had a girlfriend. My ears had pricked up so severely from across the room, they must have been like beacons on the side of my head. I hurtled around the table to join in the conversation, like a complete fool, and arrived just in time to hear him reply that he was single. Then I'd wasted no time in spluttering out that I was single too and could he recommend any dating tips. He'd shaken his head and informed us all that he wasn't on the look and he was happy as he was.

If that wasn't bad enough, half of the group then spent the rest of the meeting enquiring if I was on Tinder and encouraging me to set up my online dating profile.

I'd gone home that day hugely embarrassed and very upset. But by the next meeting, I was back to being determined. "Happy as I am" wasn't going to stop me.

Stop me doing what, though? I wasn't doing anything except acting like a fool. Why was I waiting for him to ask me out? I hadn't been in a relationship for a long time. My priority for many years had been my career. But in the relationships I had had, I'd never been shy about declaring my feelings. Yet now, when it mattered more than anything, I was a complete mess.

All right, I had to concede that maybe I was a mess

because it did matter more. I had genuinely never felt this way about anyone. It just sounded so soppy and unlike me.

'Thank you. Any questions?' Shit, Terry had been talking for twenty minutes and I'd failed to hear any of it.

Someone asked a question and I tried to listen. Insurance was important. But my brain was off again. I could smell Jake and it was intoxicating.

Stop it.

'Any more questions?' Terry asked.

We all looked at one another and I pretended to be thinking of something to say. This wasn't good.

'Thank you, Terry,' Leonard said. 'That was really useful. I'm sure we all agree.' I nodded along with everyone else. 'Right, shall we share our news?'

Now this I had to concentrate on. This was the part of the meeting where we shared testimonials and good news stories, or we pleaded for help.

We quickly swept round the room and I made sure I paid full attention to everyone. There were some really inspiring stories this week. We had quite a successful group.

About half an hour later, when we'd all said our bits, Leonard announced the meeting closed.

Wasting no time at all, Jake stood up. I couldn't just let him go. I hated that it would be a whole month before I'd get to see him again.

'What are you up to this weekend, then?' I asked as he popped his pen into his jacket pocket. 'Oh no, that's right, you said you weren't looking forward to it.' Even I had to wince at how unsubtle that was.

'You know me, Izz,' he said with a smile. 'I always find a way to look on the positive side of things. I'll survive.'

'I'm sure you will. But if ever you want to talk, I'm a good listener. I'm certainly not up to much this weekend, so give me a bell if you need to talk. I gave you my business card, didn't I?' I wanted the carpet to swallow me up. I'd replay this later and bang my head against my desk.

'Thanks. I'll keep that in mind.'

He nodded and smiled before quickly shooting off, and I sat back down with deep embarrassment. After taking a few deep breaths and giving myself a good talking to, I scooped up my things and headed out of the room. I said goodbye to a few people, but Jake had already left. Forget about alluring him, I'd completely freaked him out.

I got to my car and opened the door. I threw my bag on the passenger seat and sat down. I was already replaying the horrifying scene in my mind. Why was it when my mouth worked and words formed, they were really crap words that left me utterly mortified?

I shook my head. It was fine. It was just a general gesture of "I'm here if you need a friend." That's what people said.

I grabbed my scruffy black driving shoes from where I'd thrown them back in the car and I took my heels off.

Knock knock knock.

I jumped with fright at the sound of someone knocking on my window. I looked up.

I stopped breathing.

It was Jake.

With trembling fingers, I pressed to unwind my window.

'Hiya,' I said. I never said that. 'Good meeting, wasn't it.'

'Did you say you've got no plans this weekend?' he asked.

I just stared at him. That's all I could manage.

'Could I ask you to do me a huge favour?'

'Sure,' I said, feigning cool and laidback so hard it actually hurt.

'No. I can't. It's too much.'

'No, please. What is it?'

He paused. 'How would you feel about being my plus one at a wedding tomorrow?'

TWO

I pretended to think about it. I had to. My instinct was to climb through the open window and hug him tightly, screaming "yes" so all of Suffolk could hear. But instead I took a moment. I calmly looked up, as if to calculate in my head whether this was a good idea or not.

What would a normal person do here? I asked myself. *Find out more information, of course.*

'Tomorrow? Erm, I suppose. Can your current plus one not make it?' I asked.

He seemed reluctant to answer at first. Finally he said, 'Complete truth?'

'If you want.'

'Can this stay just between us?'

'Of course. Do you want to jump in?' I signalled to the passenger seat.

He nodded and I lost my breath again. What was happening?

He walked around and I hastily threw my scruffy shoes into the back. He opened the door and got in, and my car suddenly filled with his beautiful scent.

'Okay, full disclosure,' he said. 'One of my uni friends is getting married tomorrow. They said I could bring someone with me and - I don't know why - but I said I'd be bringing a date. It just sort of came out. But now I'm twenty-four hours away and completely dateless. I know I could just go on my own, but there's something about being the only single person at a wedding where everyone else you know is coupled up. Do you know what I mean?'

He looked at me and I knew it was my turn to say something.

'Is there... is there no one else you could ask?' I finally uttered, instantly regretting it.

'Sorry. I shouldn't have asked you.'

'No! It's fine,' I said, far too urgently. 'I can go with you. I was just... curious. Why me?'

'I know we haven't known each other for long. But we seem to get on well. We always have a laugh together at these meetings.' The image of me chuckling at everything he said, month after month, sent a wave of nausea through me. 'The other thing is... I can't ask anyone who's in a relationship. And of the single friends I've got who are female... well, they're great mates, but...'

'But what?'

'They're just that: mates. I don't think we'd convince anyone that we're boyfriend and girlfriend.'

The world stopped turning. I swear it all ground to a halt and everything fell deathly silent. All I could hear was my heart pounding away, but now ten times harder than it had been just seconds before.

'Boyfriend and girlfriend?' I asked. Either Jake was very bad at reading people or I was in the middle of an Oscar-worthy performance for my indifference.

'Sorry,' he said, shaking his head. 'This is weird, isn't it.'

'No.'

'I can't believe I've just asked you. It wasn't a plan or anything. I've been dreading this wedding for weeks, and then you just said you were free tomorrow, and I suppose I jumped onto it as a last bit of hope. We haven't got to do anything or say anything. We'll just be together and my friends can plug the gaps in whatever way they want. I'm not asking you to be my date. Or girlfriend. I don't know. I haven't really thought this through. I just don't want their pitying looks if I turn up alone.'

'Yes.' That's all I could manage.

'I don't expect you to pay for anything. Everything will be on me. The hotel, drinks, food – everything. Think of it as a free weekend away.'

'Away?' I asked, trying to stay very still and not look excited.

'Sorry, I didn't say. They're getting married in Northamptonshire. The wedding's not until four. I thought we could drive up tomorrow morning.'

'Hotel?' I asked, now far too focused on all the wrong things.

'I'll cover the costs. And it's a nice hotel. Four star.'

'I guess we'll have to share a room.' I honestly meant this as a question, but it came out almost like an order.

'No, I'm sure they'll have rooms left. I'll phone up in a minute and book you one. If you want, that is. No pressure at all. I know this is a lot to ask. I'm sorry.'

'What will your friends think, though?' I argued. 'You bring a plus one and she's in a separate room? From what you've told me, I don't think they'll believe you as the no sex before marriage kind.'

He laughed and seemed a little surprised. He wasn't the only one. My brain was getting into gear and I wasn't sure if it was a good thing or not. 'What are saying, Izz? I'm a gentleman.'

'I didn't mean...'

He laughed again. 'I'm kidding. You're completely right. But I can't ask you to share a room with me. Besides, my friends won't know what rooms we're in.'

There was no way I was going to have a night away with Jake Masters and not share a room with him. This was my big chance. Sharing a room at a wedding: that was a one way ticket to love town, I was sure of it. I was not going to let this go.

'I'm a bit confused. You said you wanted your friends to believe that this plus one was your date? So your girlfriend? Hence why you weren't asking your other friends.'

'I suppose,' he nodded cautiously. 'I've not strictly told them I have a new girlfriend. We don't have to say anything or act in any particular way. But let's just say it will make my life a whole lot easier if they think of me as... not single. Sorry.'

'Then we have to share a room. I've done this before, loads of times. Shared with friends. I mean we are friends, aren't we?'

'Yeah. Definitely.'

'Then where's the harm?'

'I see what you mean,' he said. 'So we get a twin room? We have the façade that we're sharing, but we're just mates when we're inside. Two friends, sharing a hotel room. Who hasn't done that?'

'Right. Yes. Of course. Yes.'

'So, will you be my plus one?' he asked. 'Two friends getting to know each other better. We'll have a good time, I promise.'

I paused as I counted how many times he'd said friends in thirty seconds. That wasn't good.

'It's fine if you don't want to,' he added, his trademark smile wavering.

Shit, I couldn't lose this. 'No, definitely count me in,' I said. 'I think it will be fun.'

'You're sure?' Jake said, the delight sparkling through to his beautiful brown eyes.

'Yes. Definitely. I even have the perfect dress to wear. We'll be a couple to envy!' I laughed, perhaps far too hysterically, and I knew pathetic Isobel was back. I hated her.

'You are a star. I owe you one. A big one.'

I could only smile at this.

'Pick you up at ten tomorrow?' he said. 'Is that okay?'

'Sounds perfect.'

'Will you text me your address?'

'Of course. We can plan our back story on the journey up.'

'Back story?'

'How we met. All that. We need to get our story straight.'

'But we know our story already.'

'We do?' I asked.

'We met at a networking meeting. I made you coffee and we hit it off instantly. Then one morning after a meeting I tapped on your window and asked you out. The rest is history.'

My heart fluttered. I was completely dazzled by these words. I half believed I might wake up and realise that this was all a dream.

'Are you okay?' he asked, staring at my startled face.

'Yes. Of course. I just had a moment of worrying that my dress needed dry cleaning. But it doesn't. Panic over!'

'Oh, right. Okay. Great.'

'So I'll see you tomorrow then,' I said, before adding without meaning to, 'I'll see you on Saturday. At the weekend.'

'Yes,' he said, clearly not sure whether to laugh or run for the hills. I had to stop being so weird. He opened the car door. 'Any problems, you've got my number.'

'There won't be. I'll be ready.'

'Okay then. See you tomorrow.'

'Bye.'

He shut the door and walked away. I watched him walk over to his Jaguar.

He had the most amazing car.

There was no question that Jake was wealthy. I've mentioned his polished appearance and now I'm mentioning his car, but please don't think for one second that I was attracted to Jake because of his money. I wasn't. His car and tailored suits were sexy, don't get me wrong, but it was the whole package that I adored. I had fallen head over heels for him long before I knew about his supposed millionaire status.

Yes, apparently he was a millionaire. Or so the rumours said.

The story went that he'd developed a dating app in his early twenties which he'd sold a couple of years ago for several million pounds. Whilst I had no evidence to discard these rumours as untrue, I couldn't work out why a millionaire super successful entrepreneur would come to our little networking group every month posing as a mere Business Consultant. It didn't fit.

Not that I cared either way. It was his essence that I loved, not his bank balance. I couldn't be with a man who had no flair, no ambition. Jake had that in abundance. That's all that mattered to me.

I watched as he drove away. I couldn't move. I knew I needed a good few minutes before I could function. I also knew that the day ahead of me was unlikely to be very productive now. But, hey, that was the perk of being your own boss. You could spend all day daydreaming and no one could tell you off. I could see that Jake Masters was going to be in my head more than normal over the next few days.

THREE

I didn't sleep at all that night. I don't think I'd ever been so excited. I would like to tell you that I wasn't deluding myself and I knew it wasn't a date. I'd also like to tell you that I'd been quite casual in considering where this weekend away might lead, and I was very open minded about it all.

But I couldn't say any of that. The truth was my normally grounded nature and sensible thoughts had been replaced by a totally ridiculous belief that I was now on a one way trip to happily ever after. Words like "destiny" and "fate" were fluttering through my mind, making me jittery with delight. I was practically bouncing off the walls, ready for the change that was inevitably going to happen after Jake had seen me in my stunning wedding outfit.

And every time reason or logic crept into my brain, whispering quietly that I was being a fool to think anything romantic was going to happen and I was setting myself up for a major fall, I quickly batted them away. Irrational Isobel was now in full force. It was definitely not like me, but the buzz was amazing.

I stared hard at the alarm clock the next morning, waiting for it to click to seven a.m. Even though I was wide awake and more than ready for the day, I had convinced myself that I shouldn't get up too early as it will be a tiring day. I needed to conserve my energy for when Jake and I were hitting the dancefloor that evening.

I was getting more ridiculous by the second. I had to wonder if love did this to other people, or if I was just really odd.

Seven o'clock appeared and my alarm rang. I hit the button to switch it off and I jumped out of bed. I had no time to waste. I had to perfect every strand of my hair and every fleck of make-up. Nothing but my absolute best was going to suffice today.

I opened my enormous wardrobe.

I had loads of clothes – most of them designer – and even more shoes. It wasn't that I had to have the latest fashion, and I wasn't particularly vain. It was more about how it made me feel.

Very early on in my career someone had told me to dress for the job I wanted not the job I had. Full of big ambition, I decided from that day onwards I would always look sharp, sophisticated and like a woman who was ready for anything life threw at her.

I'd translated that into stylish business attire, and every day wearing only the smartest of clothes had helped me to find the right powerful mindset where nothing would stop me from getting all the way to the top.

You may be thinking now that, like Jake, Isobel must be Little Miss Moneybags. I really wasn't. I was comfortable, definitely, but the only reason I'd been able to afford so many beautiful clothes (and even more beautiful shoes) was that I had nothing else in my life. Remember when I said earlier that I had other things to think about, not just Jake? Well, I was lying. For years I'd done nothing but work, sleep and eat. Fantasising about Jake Masters was actually a new highlight. That about summed up the life of Isobel Hargreaves.

I hadn't been on holiday in about eight years. Annual leave consisted of me going home to see my family. I had no real friends close by, so that meant no social life. Work really was the only thing I had, and it had been that way since leaving university.

I was on my own most of the time, but I'd never thought of myself as lonely. I was always too busy to be lonely. I might have lacked a calendar of social engagements, but I'd made up for that with shopping and buying nice things - including a lovely little house that was all my own. That wasn't something to complain about.

I was all packed and ready to go by nine-thirty. I knew the wedding wasn't until four p.m. and I was glammed up far too early, but I wanted to look my best when Jake arrived. I could always have a mini polish up before the ceremony.

There were elegant swirls running through my thick ruby hair. I'd opted for subtle eye make-up, and I'd balanced it out with my favourite rouge lipstick. It was soft enough not to be slutty, but still gave off sexy vibes. The perfect combination.

I was playing solitaire on my phone, trying to keep myself calm, when the doorbell chimed at just after ten.

I opened the door to my little two bedroomed house that sat on a quiet street just a couple of miles out of Ipswich town centre.

'Morning,' Jake said. His smile was there, but it wasn't as vibrant as normal. 'Is this weird?

'No!' I said.

It probably was. If any of the other men in the networking group had asked me to be their plus one at a wedding, I would have found any excuse not to go. But this wasn't a peer asking a peer to be a strange plus one. This was the start of a blossoming relationship. It just happened that Jake didn't know that yet.

'We're friends and you've asked me to join you for the day at an event,' I said. 'Let's think of it like that. That's not weird.'

'No. That's true. I think you'll get on well with my mates. They're all easy going.'

'I can't wait to meet them.'

I invited Jake in and I took a second to scan every inch of him as he walked past me. It was the first time I'd ever seen Jake out of a suit, but he looked just as sexy in jeans.

I'd been very conscious of the fact that this would be the first time he'd see me in casual attire as well. I'd opted for a summer dress that floated just above the knee. There was no way I wasn't flashing my legs. I was going to try anything to get Jake to notice me in a more sexual way. Flesh definitely played a part in that.

'Make yourself comfortable. I won't be long,' I said, as if somehow I hadn't been ready for ages.

'Is that all you're taking?' he asked, looking at the small case that rested near the door.

'My dress is separate. I didn't want it all screwed it. It's hanging upstairs. I'll just grab it and my shoes, and I'm ready to go.'

I jogged up the stairs and headed into my bedroom. I grabbed my dress that was neatly wrapped up in its carrier.

'You've got a cat!' Jake yelled up the stairs.

'What?'

I picked up the small bag that had my shoes in and I headed back down the stairs.

'Cats normally love me,' Jake said as he backed away from the grey cat that was hissing at him.

'What did you do?' I asked, having never seen a cat so angry. 'It's like it's got venom in its eyes.'

'Yeah, they're weird eyes, aren't they.'

The beautiful short haired cat before us had the most unusual sparkling blue eyes.

'I only tried to stroke it. What's its name?' Jake asked, now pinned against the wall as the hissing continued.

'I have no idea. It's not my cat. And I have no clue how it keeps getting in.'

'You've got a cat flap,' Jake responded, as if I were a little bit stupid. 'I heard it open.'

'It's not my cat flap. It was from the previous owners. And I keep locking it. But somehow this fiendish cat keeps finding a way to unlock it. He's like the Houdini of the cat world.'

'Are you sure you're locking it properly?'

'I run my own business. I think I can figure out how to lock a cat flap. The catch must be loose or something.'

The cat hissed at Jake once more before approaching me and rubbing itself up against my leg. I couldn't resist a cuddle. As much as the darn thing irritated me, it was such a beautiful creature. Luckily, I'd always loved cats in return.

'It's a boy then,' Jake said, crudely taking a look. 'My gran had a cat like that. She called it Smokey.'

'Oh, I like it. Smokey.'

'Smokey the wonder cat.'

'Smokey the pain in the arse more like.'

Smokey meowed at this as if to object. It wasn't the first time I could have sworn this cat understood me.

'If I throw him out the front, can you have a go at locking the cat flap?' I asked Jake. 'Maybe I am doing something wrong.'

'Of course. Happy to help.'

As I carried Smokey to the front door, he nestled his head into my chest. So manipulative.

'See you later, Smokey. I've got an exciting weekend ahead. You need to go and bother someone else now.' I placed him on my front lawn (patch of grass/lawn – same thing), and stepped back into the house.

'The cat flap does seem a bit loose,' Jake said, returning from the kitchen. 'You should get a new door.'

'I can't really afford that right now.'

'I'm sure it won't cost a lot. And it'll probably be worth it. Whose cat is it, anyway?'

'I have no idea. I don't really know the neighbours. I tend to keep myself to myself.'

Jake studied me for a second. 'You're quite shy, aren't

you,' he said.

'Am I?' No one had ever called me shy before. I think my family would find that quite hilarious.

'It's funny, you seem really confident and self-assured when you stand up to talk at networking, but when we're having a chat after over coffee or something, you go really quiet. Normally people are the other way around.'

Maybe I won't be getting an Oscar this year.

'I just like to listen,' I said. Which is true. 'You learn far more when you listen than when you speak.'

'Now that's an entrepreneur talking. Right, are you ready?'

I nodded. 'Let's get on the road.'

* * *

As unpleasant as the Smokey vs Jake incident was, it had certainly broken the ice. The uncomfortable tension from when he'd first stepped into my house was now all gone and we were singing along to the radio as we shot up the A14 in Jake's rather luxurious car.

'I suppose we'd better learn about each other,' I said as our dulcet tones were interrupted by an ad break.

'What do you mean?'

'I'm guessing you don't want your friends to know that you asked some random girl at a networking group to join you as you hadn't got the plus one you'd promised.'

'You're not random.'

'I know, but if we don't know a few basic things about each other, they're going to think it's a bit strange. We only know work related stuff about each other. We should share a few personal facts.'

Jake seemed concerned. 'How personal?'

I laughed. 'Not that personal! I don't need your measurements. But family, where you grew up, that sort of thing.'

'Right. Yeah, okay. Good idea. How about we do some

quick fire questioning?'

'I like the sound of that. You go first. Ask away.'

'Okay.' Jake paused for a second to consider where to start. 'Where were you born?'

'Hereford. Right over the other side of England. I then went to Middlesex University and ended up with a job as a PA in London. It wasn't my dream job, but it turns out I'm quite good at it.'

Jake chuckled.

'What?' I asked.

'The idea of quick fire questioning is that you give a quick answer. You know Hereford would have sufficed, right?'

I laughed and shook my head. 'If we do it like that, it will take forever. Doing it my way means you get a lot of information in a short space of time.'

'True,' Jake nodded, flashing that smile. 'Okay, next quick fire question with a potentially very long answer. What is your dream job?'

'That I can definitely answer quickly. I have no idea. Something with numbers I guess. I studied Economics but never quite worked out what to do with it, and now nearly ten years on all I've ever been is an assistant.'

'I think that was longer than the first answer!' Jake laughed again. I loved it.

'But in, what, eight sentences, you've learnt a hell of a lot about me. My way is actually very efficient.'

'I suppose so. And for the record, I like numbers too.'

'Really?'

'Yeah. Save you having to ask me, I studied Computer Science in Birmingham. I'm Ipswich born and bred, though, and moved right back home after uni finished. Anyway, back to you. How did you end up in Ipswich?'

'I was head hunted. How about that for quick?'

'Head hunted? Now I want you to elaborate!'

I felt quite pleased with this. 'You know PRT Insurance?'

'That's a massive company.'

'Yep. The MD heard about me through a mutual contact and offered me a too good to turn down opportunity.'

'But you don't work there anymore?'

'No. He got married about a year ago and suddenly didn't need a PA anymore. His wife looks after him now.'

'How very twenty-first century.'

'Tell me about it. I suppose there's no harm in keeping it in the family.'

'You're very understanding. I don't know if I'd be.'

'I wasn't at the time. Believe me. But within a couple of weeks, word had got around that I was out of work and a few past connections were begging for my help. It was really flattering. I thought it would keep me going until I found something new, but now nine months on and I'm quite a successful VA. It's funny how life just sort of works out like that, isn't it.'

Jake didn't respond.

'So, you're from Ipswich?' I said, thinking that maybe he was hinting that I should now be asking him questions. 'How did you end up as a Business Coach?'

'Erm, short version is that I invented an app when I was at uni, sold it a few years ago, and now I'm using the knowledge I built up to help other businesses find success.'

'I've heard about your app. It was a dating app, wasn't it?'

Jake just nodded. Something about it seemed to make him tense. My gut told me to stop prodding, but we were in a quick fire question session. This was my chance to find out as much as possible.

'There are a lot of rumours about you, you know,' I said, testing the water.

Thankfully, this seemed to pique his interest. 'Are there? What sort of rumours?'

'You don't know?'

'No. Why would people want to talk about me?'

Oh, how I could have answered that question! I took a breath to stay focused. 'They say you were hugely successful and you sold your app for like ten million pounds or something. Is that right?'

Jake paused and then he shook his head. 'I didn't sell it for ten million.'

'I did think that seemed a lot. If I'm honest, I also wondered why someone so rich and successful would now be at our little networking group working with small business owners.'

'Because it's the best place to find them.'

'What?'

'I love working with small businesses. I love finding promising young entrepreneurs and helping their potential boom. I mean, take you. I see so much ambition in your eyes when you're doing your one minute pitch.'

'I definitely have ambition,' I said.

'I have no doubt. Tell me the long term plan.'

'I don't know. Something really big. I'm still working on it.'

'We should talk sometime. I reckon I could help.'

I paused. I needed to take a breath. Working with Jake would be amazing. 'I'd love that,' I said.

'How old are you?' he asked. 'That's a basic I should definitely know.'

'I'm thirty-one. How about you?'

'Thirty-two.'

'Look at that. Not much between us at all.' I couldn't resist. 'We both run businesses, both have a love of numbers, we're similar ages and we live in the same town. It's easy to see why we're coming to this wedding together.' I chuckled as if it were all a joke.

'You're lucky you found me,' Jake laughed, totally unaware of how true his words were.

We shared more facts about each other as we left the A14 around Cambridgeshire and carried on west to Northamptonshire. I was so lost in the enjoyment of learning about Jake that I barely noticed us getting on and off the M1, and before I knew it we were pulling into a narrow road that led down to the country house hotel where Jake's friends were getting married.

It was a beautiful Grade I listed building buried deep in perfectly landscaped gardens. Such a picturesque venue. I could see why they had chosen it.

Jake parked up and we carried our bags to reception. The entrance wasn't very big, but it felt special. Modern day necessities complemented the grand features that highlighted the building's tradition. It certainly was romantic. We managed to check straight in and I virtually dragged Jake to our first floor bedroom.

I opened the heavy wooden door and we both stood still. We were both shocked, but I suspected in very different ways. Either the hotel had cocked up or my wish had been granted. Right in the centre of the room was the most enormous four poster bed.

'What the fuck! I'm so sorry, Izz,' Jake said as I tried to hide my smile. 'I asked for a twin. It's okay, I'll go and tell them.'

'No, don't!' I said, actually grabbing his arm. I knew this was wrong on every level, but we were going to be drinking and then falling asleep together in a double bed. Things were very likely to happen. That's how it worked. This was my chance.

'If you say something then you're just going to draw attention to us. Let's just leave it as it is. I don't mind.'

'This isn't right, Izz,' he said, closing the door behind us. 'Look, if we're stuck like this, I'll sleep on the chair.'

There was a quaint Chesterfield armchair near the window. It looked comfortable to sit in, but even if sharing a bed with Jake hadn't been something I'd thought solidly about for the past six months, I still couldn't have asked him to sleep in it.

'Look at the size of this bed!' I said, going over to sit on it. 'Five people could fit in this bed. We can share it no problem.'

'I suppose there are a lot of cushions. We could stuff them down the middle.'

I nodded before I found the word. 'Yes. Of course. We'll be miles from each other.'

'I don't want to make you feel uncomfortable. I know I'm already asking the world of you.' Why did I have to fall in love with the only decent man alive? I didn't know whether to hug him or slap him.

'I would only feel uncomfortable if you were stuck in that stupid chair. There's more than enough bed for the both of us.'

'Are you sure?' he said, so genuinely. 'You're very understanding.'

'What can I say? I'm just chilled about stuff.' My inner self burst out laughing. Hopefully Jake wouldn't remember me saying that if he ever got to know me well. 'We'll probably be drunk on Champagne anyway!' I added. 'No doubt we'll pass out and not even know each other is there.'

'Okay then. But if you change your mind, you must let me know. You need to be completely honest with me. You're doing me a massive favour this weekend, so the least I can do is make sure you're as comfortable as possible. So you will be honest with me, yes?'

There was no way I could agree to that, so instead I said, 'If there's anything troubling me, I'll be sure to let you know. Okay?'

'Okay. Do you fancy some lunch?'

We ate lunch, walked around the gardens, had a quick drink in the bar to relax us, and then we went back to the room to get ready. By quarter to four we were walking down to the ceremony room and I was finding it hard to stop smiling. I bet the bride wasn't as happy or as excited as I was. I knew this could very well be the best night of my life and I was determined to enjoy every second.

FOUR

I opened my eyes, relieved to know that I must have finally dozed off. It couldn't have been for long, but at least I'd got some sleep. I glanced at my phone on the bedside table. It was nearly eight o'clock. Surely I could get up soon. This had been the longest, most awful night and all I wanted now was to get home.

I lay on my back and stared at the impressive ceiling. In the centre was a small chandelier that glistened a little when it caught the light that poured through the crack in the curtains. It was a beautiful sight, but it didn't help to alleviate the hurt I felt inside.

The wedding ceremony itself had been wonderful. Jake and I had sat together, and at the end he'd grabbed my hand. He just did it and I (of course) let him. I was on cloud nine. I was sure he was falling for me too.

After the ceremony ended, we walked outside for pictures and he introduced me to some of his friends.

Then I didn't see him again until we sat down for the Wedding Breakfast.

We were naturally sat next to each other, and he turned up at the table all smiles and charm, and I thought maybe we were finally going to spend some time together. But he barely spoke to me throughout the entire meal.

We were on a table full of his uni friends and their partners, and it was clear that everyone knew everyone else very well. I spoke mainly to the couple next to me. They were nice people, and they obviously thought the world of Jake. They told me lots of stories about their university days and asked me lots of questions about myself. But Jake might as well have been in a different room for the contributions he made to any conversation I was involved in.

He made a beeline to the bar with his mates when the speeches were over with and I was left hanging around with people I'd never met before.

It wasn't a major issue in itself. His friends were all lovely and they seemed delighted to be in the company of Jake's new girlfriend, which I felt I had to let them believe. I was the centre of attention in Jake's crowd for most of the night. The only person who didn't seem to notice I was alive was Jake.

He finally made an appearance just as the first dance started. I think he'd hunted me down for it, which only pissed me off more. I had never felt so used.

However, it was when we joined the bride and groom on the dancefloor that he really began to mess with my head. He told me how amazing I was and how pleased he was that he'd had the chance to get to know me better. It was hard not to believe he was being genuine. Lust and love fizzled through me in a most uncomfortable way as he wrapped his arms around me and we slow danced along with every other couple.

At the end of the song we clapped and then Jake stopped. He was breathing me in, his eyes fixed on mine. I knew that look. That was the look I'd been dreaming about. I knew, without question, that he was contemplating kissing me. I knew it. But unlike all of my fantasies, this situation was horrible. It was all wrong.

He leaned in, now focusing intently on my lips, and the fizzle of delight morphed into nausea. I literally didn't know what to do. But before I could do or say anything, he swiftly moved to the left, kissed my cheek, whispered in my ear what an incredible woman I was, and then darted back to the bar to be with his mates.

I had been aware, under all the ecstatic joy, that there was a chance that coming to this event could potentially hurt me. But I'd never considered just how bad it could be. I was all over the place.

After a short cry in the toilets, I sorted myself out and decided that I needed to join him. He shouldn't have been making me feel this way. I stepped back into the function room and headed right over to the bar.

Before I could as much as say hello, though, I was pulled onto the dancefloor by his female friends. And Jake couldn't have been more encouraging for me to join them.

That then upset me even more. Not what Jake had done, but how his friends were treating me.

For the first time in what seemed like forever, I felt like I had friends. I felt popular and I felt as if people were genuinely interested in me. I didn't talk about work once. It was so human. I hadn't quite realised just how much I'd missed social interactions like this.

I hadn't quite realised just how much I'd missed having friends.

When "us girls" all decided to take a break from the dancefloor and head to the bar, I got to see Jake fleetingly and I had a quick check in. And quick it was. My lips had barely touched my glass of Chardonnay when his female friends swiped me away again for a girly chat, and to introduce "Jake's new girlfriend" to someone they hadn't seen in years.

After that we made a pit stop on the dancefloor for a song I'd never heard of but everyone else "just loved". Truthfully, I hadn't heard of half the songs that were playing. I had been so out of touch with so much.

I also hadn't danced on a dancefloor in about ten years. I was normally working the room if I went out, seeing what contacts I could make. I'd forgotten how much feet can hurt in stilettoes when you're on the move all night.

By ten o'clock, the party was still in full swing, but all I wanted to do was go to bed. I was loving the female company, but the knowledge that I wasn't Jake's girlfriend, these weren't my real friends, and I'd actually probably never see them again, made me want to sit down and sob.

For the first time ever I considered just how empty my life was. I realised that for all my fantasies about Jake, if he were to ask me to marry him today, I'd barely have any guests at my wedding. I'd have no one to be a bridesmaid. I'd pushed everyone away in my obsessive need to rise to the top. And what had I achieved? Nothing. I now owned my own business as a reaction to being made redundant, and some months I barely made enough to meet my mortgage.

Things were improving all the time, but I was light years away from the CEO of the year status I craved.

It seemed I was in vast denial about everything, and being at this wedding was making it hard for me to ignore it.

I excused myself from the dancefloor and hobbled over to the bar, where Jake was captivating every single person in his vicinity. He was telling some story or other and it was easy to see how much everyone adored him.

I waited patiently until he'd finished and then I fought my way to his side. His eyes lit up when he saw me.

'Izz! Having a good night?'

I opened my mouth to tell him that my feet were killing me and I might have to call it a night, when I stopped. I imagined what his response would be. He'd say goodnight and leave me to go back to the room on my own. Then I knew that I'd lie in bed wishing that I was back downstairs close to him. As I looked into his dazzling eyes that seemed so delighted to see me, I realised that, as horrible as it was being ignored by him, it still seemed a better alternative to lying wide awake on my own being depressed.

So instead I told him I hadn't danced that much in years and I asked him to order me another glass of wine.

Finally, at just after midnight, when the bar had closed and the music had ended, Jake appeared from nowhere, grabbed my hand and asked me if I was ready for bed. Those words that I'd longed to hear for so many months actually seared a hole in my heart, but I nodded.

We said our goodnights to everyone else, and all of his friends gave me such a huge hug. Then Jake and I headed back to the room.

I went straight to the bathroom to put my pyjamas on, and by the time I reappeared, Jake was fast asleep.

He had barely moved all night. I would know, I'd been awake for most of it playing the events over and over in my mind. It could not have been further from what I'd hoped for. But I had to concede that maybe it was for the best. When I'd imagined Jake as my boyfriend, I'd imagined someone who actually wanted to spend time with me. He clearly preferred the company of his mates at the bar, and that wasn't the man for me.

I knew that might not have been entirely fair. He barely saw his mates and he barely knew me. I couldn't really blame him for his behaviour. He probably thought I was happier having a dance and getting away from him. But believing that he was a bastard certainly helped me to deal with it all.

'Morning,' Jake said, turning over to find me wide awake. 'Are you okay? How did you sleep?' His voice was rough but he looked very happy.

'Morning. Really well, thank you. You?'

'Like a baby. This is a really comfortable bed, isn't it.'

'I knew it would be better than the chair.' I felt sick as I said this. Maybe I should have slept in the chair.

'Cuppa?' he said, getting up and heading over to the little tea tray near the television.

'A nice strong coffee would be lovely,' I said.

He disappeared into the bathroom to fill up the kettle and then came back to turn it on. Then he turned to face me.

'I cannot thank you enough for last night,' he said, moving over to my side of the bed. I propped myself up and he sat next to me. There was a look of pure contentment on his face and I tried to hide my pain.

'It was a pleasure,' I lied.

'My mates absolutely love you. I think they might even prefer you to me!' he laughed.

'Your friends are lovely. It's a shame you don't get to see them more often.'

He looked at me curiously. 'They told you I don't see them often?'

'Well, it's not a surprise. None of them are local. You all live all over the place.'

'Yep,' he said as he studied the kettle.

An uncomfortable silence settled on the room. All that could be heard was the kettle beginning to boil.

Jake turned back to look at me, his expression now cautious. 'There's something I need to talk to you about.'

I waited for him to elaborate, my heart thudding. It all felt like he was about to break some terrible news to me. The electric charge that he normally sent buzzing through me was now just a bleep of nausea.

'My friends loved you so much...' He shifted awkwardly. 'This is their words not mine.'

'Okay.'

'They want to see you again.'

That had been the last thing I had expected him to say. 'See me again?'

'I know we were pretty vague last night, but they all seem to believe that we are... in a relationship. They kept saying how perfect you are for me and all that stuff. I mean they're not wrong. You are special. When I said last night how incredible you are, I meant it.'

I couldn't move. My head was getting more and more cloudy and it wasn't just the hangover.

'I haven't confirmed to them that you're my girlfriend or

anything. I'm not asking for anything from you. But just... Would you mind... We'll just be like mates again... They don't need to know...'

'Jake, what are you asking me?'

'The bride and groom - Olivia and Harrison – they're coming to Ipswich the week after next.'

'Aren't they going off on honeymoon? They said they were going to Dubai.'

'They are. But they're huge Ed Sheeran fans. You know he's playing at Chantry Park - the big homecoming gig? Well, I got them VIP tickets as a wedding present. So they're coming to Ipswich to see Ed Sheeran and then they're having a night out with me before catching a flight to Dubai. And they said that they're now really excited about seeing you as well.'

I couldn't speak.

'I know. I know it's a lot to ask. It's just... I've never had a girlfriend that any of my friends liked before.'

I still couldn't speak.

Jake was an absolute shit for asking this of me. I mean, the audacity after ignoring me all night and leaving me to chat to complete strangers for hours.

But those complete strangers now felt like real friends. The idea of seeing Olivia again actually excited me.

Fuck.

The kettle clicked off and Jake stood up. It was perfect timing as I needed to think.

'It's not a surprise they like you,' he said, as he turned the mugs over. 'You're a pretty special woman. I don't deserve you in my life. I'm not taking your kindness for granted. You have to know that.'

What was I supposed to say?

Then he knocked me for six. As he poured the little sachets of coffee into the mugs he said, 'One sugar isn't it? One sugar in coffee as you find it too bitter, but none at all in tea.'

I think my jaw dropped open a bit at this. He'd

remembered. He'd listened and remembered. No one ever remembered things about me. I was the woman who remembered things about everyone else.

'Thanks,' I muttered, now utterly bewildered by my thoughts and Jake's actions.

I watched him make the coffee and he brought my mug over to me.

'What would we be doing with your friends?' I asked, deciding to get some more information before I fully committed to a response.

'It's just a night out. A few drinks. We'll head up to the waterfront for a few. Nothing special.' He sat down next to me again. 'It's just one night and then I'll tell them we're just friends. That will be it. It'll be fun. We had fun last night, didn't we?'

I found it curious how Jake viewed the night before so differently to me. I made sure not to say a word.

'Just this once more,' he said. 'I probably won't see my mates again for another six months anyway. You'll buy me a good few months where they'll stop pitying me.'

In all of our quick fire questions the day before, we'd both steered clear of past relationships, but now I was starting to realise that something in Jake's past was still lurking around in his present. Maybe I should cut him a break.

'All right. One more time can't hurt, I suppose. But drinks are on you,' I added with a smile.

'Absolutely,' he said, breaking into a smile himself. 'Whatever you want. I can't thank you enough for this, Izzy. You're a true gem. I owe you like a hundred. How about six months of business coaching completely free?' He laughed and my heart sank. I didn't want free business support. In fact I was thinking that never seeing him again after this might be my only chance of survival.

FIVE

The next week and a half flew by. It was now Thursday night, just after seven o'clock. Olivia and Harrison were off to see Ed Sheeran that night, and in just over twenty-four hours Jake would be ringing on my doorbell to pick me up. And I was sitting at my desk in the hope that masses of work would distract me from obsessing over it.

'Meow!' I heard the call from the bottom of the stairs. 'Meow!' Then I heard little paws running up my staircase. Seconds later the door to my office slowly opened and Smokey the wonder cat appeared.

I'd stopped bothering to lock the cat flap. It seemed to make no difference anyway, and frankly ever since that wedding I'd been glad of the company.

'Hello Smokey,' I said looking down at him. He sat on the floor, those beautiful blue eyes staring up at me. They were so intense, as if they hid the depth of the ocean. It was almost hypnotic.

'You can see I'm working,' I said. I carried on typing for a few minutes, ignoring him. He didn't move. It had always amazed me how cats can sit for hours just staring at one thing.

I turned around to grab a file from behind me and caught

his glare.

'I haven't eaten yet, no,' I said. I liked to imagine we had proper, full chats. 'Have you? You certainly don't come around here for the food. Does your owner feed you? Or do you bother someone else for that?'

I ran through the paperwork in the file to get the document that I wanted and then I turned back to my laptop.

'I know I'm working late. But that's what you have to do when you're running a growing business. You have to put the hours in.'

I could almost see the disbelief in Smokey's eyes.

'Are you going to make me say it?'

Those eyes didn't move an inch.

'All right, yes. I'm working late as I need to keep busy. The big date is tomorrow. A double date with the loveliest couple that I am bound to never see again, and... that... gorgeous, horrible man. My dream man who would make a terrible boyfriend. Well, they say you should never meet your idols. Not that I've really met my idol.' I looked down at Smokey. He was still watching me. 'I don't think you care, do you? Do you like me talking to you?'

As if to give his approval, he jumped up on my lap. He rubbed himself against my arm until I caved in and stroked him.

'Oh, Smokey. What am I going to do? I love who he is. I love his charisma, his intelligence, his ambition and... just about everything. Don't even get me started on how sexy he is. I think it's fair to say I'm very physically attracted to him. Ow!' Smokey sunk his claws into me. Even despite the dress I was wearing, he still reached my flesh.

'Naughty cat!' I said, knocking him on the floor. 'That wasn't very nice.'

He attempted to jump up again and I stopped him. Then he just sat and watched me, those blue eyes once again fixated on my face.

'What is it you want? You don't come here for food. You

don't seem bothered whether I fuss you or not. You just sit there, staring at me. Is it the company? I mean I know I talk a lot. It's the curse of being on your own. You need some sound to fill the room. Do you like me talking to you?'

He rolled over and stretched out, making himself exceptionally comfortable on the floor.

'Don't think you'll be here for long,' I said. 'I really should be starting my dinner. And it's not dinner for two.' My shoulders slumped. 'A double date. At least he might not ignore me so much if there are only four of us. You know he's been texting me? Yes, you do know that. I think I've had a text every single day for the past week. He wasn't that attentive at the wedding. He's probably just trying to keep me sweet so I don't back out. I showed you the texts, didn't I?'

My instinct was to grab my phone and show Smokey again, when I stopped. That was just silly.

'Olivia and Harrison are staying over at Jake's house. Did I tell you that? You know I don't even know where he lives. It's got to be around Ipswich somewhere. Maybe if we'd spent more time together at the wedding, I'd have been able to find out such basic things. God, I'm going to look so stupid if they start to talk about his house.' I suddenly felt enraged. 'Do you know what? Good. He can explain why his so-called girlfriend knows so little about him!'

Smokey sat up again, but his stare didn't leave my face for a second.

My phone buzzed. I picked it up and my stomach flipped.

'It's him,' I told Smokey.

Told O & H that you can't stay over as you have a meeting first thing Saturday. They didn't bat an eyelid. Can't wait to see you. x

I shook my head. 'Would you think it was weird that your friend's girlfriend wasn't staying over because she had a work meeting on a Saturday morning? I think that's weird.

What am I going to say if they probe me?' I slammed my phone down. 'What do I care? I'm never going to see them again. I can make up any old crap and it doesn't matter.'

I looked down at Smokey. He hadn't flinched at all at my little outburst.

I grabbed my phone again and started to reply.

Great. I will just meet you in town. That's easier.

'For all I know, Jake lives right in the town centre. It would be crazy of him to go out of his way to pick me up.'

My phone beeped again. He'd replied quickly.

I told you, it's only right we all go together. I can't let my 'girlfriend' turn up at a bar on her own. We'll pick you up on the way. x

I huffed and mumbled, 'Where was that chivalry at the wedding?' I looked at Smokey. 'Suddenly he's the world best boyfriend.'

I shook my head. I certainly had Smokey's attention. Although I imagined if he could actually understand me and communicate, he'd be telling me to shut the fuck up right about now.

'You're right!' I announced, as if Smokey had just said that very thing. 'I have to stop obsessing over Jake bloody Masters. I've just got to get through tomorrow and then never see him again. Except for at our monthly meetings. Maybe. If I decide to continue. Should I continue? I do get work from there. It would be a shame to stop going. Oh!'

I stood up. I was even driving myself mad.

'Right, come on you. Let's go and see what I've got in the fridge.'

The next twenty-fours seemed to drag. I wanted to tell myself that I was dreading the double date, but I knew inside I was getting excited again. I was convincing myself that this time it would be better, and Jake and I would finally start to grow close.

When would I ever learn?

I was ready and waiting about fifteen minutes early. I was in perhaps far too a glamorous dress for Friday night drinks in Ipswich, but I couldn't help it. There was a part of me that still wanted to fight to win Jake over. It couldn't hurt to look my best. Besides, if Jake wasn't interested, I told myself the effort was still worth it as I might grab the attention of another lovely man. There really was nothing to lose.

It was just before eight p.m. when I heard the doorbell chime. I opened the door to see Jake smiling and looking sexy as hell. He had those gorgeous designer jeans on again with a dark shirt and smart jacket. He was catwalk good looking. It really wasn't fair.

'You look beautiful,' he said. It was very kind, but I wasn't sure whether he really meant it or not.

'You look nice yourself,' I replied with the same indifferent tone.

I locked up and that was when I spotted it. We were heading down the little pathway at the front of my house when I stopped dead still.

'That's a Rolls Royce,' I said, pointing to the stunning black vehicle parked by the kerb. 'What taxi company is this?'

'It's not,' Jake said. He tried to be casual but I could detect a little embarrassment. 'With the newly-weds in town, I thought I should treat them a bit. He took them to the gig last night and I thought he might as well cater for our travelling needs tonight as well.'

'He?' I queried.

'The driver.'

'Someone you know?'

Jake shrugged. I wanted to probe more, but he opened the door of the flashy car and before I knew it I was waving hello to said newly-weds.

I sat in the back with them and Jake walked around to sit in the front passenger seat.

'How was the concert?' I asked as we pulled away.

'Absolutely amazing,' Olivia said with a beaming smile. She was far less made up than on her wedding day and I got to see how long her shiny brown hair really was. She'd looked stunning on her wedding day, but it wasn't a make-up miracle. She was very pretty.

'There's nothing like a homecoming gig,' she continued. 'It gives everything an extra bit of... oomph. Do you know what I mean?'

'Yes. Totally,' I agreed. 'I saw Lord of the Dance once in Dublin. I was over there for work and managed to get tickets. There was something magical about seeing those dancers in the heart of the place where it all began. You don't get that anywhere else.'

'Exactly!' Olivia nodded enthusiastically. 'Anyway, how are you? Jake says you've been working really hard. And you have to work tomorrow?'

'Yes. Sadly. Don't worry, I won't cut the night short or anything. But it's much easier if I'm at home.'

'You're quite safe with us. We can't do all night raves anymore. I do like to be in bed before midnight.'

'I hope not tonight, Liv,' Jake said. 'I barely see you. When we've finished in town, the party will be continuing back at mine.'

'We can't carry on partying without Isobel,' Olivia objected. I saw Jake shake his head. He probably didn't care either way.

Within ten minutes we'd arrived at the waterfront. It was a newer part of Ipswich that had been built up around the gorgeous marina, and on a summer's evening like this one it attracted hundreds of people.

The car drove down as far as it could, passed all the restaurants and bars, and the stares of the public. It was a beautiful setting with million pound boats moored up all around us, but the Rolls Royce seemed to be grabbing all the attention. I felt quite the spectacle.

The car stopped outside of one of my favourite bars –

The Kiln By The Quay - and we got out.

'I love this place,' I told Jake as he grabbed my hand. It wasn't a place I frequented very often. I used to go there on Friday night after-work drinks, when I'd be trying to establish a name for myself with the senior management team. But that was all a long time ago now.

Jake's trademark smile warmed his face. 'Me too. It's my favourite place in Ipswich.'

'Me too! But we'll be lucky to get a table on a Friday night.'

Jake just shook his head again. I went to join the small queue of people waiting to get in when Jake pulled me back towards him. He headed straight towards the bouncer.

'Jake, nice to see you. Come on in.' The tall, broad man waved us all through and Jake made a beeline for a table in the corner of the outside section. It was definitely the best table in the place with undisturbed views across the marina. I couldn't believe it was vacant.

'It says reserved,' I said as we approached it.

Jake nodded. 'For us.'

'I didn't know you could reserve tables in this place,' I commented.

He shrugged. 'I know people.'

'You know what Jake's like,' Olivia said. 'You want something sorted, he's the man to ask.'

'So I'm learning,' I said as I took a seat.

'What are we all drinking then?' Jake asked.

'Shall we share a bottle of wine?' Olivia asked me as she took the seat opposite.

'Sounds great. What do you like? White or red?' I asked.

'I think you girls should have Champagne,' Jake replied. 'We're still celebrating your wedding.'

'We also need to celebrate the two of you getting together,' Olivia sang, pointing between me and Jake.

I looked straight over at Jake and he just nodded. I felt my body tense up.

'Help me, mate?' Jake said to Harrison.

'We're having beer, right?' Harrison said.

'Yeah. And lots of it,' Jake replied.

The men walked off and Olivia immediately locked eyes with me.

'Shame you can't stay over tonight,' she said.

'I know. Next time maybe. But more room for you lot!'

Olivia started laughing. 'Yeah. Four of us would certainly be a squash, wouldn't it!' I wasn't sure what the joke was, but Olivia was still laughing. She then grabbed my hand and focused on me more seriously.

'Look, while Jake's gone, I have to tell you. I have never seen Jake this happy.'

'That's really nice,' I said, feeling quite sure that any mood changes were completely unrelated to me.

'He's like a different man. He was singing around the house earlier. Singing!'

Jake had always been so full of life at our meetings. I didn't think singing seemed like a big shift in his character. But it was dawning on me that there was a lot about him I didn't know.

'He never used to sing then?' I asked.

Olivia shook her head as a far more serious expression grabbed her face. She sat back. 'I suppose I didn't know him before Michelle.' Oliva paused. 'Harrison was his friend from uni.' She batted her hand. 'I shouldn't be saying any of this. You don't need to know all that. The important thing is that he seems really happy with you now. We're so pleased you came into his life. He deserves to be happy. He's a really great bloke. Honestly, he's one of the best.'

'He's never mentioned a Michelle,' I said truthfully.

'Oh shit. Then forget I said anything. Please don't ask him about her. I'm sure he'll tell you one day. But let him tell you when the time is right.'

'That doesn't sound good.'

'We all have baggage.'

In my case it was more like a laptop bag, but I understood her point.

'I won't say anything to him. But just tell me, is there anything I need to be concerned about?'

'Of course there isn't! He went through a bad patch. Who hasn't? But he's happy now. You're the best thing to happen to him for a long time. Believe me. You have nothing to worry about.'

The sickening feeling in my stomach begged to differ.

'Here you go, ladies,' Harrison said as a bottle of Dom Perignon was placed down before us.

'Harry, this is far too expensive!' Olivia said.

'Don't look at me. Courtesy of Jake.'

Jake placed two pints of Peroni down and took the seat next to me. 'I couldn't buy you cheap Champagne, could I,' he said. 'Not when it's a celebration.'

The cork had been pre-popped and Harrison kindly poured me and Olivia a glass each, then we all held up our drinks for a toast.

'To new starts,' Olivia said.

'New starts,' we all agreed as we clinked and sipped.

'Jacob Masters!' a voice said from the marina side.

We all turned to see who was approaching us.

'Gav!' Jake said with delight. 'What are you doing here?'

'What are *you* doing here more like! We've not seen you in ages. Not since you moved to Henstone.'

He lives in Henstone? That was a village about ten miles away. As far as I knew there wasn't much there. Why would he move all the way out there?

'My uni friends are visiting me tonight,' Jake said, pointing to Olivia and Harrison.

'Nice to meet you,' Olivia said. 'So you won't have met Jake's new girlfriend then?' she added, pointing to me.

'Jake!' a girl screamed running up towards Gav.

'Hello, Kelly,' Jake said, his smile broadening.

'This is Jake's new girlfriend,' Gav told her.

Her face lit up with wonder. 'You're Jake's girlfriend?'

All I could do was smile.

'This is Isobel,' Jake said. 'I see you've mellowed over

the years, Kell.' He laughed.

Kelly stuck out her tongue at Jake before turning her attention back to me. She was so excited. 'It's so lovely to meet you! Oh, we have to go out sometime. Get the old crowd together. Wait until we tell them we bumped into you.'

'You still see everyone, then?' Jake asked.

'Yeah, all the time. We miss you, mate,' Gav answered.

They were clearly the same age as Jake and obviously knew him very well. School friends perhaps? She was a mousy, skinny girl, but her looks defied her loud voice and bubbly persona, and Gav seemed equally as slight and equally as full of life. I really liked them. Just as I seemed to like all of Jake's friends.

'We'll get something organised,' Jake said.

'How about we all come over to yours again?' Gav pushed. 'Your housewarming is still talked about as the party of the century.'

'We saw the pictures,' Harrison said.

'It was legendary! He's got the best house for parties, hasn't he,' Kelly said, once again looking directly at me.

I nodded. That's all I could do. I was starting to build up images of a large house with bouncy castles and a bar in the garden.

'You should so arrange that,' Olivia encouraged.

'What about next weekend?' Gav asked.

'That's pretty short notice,' Jake said. 'People will have plans.'

'When they find out you're having a party - *and* you've got a new girlfriend - I can't see anything being more important.'

'Will you be free?' Olivia asked me.

'What?' I said, feeling dazed by everything.

'She has to work weekends,' Olivia explained to the others.

'Oh no, you have to be there,' Kelly said with concern. 'We can't have a party without you.'

I turned to Jake who gave nothing away. What the hell was happening?

'Depends on whether you want me there with all your mates,' I said, giving him his out. 'You probably don't want your girlfriend getting in the way. You haven't seen them all in ages.'

There was a small pause and then he said, 'If you're not working, I'd love you to be there.' What the fuck? Why was he doing this to me!

'Aww.' Kelly and Olivia made the same cute little sound simultaneously, looking at us as if we were the perfect couple. This could not get more difficult.

Did I want to continue this façade anymore?

Absolutely not. I should say I'm working.

But did I want to see Jake's house?

Hell yeah. I wanted to know exactly why he lived miles away from anyone else and what made this place the party venue of Suffolk.

I also wanted to know why one of the most eligible bachelors in the whole of East Anglia was so desperate to cling on to a fake girlfriend.

Curiosity was getting the better of me.

Okay, you know me too well now. A very pathetic need to know if anything could ever happen between us was also playing its part. I was in love with him. I couldn't help it.

'Great,' I said to Jake. 'Should be fun.'

'Yay!' Kelly bounced on the spot and clapped her hands.

'I'll text you in the week, mate,' Gav said. 'Let you know who's coming.'

'All right.'

They waved goodbye and Jake took a big gulp of Peroni.

'Sorry,' he whispered in my ear.

'I'm certainly meeting a lot of your friends in a short space of time,' I said, taking a gulp of Champagne myself.

'I wish we could join you, mate,' Harrison said. 'Send us some photos.'

'Will do.'

SIX

For the rest of the night, we didn't move anywhere. We had the perfect spot to sit and drink on a perfectly warm night. If only everything else had been perfect.

After Kelly and Gav had left, I had to listen to about two hours of Jake, Olivia and Harrison all sharing stories of the old days; completely excluding me.

I'd excused myself to go to the toilet when I could take it no more. It was so boring listening to in-jokes and tales of people I'd never met. I took my time, amusing myself with a quick game of Spider Solitaire to waste away a few minutes, and when I returned I think they'd got the hint. I'd lied about how massive the queue had been to justify my long absence, and Olivia quickly began to ask me questions about my job, to make sure I was finally involved in the conversation.

Whilst that was incredibly nice of her, my pretend boyfriend switched off after five minutes. He turned to Harrison and began telling him about all of the woes of being an Ipswich Town football club supporter.

Just like at the wedding, I barely got his attention all night. Every now and then he'd smile my way and make a weak attempt to check I was okay, and then he'd go back to ignoring me again. It was really irritating.

At just before midnight, as the place was closing up, the Rolls Royce reappeared and we climbed in.

The laughter between the three friends was so joyful as we drove back to my house, but I was finding it hard to raise a smile. I was utterly fed up.

When we pulled up outside my house a few minutes later, I couldn't wait to get out of the car.

I quickly said my goodbyes and then fumbled for my key as I made my way directly to my front door.

'Are you okay?' Jake asked, suddenly appearing next to me.

'Yes, are you?' I said as I opened up.

'I'm really sorry about Kell and Gav and having that party next week.'

I was just about to respond when Jake yelled, 'Shit! Ow! What the fuck!'

We both looked down to see Smokey wrapped around Jake's leg, digging his claws and his teeth into Jake's jeans.

'Smokey!' I said, trying to pull the cat off. He eventually gave up and Jake winced at the pain.

'Are you okay?' I said, throwing the cat aside. 'Bad boy!' I yelled before turning back to Jake. 'Come in, let's take a quick look at you.'

Jake hobbled inside and I slammed the door shut before Smokey could follow us. Jake sat on my cream settee and we pulled up his jeans as much as we could. Thankfully, there were just a few scratches. Not too much damage. Well, except for his pride.

'That bastard cat. I think he's jealous,' Jake said.

'He's been exceptionally needy lately. He's here all the time. I might have to look into that new door.'

'I can probably fit it for you.'

'No, it's fine,' I said quickly. Jake looked at me, clearly confused by my sudden snap. I added, 'If we're not careful you'll be over here all the time as well and we really will be boyfriend and girlfriend.'

'Again, I am sorry about next weekend. You don't have to play along. I'll say you're working.'

'No, it's fine. It's not like I have anything better to do. Besides, I'm quite curious about your house. You live in Henstone?'

Jake shrugged. 'It's a nice place. You ever been?'

'I don't even know what's there. What is there? Why did you move?'

'It's quiet. I like how remote it is.'

'You can say that again.'

'There is a pub, though. We can head there first. We won't be stuck in my house all night, don't worry. Give you chance for a break.'

'Are we going to have to share a room again?' I asked, this time nowhere near as happy about the concept.

'It'll be fine this time,' he said. 'I have a sofa in my bedroom. I'll sleep on that.'

I felt relieved. I didn't know how much more my heart could take. These nights out were killing me, but I just couldn't form the word to tell him no. I knew I was fooling myself into the notion that eventually he'd fall in love with me. Of course I was. But somewhere deep inside I also knew the truth that it was never going to happen.

Yet still I kept torturing myself.

I caught him studying my face.

'What are you thinking?' he said.

'I'm thinking about you. Your friends seem so pleased that you've got a girlfriend. What's that about?'

He shrugged. 'I'm just the bachelor who seems to have settled down. They think you've tamed the beast.' I knew this was a lie. Olivia had warned me not to ask him. As much as I wanted to, I felt it best to respect his secret. I'd given him the opportunity to tell me and he hadn't. I needed to leave it there.

I tidied up the leg of his jeans and helped him to his feet.

'I'll see you next week, then,' I said.

'I'll come and collect you on Saturday afternoon, if that's

all right? Give you chance to get to know the place before the others arrive. Can't have my girlfriend not even knowing where the toilet is, can I.'

'No. Good thinking. Text me what time. I really won't be working.'

'I can't thank you enough,' he said. 'We'll set up a time to talk about your business. I owe you that much. I have some ideas that I think could really help you.'

'Yeah. Let's set that up.' I wasn't remotely interested in that. I wanted to get this weekend out of the way and then I knew I'd have to say goodbye to Jake once and for all. I was even considering leaving the networking group. It was just too hard and too painful.

'See you soon,' I said, opening the front door.

Smokey was sat on the lawn and as soon as Jake stepped outside Smokey hissed at him. It made me laugh but Jake seemed quite shook up.

'You'd better look after me or Smokey's coming for you,' I joked.

Smokey lurched forward to attack Jake again and Jake ran to the car.

'Goodnight!' he shouted before jumping in the back seat next to his friends.

'Goodnight,' I said waving goodbye as my heart tore into shreds.

This was absolutely the worst thing I could be doing. But I knew I wouldn't back out. I had to see Jake's house.

I closed the door and locked it up and then I turned around to see Smokey sitting in the middle of the floor staring at me. He didn't look impressed.

'Go home,' I said to him before I headed upstairs full of self-pity.

I fell straight to sleep after all that fizz, but it was far from a restful night. By the time I woke up at around seven o'clock, I felt absolutely rotten. And it wasn't just the hangover.

I sat up to check my phone when I saw Smokey glaring

at me from the end of bed. The cheeky cat had probably been there all night.

'Go away,' I said to him. But rather than him listen to this – when I know he understood me – he had the nerve to saunter over my duvet and snuggle up next to me.

I pushed him off the bed and got up, but still he didn't get the hint. He tried to follow me into the bathroom.

I slammed the door shut as I turned the shower on. I needed to wash off the night before.

I stepped into my tiny shower cubicle and I enjoyed the feel of the steamy water. I was in no rush that day, so I spent about forty minutes pampering myself and trying not to think about Jake and how painful this experience was turning out to be. Although, inevitably, that was all I could think about.

I switched off the shower and put my hand out to grab the towel that hung on the rail, but as I reached forward I noticed the door wide open.

I shrieked when I saw Smokey sitting there staring at my fully naked body. I swear he was smiling.

'Get out!' I shouted. 'You horrible cat! Get out!'

How he'd opened the door was beyond me. He really was a clever cat. If one day I found there to be a secret utility belt underneath his fur, it wouldn't have surprised me.

I quickly dried myself, got dressed and blasted my hair with my hairdryer.

I threw Smokey out of the front door, but he didn't go far. He sat on my front pathway looking indignant, as if he were the best behaved cat in the world and I was being particularly cruel with my treatment.

I knew it wouldn't be long before he'd find a way back in. I could see those blue eyes concocting a plan right before me. I really was left with no choice. My first task that day would be to find a replacement door. And my second task would be to find someone to help me replace it.

I tried to shoo Smokey away just as a voice startled me.

'Morning!'

It was my next door neighbour. She was a lady around retirement age who I think lived on her own. She was always out tinkering with her garden.

'Morning,' I replied, and then I grabbed the chance. 'Is this your cat?'

'No, love,' she said.

'It's constantly in my house. I don't know where it's come from.'

'It's that man's across the road,' she said, as if this were completely obvious. 'Number eighteen.' I looked at the large house across the street. It was much bigger than mine, with three floors. It seemed to loom down over me. 'He owns it, but you're the one that seems to look after it.'

'Not through choice.'

She shrugged as if she didn't believe me and I felt a rush of indignation. Why would I be desperately shooing away this irritating cat if I was secretly trying to make it my own? Some people never applied logic to their thinking.

'I think I'll go and have a word,' I said, making a point that I did not want this cat in my life.

'I bet you will,' she said with a knowing smile. I didn't know what she thought she knew, and I wasn't interested enough to probe. I had located Smokey's actual home and that was my main priority.

Ignoring her comment, I headed back inside to grab my shoes and keys. When I returned to my front door Smokey was still sitting there. I picked him up and carried him across the road to the mystery man's house. I don't recall ever seeing this man, but that wasn't strange. Even though I worked from home now, I was still chained to my desk most of the day, or out at meetings. The only reason I knew my neighbour was that she was always outside, come rain or shine. And I still didn't know her name.

Maybe I should have asked.

I walked up the little pathway next to the slightly overgrown lawn and I rang the bell.

No one answered. I gave it a few more minutes and still

no one answered.

I couldn't resist taking a quick peek through the window just to the left of the door. I wasn't normally nosey, but it was just there, inviting me to look through. I couldn't see much, just an immaculate living room. It didn't appear as if anyone was home.

Although actually, it was about half eight on a Sunday morning. Maybe he was still in bed?

Feeling bad that I was bothering someone so early, I put Smokey down.

'Stay here. This looks like a nice house. Much better than mine. Will you stay now?'

He didn't move. He sat on the doorstep glaring at me.

I walked back over the road and thankfully Smokey didn't follow. Maybe he'd finally got the hint.

'Is he not in?' my next door neighbour asked.

'It would appear not.'

'I'm sure you'll try again.'

I paused, still unsure what her meaning was, but I decided yet again to ignore it. It was probably better that way. I had no time to get drawn into idle gossip. I'd seen her chatting to enough people to know this lady liked a good gossip.

I let myself in and made a beeline for my little home office upstairs. I switched my laptop on and began my search for a new door. If nothing else, it was a welcome distraction from the taunting thoughts of Jake.

About ten minutes later my doorbell rang.

My doorbell never rang unless I was expecting a parcel. I knew no one socially in the area and even sales calls tended to be few and far between.

I headed down the stairs, curious as to whom it was. I opened the door to find a stunning man staring back at me. He was like a God, with brown floppy hair, a chiselled jaw and glistening blue eyes.

'Sorry, you rang on my door,' he said very politely, maybe with a Home Counties accent? He definitely wasn't local. 'I live across the road. I was in the shower but I saw you head back over this way. Thought I'd be courteous and return the call, so to speak.' He laughed and I clocked his brilliant white teeth.

'Hi,' I said, momentarily flummoxed. I had expected an older gentleman whose cat was his only friend. You don't expect someone with movie star looks to be living across the street from you. How had I not noticed him before?

'I was bringing your cat back,' I said, before realising that I didn't actually know for sure if Smokey was this man's cat. 'Sorry. The grey cat. The lady next door said he was yours.'

'Yes. Smokey. He hasn't been bothering you, has he?'

'He's called Smokey?' I asked with surprise.

'Yes. Why?'

'That's what I nicknamed him. Well, Smokey the wonder cat actually. If you're ever wondering where he is, he's most likely in my house. I keep locking the cat flat but he keeps finding a way in. I don't know how he's doing it.'

'Oh, well he used to be a cat detective, working with Scotland Yard. He was trained to break into almost anywhere. But when they get to about six years' old they have to be adopted out. He's my third cat from the police.'

I was gobsmacked. 'Really?'

'No.' The gorgeous man started laughing. 'Just kidding. He's a devil of a cat. It's probably a loose cat flap and he's worked it out. They learn quick.'

'Oh right.' I laughed too. 'He certainly is a clever cat.' Despite the apparent jovial nature, something about this exchange was starting to unnerve me. As good looking as this man was, he was also a little creepy. He kept staring at me intently.

'Sorry if he's bothersome,' the man said. 'Do you like cats?'

'Oh yes, I love cats. But I know he's yours. Please don't worry, I'm going to get rid of the cat flap.'

'No! Don't do that,' he said, rather urgently.

'Why?'

'The doors in these houses. They're made to measure. It'll cost you a fortune to replace it. I had to. Had a break in. Cost me nearly a thousand pounds.'

'What? You had a break in? When was that?'

'Don't worry. It was targeted. I deal in finance and they were trying to... long story. Anyway, the doors are very expensive to replace. Maybe you could just get a new cat flap? That would be much cheaper. And I'd be happy to foot the bill seen as it's my naughty cat who's causing you all these issues.'

'Erm. You don't have to do that. Don't be silly. I'll check out a few options. I'm sure he'll get bored eventually, anyway.'

'I wouldn't be so sure. A beautiful girl like you. It's not hard to see why he's hanging around so much.'

If Jake had said something like that, I would have been putty in his hands. But this man's attempts at seduction made my skin crawl. Although I couldn't work out why.

'Sorry, I should introduce myself,' he said. 'I'm Nicholas.'

'Nice to meet you. I'm Isobel.'

'Lovely to meet you. I don't know how we've missed each other before. I must apologise. I work from home, but I'm normally chained to my computer, barely seeing daylight.'

'I'm exactly the same. I work from home too, but I've never been able to get the work life balance quite right.'

'Fancy that. What do you do?'

'I'm a Virtual Assistant. You said you work in finance?'

'Yes. I consult mainly, although I am an FD for a few businesses. Non-executive. You know how it works, I'm sure.'

'Yes. Sounds interesting.'

I knew this meant he was on the board of a business but not part of the management team. To do this for a few companies certainly seemed to suggest that he was good at his job. He was handsome, ambitious and successful. Why was I not swooning?

Jake Masters. That's why. Bloody Jake Masters was in my head, ruining me for any other man.

'Excuse my forwardness. I know we've only just met,' he said, his voice softening. 'But both being the workaholics that we are, perhaps I could take you out for a drink sometime? Force us to get out of the house? It would be lovely to get to know you better.'

This could be it. The perfect chance to get Jake out of my system. This is exactly what I should be doing: dating other men. Even though I was strangely not at all attracted to the man before me who ticked every single box, I knew I would have been crazy not to accept this offer to get to know him better. Put Jake behind me. Move on. This was the best decision.

'That's very kind of you to ask,' I said. 'But I have a boyfriend.'

The words just came out. I don't know where from. What the hell made me say that?

I told myself in that instant it was just the complicated nature of my situation and I should 'break up' with Jake first before I started to date other men.

That may have been an element of it, sure. But I was holding out for Jake. I was. And it was probably going to kill me.

'Right,' Nicholas said. He seemed quite surprised. 'Boyfriend? What a lucky man he is.'

'It's early days,' I said.

'Well. Best of luck. If anything changes, do let me know. I'd be very keen to get to know you better.'

'That's very sweet. Of course I'll let you know. I know where you live.' I laughed. This was now getting very awkward.

'And if Smokey becomes a lot of trouble, please don't hesitate to drop by and let me know. The last thing I want is to cause you any problems. I can always lock him indoors for a few days to see if it'll calm him down.'

'I don't know if that will work. I bet that cat could pick a lock!'

Nicholas laughed heartily. It wasn't that funny.

'Nice to meet you Isobel. Have a good day.'

'You too. Bye.'

I closed the door and stood still for a moment. That had been quite bizarre. I didn't know whether to feel flattered or creeped out. Although why he made me on edge was a mystery. It had to be some sort of weird guilt about Jake.

This was becoming increasingly bad for my health. I had to get this house party out of the way and then I needed to end this cycle once and for all.

I nipped back upstairs and returned to my laptop.

Nicholas's advice about the doors echoed through my mind. Made to measure? It was just a simple house.

Maybe I could ask Jake his thoughts on that. He seemed to know about doors. More than I did. I might as well use this fake relationship to my advantage while I could.

I closed down the web pages about doors and opened up my email. I had nothing better to do. I might as well do some work.

SEVEN

Another week of hard work flew by. I'd worked very long hours, even for me. Mostly to distract myself from the nausea of considering the weekend ahead, but also to stop myself from over-analysing why I'd told the gorgeous man across the road I had a boyfriend when I was perfectly free and single to date anyone I wanted.

Since Nicholas had visited me, I'd seen Smokey a little less. He still popped by, but just for day visits. He wasn't watching me sleep anymore, so that was good. I had imagined Nicholas sitting him down and giving him a stern talking to.

On the plus side, burying my head into my work even more than normal had certainly paid off. I'd gained two more clients that week. Business was indeed booming.

If only my excitement levels were.

It was now Saturday afternoon again and I was pacing around feeling sick as I waited for Jake to collect me. I was both dreading seeing him whilst also jittery with eager anticipation. It was torment. I didn't know what to do with myself.

The bell chimed at just after half two and I opened the door.

Jake stood there full of smiles. Forget the stud across the road, Jake was five times more attractive. He oozed charm and warmth, and it was very hard to resist him. I could never tell Jake I had a boyfriend. Even if I had got one.

'Hi. How are you?' he said. 'Had a good week?'

'You know. The usual. Working hard. I got two new clients.'

'Good for you!'

'Thanks. I'll just grab my bag.'

I nipped inside to collect my things. I was gone for like half a minute, but by the time I reached the front door again Jake was battling with Smokey.

'Fuck off!' Jake said, trying to prize Smokey's vice-like grip from his leg. Those poor well-fitting jeans were going to be in shreds before long.

'Smokey, get off!' I shouted, running forward. I clutched the cat and gently tried to encourage him off. I didn't want to hurt the furry little thing, but I couldn't let him hurt Jake either.

'Ow, he's really digging his claws in,' Jake whimpered as he shook his leg. Smokey hissed up at Jake before taking another bite.

'I know whose cat he is now. Hang on.'

I raced across the road and knocked on Nicholas's door. 'Nicholas?' I shouted through. 'It's Isobel from across the street. I need your help with Smokey.'

There was no answer. I looked through the window again, being uncharacteristically nosey for the second time, but the house seemed totally empty.

I raced back to Jake, but all I saw was my front door closed and Smokey jumping up against it, hissing and screeching. I'd never seen a cat dislike someone so much.

'Smokey!' I shouted as I joined him on my little pathway. 'Bad cat. Leave Jake alone.'

Smokey sat very still and glared at up me with clear disapproval.

'What has Jake done?' I asked. 'He's been nothing but

nice to you. I won't stand for it. Go back home this instant. I'm warning you.'

Smokey didn't move. Not that I had expected him to.

'Jake,' I said, knocking on my own door. Jake opened it a crack.

'Sorry,' he said. 'This is crazy. He's actually shed blood this time. It's an evil cat.'

'I don't know what's got into him. He's normally so nice.'

'I told you. He's jealous. He wants you all to himself.'

I looked down at Smokey who was sitting firmly on my front step. It certainly did appear as if he were jealous. But I wasn't even his owner.

I'd have to speak to Nicholas about this. This couldn't go on. It wasn't fair on me or Jake.

'Hang on,' I told Jake. 'I'll take him back over. Grab my bag and I'll meet you in the car.'

'Thanks,' Jake said. 'And sorry.' He sounded very unnerved. It probably should have been amusing, except Smokey clearly meant business.

I picked up the cat. Not once had he ever even slightly objected to me handling him, which I knew was most unusual for cats. I may not have ever had a pet cat, but they weren't strangers in my life.

There was a time growing up when I'd wake up in the morning and there would be a line of cats sitting outside the window waiting for the curtain to open to catch a glimpse of me. It had made me laugh. I'd never been bothered by it. It had freaked my parents out, but I used to go out and play with them. They seemed to adore me. But even then, if I tried to pick one up when it wasn't in the mood, it would soon let me know.

Smokey, on the other hand, seemed to relish the attention, regardless of what mood he was in. And he was certainly in a bad mood right now. He had venom in those sparkling blue eyes.

I took him across the road and turned around to check

that Jake had made his escape. Jake nipped out with my bag and safely accessed his car.

I placed Smokey down and told him to stay put. I then raced back, locked up and jumped in the passenger seat.

Smokey hadn't followed me. Well, not with his legs. But his eyes watched my every move, intently staring until we were completely out of sight.

'That cat is nuts,' Jake said, rubbing his leg.

'Make sure you wash your leg when you get home. You got any plasters?'

'I'll be all right.'

'You don't know where he's been. That cat could have been anywhere. Making weapons or anything. He's clever enough.'

We both started laughing.

'I'm telling you, he's jealous. He must think we really are boyfriend and girlfriend.' Jake laughed again but I was silenced by the sting in his words.

Smokey might be fooled, but I wasn't. Jake was everything I wanted in a man and nothing I wanted in a partner. It was devastating.

I just had to get through this weekend and I was home free. I would absolutely not be agreeing to any more dates. Ever again. This was it.

Jake chatted away as we made the twenty-five minute journey to his house, but I mainly ignored him. Not deliberately, but my mind just wouldn't stop wandering elsewhere.

As we moved further away from Ipswich, the land became more and more rural, and as we finally entered Henstone I couldn't see what the appeal was at all.

I was far from a city girl. I'd been happy to leave the chaos of London behind. I much preferred fresh air and space than the buzz of the urban jungle. But this was too rural, even for me.

There were a few houses, one shop, and then we drove past "The White Lion", the pub that Jake described as

Henstone's one and only form of entertainment.

We carried on for a couple of minutes more until we reached a single track road. Jake's Jaguar seemed at odds to what really should have been reserved for farm vehicles only. But on we went.

And then it appeared. At the end of the road was a gate, and behind it was the biggest house I'd ever seen.

It wasn't new. The heart of the property was mainly stone and it was clearly drenched in history. But across the land were more modern features, like a conservatory, a double garage and an extra little building that was probably a games room or something. We parked outside the front and I was in absolute awe.

'You live here?' I said.

'Yeah.'

'Alone?'

'Yeah.'

'No wonder your friends wanted to come here. How many bedrooms has it got?'

'Seven,' he said. His answers were clipped, bordering on embarrassed.

'Good for you.'

I decided to bring my awe to an end. He clearly didn't want to talk about it, and I'd have to insist upon a tour anyway to make it seem like I knew the ins and outs of the place as his girlfriend. So I'd quietly take it all in when he showed me around. I didn't want to embarrass him anymore.

Although how you could be embarrassed by this place was beyond me. It was incredible.

He grabbed my bag from the boot and led me to the front door. He opened up, fiddled with his security device and I stepped in.

The entrance wasn't big, but there were doors in all directions. We headed right, into his enormous living room. To say it was light was a vast understatement. The sun poured in through the giant windows, giving the modern décor an extra special uplift. The wooden floors were perfect, with just a navy rug across the middle that looked so sumptuous I wanted to whip off my sandals and bury my toes in it.

Maybe later.

'So this is the living room,' he said, putting his car keys on a little plate on a shelf.

I scanned the room some more. The TV that hung on the wall was more like a cinema screen, and below it was an enclosed black unit that I guessed hid a million gadgets.

On the other wall there were two dramatic pictures of the sea. As I took it all in, I noticed how the paintings complemented the giant blue sofa, making it somehow look like the depths of the ocean.

'You like the sea?' I asked.

'Very much so. Whenever there's nice weather you'll find me in Dunwich or Felixstowe, or pretty much anywhere else there's a beach.'

'I love Felixstowe.'

'I only ever go to the top end, where you can escape the crowds and just listen to the waves.'

'Yes. I know exactly where you mean. There's this little bench on the cliff top and I sometimes sit there for hours, watching the world go by. It's so relaxing.'

'Yes!' he said, smiling.

I continued to stare at everything, relishing in this new view of Jake all around me.

'You're very tidy,' I said.

He smirked and mumbled something about a cleaner, but again he seemed quite sheepish.

'I suppose you'd better show me every inch of this place,' I said, making it out as if it were a chore. 'Someone's bound to ask me something later, assuming I'm here all the time.'

'Of course. This way.'

He led me through a door towards the back of the room which revealed what looked like another living room, but this one faced the acres of land that stretched outside.

'That's your garden?' I asked with amazement.

'Not all of it. There are other farms in the area. I just have what you see directly leading from this house.'

'Wow. Even so. That must be a bitch to look after.'

He mumbled something about a gardener, but I didn't pick up exactly what he said.

'Can we look outside?' I asked.

'Sure,' he said, opening the patio door. I stepped out onto the paving stones and got my first real look at it.

To the right was a whole area of decking next to a paved section that held a barbecue.

'Look at that! Are we having a barbecue later?' I asked.

'No. It gets messy with my mates, trust me. I've ordered some catering in.'

'Like a take-away?' I asked.

'Of sorts.'

Then I turned to the left and my jaw dropped open. He had a swimming pool. An actual swimming pool!

'This is the best house I've ever seen!' I said.

My mind flicked back to the rumours I'd heard about him. He might not have sold his app for ten million pounds, but he certainly must have made a decent sum of money out of it. Why on earth wouldn't you move here if you could? I was in heaven.

I ran onto the perfectly mowed grass and took in the house from the back. It was so big but so homely. I should have been intimidated, but I was the most relaxed I'd ever been in Jake's company.

I looked over at him and noticed how he seemed the complete opposite.

'Shall we move on?' he said, eager to get the tour over with.

'Two more minutes,' I said, turning around to take in the landscape, loving the combination of perfect sun and perfect silence.

But as I let my surroundings soak in, that niggling

thought I'd had about why a millionaire would come to our networking meetings and faff around with one man bands re-entered my mind.

He clearly was a millionaire. Yet he still spent his time helping small businesses find success.

Was he really just Mr Absolute-Nice-Guy? Or was there something I was missing?

'Where have they come from?' Jake asked, sounding concerned.

I turned around to find his face just as concerned as his voice.

'Look.'

I followed his glare to see four cats sitting by my side. I laughed.

'What can I say? Cats adore me. I've had this all my life. I think my sweat must smell of catnip or something.'

'What do you mean all your life?' Jake asked.

'I'm like some sort of cat magnet. They always seem to flock around me.'

'I didn't even know there were cats in the area.'

'Yeah. They sniff me out.'

'Doesn't that bother you?'

'Not at all. It's a bit annoying when they come into your house. But that's only ever been Smokey. Other than that, they've just always watched me or played with me. It's like having groupies. I see it as flattering.'

'I think it's a bit disturbing. You don't really smell of catnip do you?'

'You tell me.' I stepped over towards Jake, being more confident than usual around him.

I stood before him, glad of the perfume I'd drenched myself in not an hour before. He took a very subtle sniff and everything went very quiet.

Jake looked me directly in the eyes, and neither of us said a word for a good minute or so. Then he uttered, 'You smell beautiful.' He took a step away from me. 'They won't follow us in, will they? I like cats, but I don't want to wake up next to one.'

'Don't worry. I'm sure they'll just watch us from afar.'

'Let's hope these aren't as protective of you as Smokey is.' Jake studied them and I could see a drop of fear in his eyes. Although after Smokey's antics, I thought that was fair enough.

'Right, next stop then,' he said.

Next he showed me his enormous kitchen full of mod cons, followed by his separate dining room that could easily sit ten. Ten!

After that we visited his secret building outside. It was originally a practical place for the farm, but he'd turned it into his home gym. Of course.

Then he showed me upstairs, taking me through all of the bedrooms (including the one that was his office) and the bathrooms.

But he saved the best until last. After we'd seen everything else, I finally got to enter the master bedroom - the room where Jake slept. Where I'd be joining him that night.

As expected, it was huge. The bed could probably sleep eight. There was a desk in the corner, a huge fitted wardrobe, a door to the side that I guessed led to the en suite, the large, comfy sofa where Jake said he'd be sleeping that night, and then, totally to my surprise, a free standing bath near the window.

'A bath?' I said.

He couldn't look at me.

There were two other baths in the house. The fact that he had a separate one in the bedroom was very unexpected.

'What a lovely idea,' I added when he didn't respond. I didn't want him thinking I was criticising him. Far from it. 'Do you use it often?'

'Never,' he said in that clipped tone again.

'So it was here when you moved in?' I asked.

He shook his head.

'I'll just grab your bag and bring it up,' he said. 'Feel free to keep nosing around.'

As much as this open invitation delighted me, all I found myself doing was sitting on his bed and staring at the bath. I had been so eager to find out what sort of house Jake lived in, it hadn't occurred to me just how much I'd get to see into his world. I felt as if I knew him better now, but this insight into his life had also left me with a million more questions that suddenly needed answering.

There was one thing I knew for sure, though. I was head over heels in love. I loved his house, I loved how he'd decorated it, I loved all the choices he'd made, and I loved him.

His friends were probably all setting off soon for what they were imagining to be the party of the year. All I could think of was how I was going to survive it unscathed.

EIGHT

It was shortly after five o'clock when the first of Jake's friends arrived, and then by five-thirty all eight of them were there. We made up five cosy couples in total, and I could see why Jake was so reluctant to be viewed as the single friend.

As each person entered, they all made a point of saying hello to me, eager to find out who Jake's new girlfriend was. Having been so out of touch with any sort of social scene in such a long time, I automatically adopted the formalities of business, and for every person that approached me, I stuck out my hand to shake. And every one of them ignored it and moved in for a hug.

Yet again, all of Jake's friends were thoroughly lovely, and they all seemed thrilled by the notion that, not only did he have a new girlfriend, but I seemed nice and he seemed happy.

I'd rarely ever seen Jake without a smile on his face. To know that his friends were so relieved that he was happy – as if this weren't the norm - was quite a revelation. I knew I'd have to dig deeper into this as the night went on.

After a drink outside on the decking, Jake suggested that

we go to the local for a couple before the catering arrived. I got the feeling that it was going to be far more impressive than pizza or a Chinese, but whenever I'd broached the subject with Jake he'd been coy about it. I guess I'd find out soon enough!

We all got ourselves ready and then we sauntered down the long single track road and off into the village of Henstone.

It took about twenty minutes to get to the pub and it was such a pleasant journey. Jake even walked by my side. He didn't say a word to me, he was too engrossed talking with his friends, but it was nice that at least we were together.

We arrived at the pub and one of Jake's friends opened the door. We all poured in and I was instantly stunned by the reception.

It was a proper local pub, with wooden beams, a paved floor and a real rustic feel. But I had flashes of old Western movies when every punter in there turned to us and glared. The whole place fell silent as they watched us enter the establishment. They seemed hostile and suspicious, as if we could be aliens from another planet and they were yet unsure as to whether we came in peace or not. I'd never felt so unwelcome anywhere.

'Hi Kim,' Jake announced, heading towards the bar. 'Got my old school mates here. I promise we'll behave ourselves.'

His words seemed to knock the tension down by about ten percent, but we were still being glared at.

'You always behave yourself,' the lady behind the bar said with a true Suffolk accent. She offered a cheeky smile in Jake's direction and I could tell she was used to flirting with him. I couldn't help but burn with jealousy. How ridiculous was that!

Jake leant against the bar. 'You're looking really well. The holiday's done you the world of good.'

'At least forty degrees every day and we did absolutely nothing. Heaven. Can't thank you enough.'

'Anything for my favourite landlady.'

'Usual?' she asked, but my brain was still processing why she was thanking Jake.

'Yeah, I think I will.' Jake then turned around. 'What's everyone else having?'

The orders came flying in and Jake paid for it all. He was so generous.

Although as I shot an unintentional death stare at Kim the landlady, I considered that maybe he was too generous.

We took our drinks towards the back where there were two tables near each other. We were still being periodically watched by the fellow drinkers, as if they needed to keep an eye on us in case we did something crazy. It made it very hard to relax.

I sat down and Jake sat near me, sort of hovering between the two tables. As the host, this made sense. He wanted to be sociable. I tried to make peace with it.

My eyes were momentarily drawn to the darts board near us. It had been a long time since I'd played darts. I found myself transfixed by the two men playing, remembering the good times I'd had on the university darts team.

'You live in Ipswich, don't you Izz,' Jake said, pulling me back to the crowd.

'What?' I asked. 'Sorry, yeah.' He was telling his friend, so I thought I'd elaborate. 'I'm from Hereford originally, but I've lived here for a few years now.'

'Do you like it here?' the man asked me. I couldn't remember his name. There had been too many people to meet in too short a time.

'Yeah. I do. I've made some good contacts in the area.'

'Izz is a Virtual Assistant,' Jake said. 'Which reminds me, how is your business doing?'

And that was it. That was the extent of my involvement in the conversation.

Before long, the catch ups were over with and the stories of days gone by were being shared. In-jokes were relayed, laughter was aplenty, and all I could do was smile and nod.

Jake was pulled into chats from every angle, and the only

person he didn't make any eye contact with was me. I was yet again left completely out of it. There really was no point in me being there at all.

I finally got a respite from the boredom when Kelly, the girl we'd met at the waterfront, jumped into the seat next met.

'You must come here all the time,' she said. 'It's such a lovely pub.'

I spent a few seconds considering my answer. The lies were very easy to tell, but I figured if the flirty landlady – the one that clearly knew Jake very well - announced that she'd never met me before, things would start to unravel. So I decided to keep things as close to the truth as possible.

'No, actually, I've never been here. More often than not, Jake comes to mine.'

'Really? What's your house like? Is it like Jake's?'

I shook my head. 'I don't think many people have a house like Jake's.'

'Yeah. It's pretty incredible, isn't it.'

I nodded.

Kelly fell silent. I could see she wanted to speak some more, but she clearly didn't know what to say. So I took the opportunity. Jake was out of ear shot, nattering away to his friends, and I had a burning question.

'Can I ask you something?' I said.

'Of course,' Kelly replied, full of smiles.

'You don't have to tell me. You can say you don't know or you feel wrong telling me or whatever. That's fine. But I'm going to ask.'

'What?' she said, now more cautiously.

'Jake's friend, Olivia – the girl we were with the other night - she said something about Jake's ex, Michelle. I got the feeling that something bad might have happened. Do you know anything about her? I'm only asking because Jake hasn't said a thing about his past and I worry there's something I should know. I just want to know he's all right.'

'He's not told you about Michelle?' Kelly asked with

surprise.

'Not a word. When I ask him about his past, he gets very quiet.'

Kelly hesitated. 'Okay, I'll tell you about her. But don't tell him you know.'

'I promise, I won't say a word.'

Kelly took a breath. 'Okay. You must know Jake is super clever, right? He was the comedy character at school. He'd always have us in fits. But he took school work very seriously and he got top marks in everything. He was so driven. Still is, I guess. Anyway, you must know about his app?'

'Yeah. A dating app?'

'Yeah. He came up with the idea for Coupled With-'

'He invented Coupled With?' I said, astounded.

'Yeah. He didn't tell you?'

'No. He just said it was a dating app. An app that he'd sold a few years ago. Coupled With is one of the biggest dating apps... well, in the world.'

'I know. He was robbed, right. That was one of the problems. He could have probably got about a billion pounds or something, but he settled for a quick sale. Just four hundred million. Makes me so mad.'

My mouth dried up. I clearly hadn't heard correctly. 'Four hundred million pounds?' I said, aghast. 'He got four hundred million pounds for selling his app?'

'I know, right. It's worth about three times that amount. Another reason why he's so crushed now.'

I had so many questions, but one thing at a time. I took a moment to let my head calm down, then I said, 'Okay, so go back to what you were saying. He invented the app.'

'Yeah, and it was a mega success. As we all know. He's so smart. He's always just understood people and found ways to make things work. So he left uni, started his company, was commuting to London every day-'

'He commuted to London from Ipswich?'

'Yeah, he had like a mega office somewhere and loads of

staff. He was making a fortune before he sold up. He'd struck gold.'

'So why did he sell?'

'Because of her. That bitch.'

'Michelle?'

'Yeah. He met her at a convention or something. She was into tech too, and happened to live in Norfolk. They got chatting, starting dating, and before long she moved in with him. I don't think she was happy to leave Norfolk, but he had to commute to London, and Ipswich is a much shorter train journey.'

'Why was she a bitch?'

'Because she was. Jake was madly in love with her, but none of us could see why. She was glamorous and sparkly and all that, but she had this way of putting you down even when she was pretending to be nice. We all instantly hated her. Every one of us. She was poisonous.'

Things were starting to make far more sense.

'The thing is, though,' Kelly continued, 'we all could have lived with her bitchy ways if Jake had been happy.'

'He wasn't happy?' I asked.

'He said he was, but we knew him. That glint in his eye. What he's got now. What you've restored. She took that right away. She stamped all over him. He was like an echo of himself. All the joy was zapped from him. She was horrible.'

'And she made him sell his app?' I asked.

Kelly shook her head. 'Worse. She implied that the reason he'd invented a dating app was so that he could go on dates on the side and she'd never know. He had the app on his phone. Of course he did – it was his app! But she accused him of cheating. Like every day. He was working such long hours, commuting to London all the time to make things a success, but all she did was moan at him and accuse him of cheating on her. It was awful and it slowly wore away at him. There was nothing he could say or do to make her believe he was utterly faithful. And, believe me, Jake is nothing if not loyal. You must know that. It got to the point where it was give up his business or give up Michelle.'

'He sold the app for her?'

'He barely saw there was another option. He wanted to make it work with her and he convinced himself that it was his fault that she didn't trust him. Like somehow he'd been a bad boyfriend. Which only made us all hate her even more. You know, he was paying for everything. Keeping her completely. She was such an ungrateful cow. So he sold up and took the first deal that came along to get it over with quickly. It was so unlike Jake. As you know, he's a shrewd business man. To take such a stupid deal stunk of desperation and pressure.'

'Was she happy then?'

'You're kidding, right? I tell you, she was an absolute money grabbing bitch. Jake was suddenly out of a job and moping around the house. He was used to working silly hours and now had nothing in his life. So she started moaning about that. Then she started fretting about how he was going to support them. As if four hundred million was just bordering on the breadline.'

'Tell me he then broke up with her.'

'No. He spent all his time trying to make her happy again. As you must know, he's invested in quite a few companies. I don't know it all, but he's more than set up for life I reckon. But she still wasn't happy. That's when he bought the massive house. He didn't tell her, he just bought it. I think he was trying to give her stability or something. He held the most epic house-warming party imaginable. All of us came, and he invited all of her friends too. He hired pop stars, magicians, we had fireworks. You name it, the party had it. It was epic! But she still wasn't happy. She moaned that it was too far away from her family.'

'Was that the final straw?' I asked, my heart breaking for him.

'To be honest, none of us know for sure. All we know is that she never moved in. He never told us officially that they'd broken up, but I never saw her again. That's when he stopped coming out with us. Stopped doing anything. We've barely seen him in two years. We thought we'd lost him for good. But when we saw him with you last weekend - wow. He was like our old Jake. He had that smile back. That sheen. You could feel his joy again. That's got to be thanks to you. We're all so grateful he met you. Thanks for bringing him back to us.'

I smiled. What could I say to that? I was hardly the person who had restored Jake, but I couldn't very well tell her that.

Instead I sat back in my seat and I let her story sink in. It explained so much about why he was looking for a fake girlfriend and why he was so coy about his house.

Poor Jake.

I turned to see him laughing with his mates. Mates he hadn't seen in a long time. No wonder he was so engrossed in chatting with them. It must have been very hard for him to get back into his life. Somehow I must have helped him open a door.

For a small moment I forgave him for ignoring me.

'Kell, you want another drink?' Gavin asked.

'Yeah,' she said, standing up. 'I'm going to see what they've got. You want anything?' she asked me.

I shook my head. 'No. I've still got most of my gin and tonic.'

'All right. Catch you in a bit.'

She left and the seat next to me remained vacant.

I sat alone for quite a while, not a person in the room seeming to notice me. Not even Jake. Not once in half an hour did he look my way. Not once did he even seem to remember I existed.

As time stretched on, my forgiveness waned. He might have been happy to reconnect with his mates again, but this had all been made possible because of me. He had used me to reconnect. The least he could do was acknowledge me.

As the minutes ticked by, I became more and more

angry. So much so, I eventually turned my chair around and turned my back on them all. Sod him and sod his friends.

Whatever sad story he had in his past, I didn't deserve to be used like this, and no man I could ever love should treat me like this.

Then and there, I decided Jake Masters could do one.

NINE

As I sat there stewing over how Jake was treating me, I contemplated my options. I couldn't drive home. Putting aside the fact that I'd had two drinks, my car was in Ipswich. And that was ten miles away. Could I order a taxi? No. We were so far out in the sticks, I imagined that any taxi around here would have to come from Ipswich, costing me twice the price.

As much as I was hating every second of this night, I realised I had little option but to stay put and find a way to get through it. I needed to keep my head down and not look upset. It hurt like hell that my fantasy had ended, but at least I knew where I stood now. I had to take solace from that. This would be far better in the long run. At least I was no longer stuck in that limbo.

My eyes were drawn to the dart board again. Two different men were now playing, but they weren't very good.

'You think you can do better?' one of them said to me as he caught the wince on my face when he scored the huge total of three in his go.

'I'm just watching,' I said.

They carried on playing, but between shots both men were now glaring at me. At any other time I would have looked away as they clearly weren't happy having an audience. But if I turned around now I'd have to re-join Jake and his friends and be ignored all over again. Sticking to my guns and enjoying the darts seemed like the more dignified option. As uncomfortable as it was now becoming.

'You like darts?' one of the men suddenly asked me. He was a tall, broad man, perhaps in his late twenties.

'I've played once or twice,' I replied. I'm not going to lie, he was a bit intimidating. I was clearly encroaching on his space and he didn't like it.

Then, to my complete surprise, he turned to his mate and said, 'I'm going to play with her next.'

'If you're so interested in darts,' he said, now focusing back on me, 'it seems only right we let you play. You never know, you might enjoy it.'

I caught him smirk and my stomach churned. Was this supposed to be a new way of chatting me up? Was I supposed to swoon when he touched my hand to help me point the dart at the board? That's all I needed: another man thinking he could get one over me.

I really was reaching saturation point.

My fiery competitive nature kicked in and I stood up.

'All right, let's see,' I said, taking the darts from his hand. He seemed to like my forward approach. He grinned broadly and stood back.

I took my place at the end of the makeshift oche (a bit of tape on the wooden floor) and I aimed at the board. I knew I'd need a bit of time to get my eye in again.

'Can I have a few practise throws before we start a match?' I said.

'Sure,' he said. 'Do you need any tips?'

'No. But thanks.'

I focused on the 20 on the top of the board and aimed the point. The dart flew out of my hand and I forgot how good it felt.

It landed just to the left hitting the 5.

With the second dart, I edged more to the right to make

up for it, but it went too far over and hit the 1. Off again.

For my final throw, I felt it all come together. It felt right. The dart sailed out of my fingers and landed square in the middle of the 20.

I turned to the man, chuffed with myself. I might have only scored 26, but I was in very close range of just where I needed to be. For my first darts in years, it was an extremely good effort. The man, however, just shrugged.

'You hit the board,' he said. 'That's a start.'

I could see how this was going to be played. The little woman was going to be put in her place while the man showed her just how the game was won. I could see it all over his smug face. Then he'd tell me how well I'd done and offer to buy me a drink, and I'd be all impressed because in one go he'd scored 42. I'd seen it all before and I just wasn't in the mood.

'I think I'm ready for a game,' I said. I edged forward and wiped the chalk scores of the previous game off the board.

'What's your name?' I asked.

'Allow me,' he said, sliding the chalk from my fingers.

He wrote "Jambo" on the top of the board. I assumed that wasn't his real name, but I resisted asking.

'And your name?' he asked.

'Isobel,' I said. He put "Izz" on the board and that annoyed me even more. Only Jake called me Izz and he wasn't exactly my favourite person at that moment.

I was becoming moodier by the second. It was most unlike me. I had hoped this distraction would chill me out.

He then wrote 301 under both our names.

'You can't hack 501?' I queried.

'Come on. It's your first game. 501 is very hard.'

'If I'm going to learn, then we need to play by the proper rules,' I said. 'So we'll play 501. I also believe you need to start and end with a double. Unless that's too hard for you?'

He stood back, amused. 'If that's what you want. But don't blame me.'

'Likewise.'

'Shall we throw for the bull to begin with?' he asked. 'That means whoever gets closest to the bullseye in the middle starts.'

I held back saying what I really wanted to. Instead I answered, 'If that's how the game should be properly played, then let's do it.'

He took the darts from my hand. 'These are mine,' he said. Then he took the darts that his mate was holding and handed them to me.

'They're your own darts?' I queried with surprise.

'Certainly are. My lucky babies. Helped you hit the board.'

My rage flared up that little bit more.

'Right. You go first,' I said.

He lined up his shot and hit the bullseye dead centre. Maybe he was better than I'd given him credit for. Still, I had no intention of backing out.

I took to the oche and had my turn. I skimmed the edge of the outer bull. Damn it. I still needed to get my eye in. But I didn't show my frustration. All in all, it still wasn't a terrible shot.

'You first then,' I said.

He edged forward with his smarmy grin and threw a double three instantly. He really was much better than I'd expected. After three darts he was at 456.

I stood forward but failed to get a double on any of my first three darts. My hands were shaking. I had to calm down and do better.

As he played his next three darts, I turned around to have a sip of my drink. Jake was still chatting to his friends. None of them had even noticed that I'd moved and was now playing darts with a strange man. That said it all.

I turned back to the board to find Jambo had scored 41. He was grinning inanely.

A flash of all of those nights I'd dreamt about Jake and what an incredible boyfriend he'd be sparked in my head.

'You don't have to get a double if you don't want to,' Jambo said in a terribly patronising tone. 'Just give it your best shot.'

That was it. My anger went supersonic. That spark in my head went into overdrive. It sent waves of determination right down to my hand and made everything suddenly crystal clear.

I swiftly hit double 20, and then followed that with another 40 points from the remaining two darts.

Jambo's mate laughed. 'You want to watch her!'

I smiled and headed to the board. I crossed out 501, wrote 421 in chalk, and then pulled my darts away.

'Your turn,' I said.

He scored 43 and I scored 60. That's when things started to tense up.

'I take it you've played more than once before,' Jambo said.

'When I was a kid,' I replied. 'Not for a long time.'

'Right.' The smile had now been wiped from his face, but it wasn't enough. This man now represented all the pain that I was feeling and I was ready to annihilate him.

He threw a 60 this time, slightly upping his game. He seemed to thrive off pressure as well. I needed to do better.

I stood at the oche, took a calming breath, and recalled his patronising tone from not minutes before. Then I imagined Jake behind me buying another round for his mates, completely forgetting that I even existed. I hadn't looked back again. I couldn't. It hurt too much. But at least I could put that pain to good use.

I zoned in on the treble 20 and I blocked out everything else in the room.

The dart zipped from my fingers and hit my target exactly. There was a huff from Jambo and a snigger from his mate. I put them out of my mind and zoned in again. The second dart also smacked into the treble 20 with force. Feeling the flow, I didn't hesitate, and the final dart gave me the maximum score of 180.

Applause erupted from behind me.

I turned around to find Jake and all of his mates standing in awe and cheering.

'That's my girl!' Jake shouted.

'Is he your boyfriend?' Jambo asked me.

'I certainly am,' Jake replied.

I'm not sure what pissed him off more: the 180 or the fact that I had a boyfriend.

I collected my darts and scribbled 181 on the board. I was more than 100 points ahead of Jambo, and I realised that I needed to bring this game to a close, and fast.

'Are you hustling me?' Jambo said.

'You invited me to play!' I argued back. 'And I was honest with you. I haven't played in a long time. I'm just finding an unexpected flow.'

'Is everything all right?' Jake said, coming forward as he sensed the tension.

'We're fine,' I snapped, unable to believe the nerve of his sudden knight-in-shining-armour act after the way he'd treated me. 'Jambo here is just giving me some tips. Aren't you?'

Jambo looked at Jake and then me.

'It's fine, Jake, mate,' he said. 'Just having a nice game. Didn't realise it was your Mrs.'

'Well, she is,' Jake said. He might as well have peed up my leg for how territorial it all began to feel.

'Can we get on with this?' I urged.

I stood back and pulled Jake away. He was glaring at me. There was an intensity to his eyes that I hadn't seen before.

Jambo lined himself up and threw his darts. He scored just 21. One of his darts even missed completely. I was clearly getting to him. Good.

I edged up to take my turn. I scored two 20s and then found that laser sharp focus again and scored a final treble, taking my score to just 81.

I knew I could end this on my next go. It would take some very good shots, but I needed this to end now. This was the least enjoyable game of darts I'd ever played.

Jambo was all over the place. He'd managed to get his score down to just 243 and I saw my chance.

I focused in and scored 1, just as planned. I took my time on the next shot. I couldn't mess this up. After a calming breath, I went for it.

'Yes!' I heard echo around me as I hit the double 20.

'You need to end on a double, don't forget,' Jambo demanded, the strain in his voice highly apparent.

'I know,' I said. I took that breath again and aimed at the exact same place as before.

The dart landed perfectly in the centre of the double 20 giving me exactly 81 and the win.

I turned to Jambo. 'Thank you for the game.'

'You bitch,' he said and the whole atmosphere seemed to crack.

'What?' I asked.

'Time to leave, I think,' Jake said. 'Come on guys, let's go back to mine.'

I turned to Jambo's friend who was trying to hide his laugh.

'Thanks for the darts,' I said, nodding towards the three Union Jack decorated darts that I'd left in the board.

'No problem,' he said.

Jake grabbed my hand. 'Let's get out of here.'

His friends were all cheering, laughing and saying how amazing I was as we swiftly headed out of the pub.

'See you soon,' the barmaid said as we passed. 'Although maybe give it a couple of weeks.' She winked before she turned to me and dropped her voice. 'Well done.'

I smiled and thanked her quietly and then we left.

Jake's friends were well ahead of us, finding their own way back to the house, while Jake and I trailed behind, his hand firmly gripped around mind.

As we walked on, I looked at him. I could sense that intensity still there as his eyes met mine, but he said nothing.

We carried on down the very quiet road. The only sound

that could be heard were the voices of Jake's friends who were quite far ahead.

I wanted to say something. I wanted to break this cold silence between us. But I simply had nothing to say.

Suddenly Jake pushed me against a wall. It was gentle but totally unexpected. My heart began pounding.

'Every time I think I've got you figured out,' he said, 'you do something incredible and confuse me all over again. You're like no other woman I've ever met.'

His face was now just centimetres from my own. I could smell his divine after shave and every inch of me began tingling. There was no denying how much I loved him.

I saw his eyes focus on my lips and my heart stopped. Was he about to kiss me?

Everything around us seemed to disappear as I felt his soft breath against my mouth. It was tantalising.

'No one has ever...' he said before trailing off. 'I've not...'

He took in my lips again and I felt myself curl inside. I was still mad at him, but I had also never wanted to be kissed more. All I became aware of were his face and the sound of my heartbeat throbbing in my ears. It was throbbing so loudly he must have been able to hear it.

We stood like this for a few minutes more, neither of us moving. I couldn't be the first to kiss him. Not after everything we'd been through. It had to be him, and it had to be now. This had to be the moment it all changed. Surely.

Finally the tension split as Jake stood back.

I wanted to grab him, to bring him back to my lips, but he took my hands and studied them for a moment.

'There is no one in this world that I'd be more proud of to call my fake girlfriend than you,' he said.

My heart slammed down towards my feet with disappointment.

He looked back up at me with his charming smile.

I was on the verge of tears.

'You like a girl who plays darts then?' I said in an attempt to brush off the terrible pain I felt.

'Turns out I do,' he said. Then he laughed. 'Who knew.'

I looked up at the sky as I tried to control my emotions. I couldn't cry. I still had a whole night of this pain to endure.

'We'd better get a move on,' I said. 'You're the only one with a key.'

He looked up the road to find all of his friends now out of sight. 'Shit, yeah,' he said. 'Come on.'

He helped me forward and we headed back to his house. We remained holding hands but neither of us said another word.

TEN

The rest of the night was perhaps five percent better. We got back to the house, the music kicked in and the party properly started. We sat outside until after dark, some people on the decking, others in and around the pool. The drinks flowed easily and the catering was out of this world. Jake must have hired some fancy chef. They looked like general party nibbles, but they were like nothing I'd ever tasted. Every mouthful was so rich and full of flavour.

Jake still barely said a word to me, but I noticed how he had started watching me. He never seemed far all night, and I felt his eyes constantly on me.

By three a.m. people finally began drifting off to bed, and Jake asked me if I wanted to call it a night. As we were sharing a room, it seemed only right that we went to bed at the same time.

We took it in turns to go into the en suite to get ourselves ready, and then I curled up in Jake's enormous bed while he made himself comfortable on his sofa. Perhaps I should have felt guilty for taking his bed, but I figured after the way he'd been treating me it was the least I deserved.

Not that I'd have been willing to give up this bed in a hurry. It was heavenly. It was like sleeping on clouds. If it wasn't for the fact that I was such an emotional wreck, I probably would have had the best night's sleep ever.

I did manage to get some sleep, but generally it was another restless night. I was so grateful when Jake rose at just before nine. I was more than ready to go home.

The first thing he did was make a full English breakfast for everyone. Of course he was also a tremendous cook, just to add to the things that made him so irresistible. The bastard.

When the food was eaten and a few people had enjoyed a final dip in the pool, slowly, one by one, Jake's friends started to pack up. By early afternoon everyone was gone and I told Jake I needed to get home too. It should have been a dream, him and me in this enormous house together. But instead it was just awkward and uncomfortable.

We barely spoke on the journey back and that said it all. There were no more dates planned and there was no reason for this pretence to carry on. We didn't need to spell it out. It had come to a natural end and that was that.

I wanted to be relieved. I wanted to say good riddance. But I couldn't help but feel gutted. I'd never sleep in his bed again. I'd never hold his hand again. I'd never get to kiss him. It had all fallen apart in the most horrible of ways. I was devastated.

He pulled up outside of my house and helped me with my bag. I didn't invite him in and he stood politely on my doorstep. Both of us knew something needed to be said, but it seemed neither of us wanted to be the first to say it.

Just as I was finding the words to say goodbye, Smokey appeared, making Jake jump.

Luckily, Smokey didn't do anything this time. He just sat on the grass and stared at Jake carefully.

'I think that's my cue to go,' Jake said.

I felt my shoulders droop a little. I didn't want him to go, but I also knew I'd never get what I really wanted so he'd have to.

'Yeah. I guess so,' I said.

'I had a good weekend. Thanks.'

'I think everyone had a good weekend. You certainly have an amazing house.'

A sadness cast itself across Jake's face and I knew I'd said the wrong thing.

'Thanks for all the food and everything,' I added.

'It's the least I could do. Thank you for everything. You've been very kind to me. The perfect girlfriend.'

I instantly tensed up.

'So I'll see you next Friday?' he quickly followed with, sensing that he'd now said the wrong thing.

'Next Friday?' I checked as my stomach flipped.

'Networking.'

Oh fuck. I still hadn't made my mind up about whether to continue attending or not. I had a lot to consider. 'Is that next Friday?' I said. 'Where does the time go?'

'Flies by when you're having fun.'

'Yeah. I guess so. I'll see you next Friday then.'

'See you then.'

Jake hesitated before turning around and heading back to his car. He waved, almost reluctantly, and then got in and drove away.

I watched until he was out of sight, and then my attention was caught by Smokey who was sauntering into my living room.

I closed the front door and flopped onto my sofa in despair.

'You're so lucky you're a cat,' I said to him as he jumped up next to me. 'I hope you've been snipped because chasing after the opposite sex brings nothing but unhappiness.'

I curled myself up and grabbed the remote. I wanted crap TV and for the day to fade away. Within minutes I was asleep.

I threw myself into work on Monday morning. I had three client newsletters to get out, five social media accounts to update, some market research to go through, and then I needed to do some of my own marketing as well. There was barely time for lunch and I was glad of it.

By Tuesday I'd bagged myself two more clients and I was starting to think I'd need a Virtual Assistant to help me. Business was soaring and it was becoming close to the point where I was struggling to keep up.

Jake's offer of help had bounced around my mind a few times. He'd said he'd got ideas and I was very keen to find out what they were. He was obviously a hugely successful business man and I was sure he'd have some very savvy advice to share. I also knew that he'd honour helping me for free. But I couldn't take any more heartache. I needed a break from him for a while. I needed closure on that part of my life, and I wasn't going to get that if I attempted to start working with him.

By Thursday afternoon, a solution hit me. Moping around was not going to help me move on. What I needed was to actually move on. I took one look at Smokey who was curled up next to me in my office and the perfect idea came to me. A very attractive man had already asked me out. Maybe a date with him was the answer I'd been looking for.

Leaving my work aside, I ran to my bedroom. I freshened up my face with a bit of make-up and I brushed my hair. I picked up Smokey, popped on my beautiful heeled sandals (which looked super with the pink dress I was wearing), grabbed my keys and left my house.

'You're looking very pretty today.' I jumped at the sound of the voice. It was my neighbour. She was in a sun hat and gardening gloves, snipping bits of her bush that hadn't even been given a chance to grow.

'Thank you,' I said.

'I know where you're going.'

'Dropping off Smokey again.'

'It's convenient how he keeps on dropping by, isn't it.'

'Believe me, it's far from convenient.'

'You feed him, don't you. Gives them a reason to come back.'

'I actually don't.'

'Of course you don't.'

Her lips curled into a smug smile, but I decided to not even begin trying to work out why.

'Have a nice day,' I said, heading over the road.

'I'm sure you will,' she called back.

I walked up to Nicholas's door and rang the bell. I was holding Smokey in my arms but he was desperately trying to wriggle free. It was the first time I'd ever known him resist me. Maybe he was concerned about being in trouble with his actual owner. I placed him on the ground and he scuttled off towards the back garden.

I tried the bell again and waited a few moments more.

When nothing happened, I couldn't resist a little peek through the large window. It was like it was calling to me. I stepped carefully to the left and had a sneaky glance through the glass.

The house looked empty and I sighed. His car was there on the drive, but I figured he could be on his head phones in his office, completely distracted. I could always call back later.

Feeling a huge wave of disappointment after psyching myself up so much, I strolled back across to my house. I kicked my heels off in the hallway and I trotted back upstairs to carry on with my work.

Not ten minutes later my doorbell rang and my heart throbbed.

I took a breath, saved the budgeting spreadsheet I was working on, and headed back down the stairs.

I opened the door to find Nicholas standing there. He was dressed in a suit. A gorgeous tailored suit. He looked extremely handsome.

'Sorry I missed you again,' he said. 'I was on a call. I tried to wave to you through the upstairs window, but I don't think you could see me.'

'Oh, sorry. I never looked up.'

'You know what it's like working from home.'

'Clients come first,' I said, nodding.

'Anyway, how can I help? Is Smokey bothering you again?'

'No, but I do worry that you never get to see him. He's here all the time.'

'He's certainly taken quite a shine to you. But cats will be cats. They're very independent.'

'I probably should confess something. This is going to sound weird, but I've always had an affinity with cats. I think my sweat must smell like catnip or something.'

This comment normally made people chuckle, but Nicholas just stared at me as if I'd said something quite alluring. I swear his eyes began to undress me.

'Cats do like catnip,' he said after a moment.

I nodded. It was all getting creepy again.

No. No it wasn't. I quickly told myself that I was probably only feeling that way because no man compared to Jake. I wasn't being fair to Nicholas and I needed to give this exchange a chance. He was truly handsome. He was also very clever and ambitious. I could do a lot worse.

'So yeah...' I mumbled. 'Erm... I didn't actually want to talk about Smokey.'

'No?'

'No. Actually... I wanted to see you.'

His eyes lit up. 'Yes?'

'I wanted to follow up on that kind offer of yours from last week.'

A short pause. 'What offer was that?' He said it slowly. It was obvious that he knew exactly what I was talking about, but he was going to make me say it. I wasn't sure if that was annoying or sexy.

My irritation levels told me annoying.

'You said you'd like to go out for a drink sometime. If that's something you'd still like to do, I think that might be nice.'

He studied me. 'I thought you had a boyfriend?'

'We broke up. It wasn't very serious. I thought

something was starting, but it wasn't. He wasn't the man for me. So...'

This made him smile. Nicholas had a lovely smile.

So why did my stomach churn?

'It seems we're both free and single then,' he said. 'Another thing we have in common. I think we owe it to ourselves to get to know each other better.'

I hesitated. 'I agree.'

'Wonderful. Are you free Saturday night? I could order a taxi for seven to take us into town?'

'Sounds fantastic. I look forward to it.'

'Me too. I'm glad you called by.'

'And I'm glad you called back!' I laughed. This was so awkward.

'I'll see you Saturday then.'

'Yep. See you then. Unless I see you around before that. I mean, we do live on the same street!' I laughed again, although I was starting to cringe inside.

He smiled. He seemed to enjoy me wittering on. 'Yes. Well, have a good rest of the week, Isobel. I'll be counting down the minutes to Saturday night.' His voice dropped. I think maybe he was trying to be sexy. I don't know. And truthfully I was too jittery to care.

I smiled as he sauntered back across the road and I waited until he was at his driveway before I closed my door.

I dropped straight on the stairs and caught my breath.

This is going to be great, I told myself. Now I just had to start believing it.

ELEVEN

By half past six on Saturday night I was ready. I had gone all out. I was dressed in my favourite little black number and my killer red heels. My hair was curled to perfection and I'd opted for pure sex appeal with my make-up. Forget the girl next door (or over the road), I was going for the full on knockout punch.

There was no question that I was vastly overcompensating for how little I was looking forward to the date, and the impression that I was about to make on Nicholas hadn't once occurred to me. I had been so focused on the things that I mustn't do, such as think about or – worse – talk about Jake, that I hadn't at all considered the important things, such as how Nicholas was going to interpret my excess of bare flesh.

I sat on my settee and played solitaire, trying to flitter away the minutes. At ten to seven my doorbell rang.

I opened up and Nicholas's eyes nearly popped out of his head.

'Wow,' he said. 'You look absolutely stunning.'

'Thank you,' I replied, a little embarrassed. I suddenly realised just how much leg I had on display and I felt a terrible urge to pull my dress down. But it was too late.

He was dressed in a suit and he looked absolutely gorgeous himself. Although I didn't feel the urge to tell him.

'I thought we could wait together for the taxi,' he said.

'I suppose that makes sense.'

'Is Smokey here as well? It might be nice to actually see my cat.'

I laughed. 'No. I haven't seen much of him today to be honest.'

'Oh well. He's off causing trouble somewhere no doubt. But he always comes home eventually.'

I was just about to invite Nicholas in when the taxi arrived.

'That must be ours,' I said.

'Yes. Looks like it.'

'I'll just grab my bag.'

I totted back into the living room, grabbed my bag, checked my keys were in it, and then locked up.

'Are you two going out on a date?' I stopped in my tracks as I saw my next door neighbour. She was grabbing bags of shopping from her car boot and her smile was smugger than ever.

'We certainly are, Vivian,' Nicholas replied. He knew her?

She smiled sweetly at Nicholas. 'Such a lucky girl. Enjoy!'

She disappeared inside her house and I walked towards the taxi. Nicholas opened the door for me before walking around the other side to let himself in.

'You know her?' I asked as I buckled my seatbelt.

'Vivian?' he replied.

'Yes.'

'How can you not? She's always on the street looking for someone to gossip with.'

'Where to?' the taxi driver cut in before I could explore this more.

'To The Kiln, please. By the waterfront,' Nicholas replied. As he leaned forward I got a whiff of his musk. He smelt very nice. He looked very nice. He seemed very nice.

But none of it excited me.

'I love The Kiln,' I said. 'It's my favourite bar in Ipswich.'

'Yes, it is rather nice there isn't it. The perfect place to go on a warm summer evening.'

'Yes.'

We didn't say much else until we got out of the taxi on the heaving waterfront. We stood in the small queue to enter the bar and we tried to find a seat out the front, but it was just too busy. Instead we had to head inside.

The venue was full of nooks, crannies and different rooms, and normally you would spend ages poking your head into different areas to see if there was a free table. But that night there were plenty of seats. Most people were opting to stand outside to soak up the glorious weather.

We grabbed a table near the window to feel some air and Nicholas went to the bar.

He came back with a glass of red for me and a pint for himself.

'Here's to a good night,' he said, clinking my glass.

'I hope so,' I replied.

We took a sip and the conversation dried up. I had to think of something to say.

'Are you from Suffolk originally?' I asked, knowing he couldn't be with his lack of a local accent.

'No. Kent originally. I grew up in Canterbury.'

'What brought you to Ipswich then?'

'Work mainly. That's the reason most people seem to move, isn't it. I can tell you're not a local either.'

'No, I was born in Hereford. Then I worked in London for a while before getting a job in Ipswich. So work has brought both of us here.'

'The similarities keep totting up.'

'It would seem so.'

The conversation dried up again.

'Tell me more about this boyfriend,' Nicholas said. 'I don't want to be treading on anyone's toes.'

'You aren't. That's completely over with. It barely even started.'

'Okay. Good to know.'

'What about you? When was your last relationship?'

He paused. 'It's been a while, if I'm honest. I've had a few flings here and there, but work commitments have always made a full time relationship difficult. Well, before now. I'm far more settled in my life now and I've been looking more to the future lately. And then I meet the most beautiful woman in the world who just happens to live across the street.'

I forced a smile but his words made me deeply uncomfortable.

'You never seem to have any visitors,' he noted. 'I guess your family is still back in Hereford?'

'Yes. Pretty much all of them. And my uni friends are all scattered here, there and everywhere. That's the problem with Ipswich, it's so far away.'

'I know what you mean. Kent's much closer than Hereford, but it's still a fair journey. So you have no local friends?'

'Not really. I had a few acquaintances at my old job. Before I started freelancing. We used to come here for Friday night drinks quite a lot. But we never swapped numbers or anything. I couldn't call them friends. When I got made redundant, other than a few LinkedIn messages to say sorry to hear the news and best of luck for the future, that was it. It's the curse of being such a damn workaholic. Even on those Friday nights, I still tended to hang around with management, talking about work. It was my life. Turns out I have very little else.'

'I've had very similar experiences. If you don't let people in, they keep their distance. It seems the right choice at the time, but when you look back it can be quite lonely.'

'Yes. Totally.'

'Lucky we found each other.'

I took a sip of my drink so I didn't have to respond.

I needed to lighten things up.

'So we've talked work and exes. What about fun stuff? Any hobbies?'

He smiled. 'Does hunting down that pesky cat of mine count?'

I laughed. 'That does not count, because when he's not with you, he's most likely with me.'

Nicholas laughed. 'Then no. I hate to say it, but Smokey and work take up pretty much all of my time. I try to see family when I can, but... you know. What about you?'

I took a second to think. 'I like to read,' I said.

'What are you currently reading?'

'I read mainly business books. I'm working through this great book at the moment about sales pitches and how to win new clients. It's full of really good advice.'

'Sounds interesting. Do you read fiction as well?'

'I have done. But I get bored. If I'm not somehow progressing or improving myself, I get twitchy. I end up grilling myself about whether what I'm doing is a good use of time or not. You know...' I stopped.

'What?' Nicholas asked.

'Nothing.'

'Go on. What were you going to say?'

I leaned in. 'If I tell you something, will you promise not to laugh? I'm deadly serious so you can't laugh.'

'I won't.'

'My greatest ambition is to one day be named business person of the year.'

He studied me. 'That's amazing. That's not funny.'

'It sounds like one of those silly fantasy ideas. But I want to get to the top of the ladder. I know I need to become more than just an assistant to achieve that, but I'm now running my own business. I already feel a lot closer to that dream than I did a year ago.'

'So you're a career woman through and through, then?' he asked.

'One hundred percent. It's in my bones.'

'Do you ever think about settling down? Having a family? I know that can be hard for a working woman, so I was just curious if you've ever considered it.'

This question threw me. Until I'd met Jake I'd never considered any such thing. But over the past few months my mind had certainly been opening up to the idea of settling down. It wasn't a conscious thing. It had just sort of happened.

'I don't think women have to choose one way or the other these days,' I said. 'Why can't I have it all?' I smiled broadly and lifted up my glass. 'To having it all,' I added and I clinked his glass with mine.

He smiled and lifted his pint up. 'To having it all. You're right. There's no reason why that's not possible. Life should be whatever you want it to be.'

Nicholas leaned in and rested his hand on mine, and I shifted awkwardly in my seat. There was absolutely nothing that I didn't like about this man. On paper he was completely perfect. But I just couldn't find it in myself to fancy him. It just wasn't there. His touch left me cold.

'What the hell do you think you're doing?' a voice said next to us. It was a voice I knew all too well. A voice that shot goose bumps across my skin

I glanced up and Jake was standing above me. He looked furious.

TWELVE

'What are you doing?' Jake said, full of rage.

'I'm enjoying a night out with this lovely man,' I snapped, sizzling from the anger that was now burning through me. I had no clue if this is how I should have felt. If I'd stopped for a second to consider why I was so annoyed, I might have realised that it was as much to do with the fact that I was stuck with Nicholas when Jake was here as it was to do with the nerve of Jake interrupting us.

'But... My mates are here. You're supposed to-'

'I'm supposed to what?' I growled. 'Am I not free and single to date any man I choose?'

I turned to Nicholas but his eyes were firmly fixed on Jake. Eyes that were now more of an angry green than their usual glittering blue.

'Can we have a word in private?' Jake said, his tone quite demanding.

I should have said no, but of course I answered, 'You've got two minutes.' I turned to Nicholas as I stood up. 'I'm very sorry about this. Let me just sort it out. It's nothing for you to worry about.'

'No problem,' Nicholas said in a tone that told me he had a huge problem with it. Quite understandably.

When I was at full height, Jake's eyes absorbed every inch of me, head to toe and right back again. He took a breath and then grabbed my hand. I can't deny this didn't give me a little kick. But I didn't show it.

He led me to the back of the room, where it was slightly darker and quieter, but Nicholas was still in sight.

I stood against the wall and Jake stood directly in front of me, his face just centimetres away from my own. For the first time that night my body began tingling with desire. This was how you were supposed to feel on a date. It was so frustrating that I couldn't feel anything even remotely like this with Nicholas.

'What are you doing?' he said to me.

'I'm on a date.'

'But my mates are over there.'

I glanced over Jake's shoulder to find three of the lads who had been at the party last week leaning against the bar and pretending not to look at us.

'So?' I said, focusing back on Jake. 'What do want from me? You want me to only pretend to be your girlfriend, but at the same time you want me to also be faithful to you and not date anyone else? So ultimately I get absolutely nothing from anyone. Is that what you want?'

'That's not what I want.'

'Oh, I see. So you want me to go to Norfolk? Not flaunt my dates anywhere locally on the off chance that one of your mates might see. Is that it?'

'No. Of course not.'

'Then what?'

Jake stood back and rubbed his head. 'It's just my mates now think that you're cheating on me.'

'Well, there you go. The perfect way for us to break up. I'm a bitch and I don't deserve you. Tell them what you like. I don't care.'

'That's not the point. I don't want them to think you're a bitch.'

'What does it matter? I'm never going to see them again.'

Jake took a deep breath. 'What if I want them to see you again?'

'I can't keep going on like this.'

Jake couldn't look at me. He appeared to be going through some sort of internal anguish.

I glanced over at Nicholas who was staring back at me. Even from a distance his eyes were burning into me, just the way his stupid cat looked at me. So intense without me being able to understand the thought process behind it. Was he angry? Was he about to walk out? Was he just confused? Who could tell?

'What about if we change things slightly?' Jake said, his voice softer.

I turned back to look at him. The usual bright spark on his face was gone. He seemed more serious; more vulnerable.

'What do you mean?' I asked.

'Let me take you out on a date. A proper date. Just the two of us. No mates around. No pretence. I...' He looked over at Nicholas who was still staring intently our way. 'I don't want to lose you.'

'You want to take me out on a date?' I asked. I was completely unprepared for that.

'Yes. If you want. I know you're on a date with that other bloke, but... How about we give us a proper try?'

The tingling across my body intensified and my heart began to pound, but I refused to get excited. Everything with Jake had been too good to be true so far. 'A proper try?' I checked.

'Yes.'

I had no words. I found myself lost somewhere between immense jubilation and caustic cynicism.

However, before my brain could even begin to process which side of the fence I wanted to opt for, Jake edged in closer to me. He looked at my lips, just as he had done several times before, but this time there was no hesitation. I didn't even get a chance to catch my breath before he kissed me.

Within seconds, I'd lost touch with reality.

That familiar electric charge transcended into overdrive. I swear you could hear my body fizzle with the sensational pleasure of his touch.

I'd fantasised about this moment more than I'd ever care to admit, but the reality surpassed anything I could have imagined. It all felt like absolute perfection.

I began to sense myself trembling like a rocket that was about to take off, and that's when Jake deepened the kiss. I think I actually stopped breathing.

His tongue brushed against mine and fireworks began exploding through me.

I never wanted it to end.

But it did. All too soon.

He stepped back and I licked my lips that were now raw with passion. For a moment our eyes were locked together and the world stopped turning.

Then Jake looked around. I watched as he sought out his friends behind him. He nodded at them.

He nodded at them!

'What are you doing?' I snapped.

'What?' he said, spinning his head back to look at me.

'I don't believe it. You don't want to date me at all. You're just playing this stupid part again so your mates will think we're still going out.'

'That's not it.'

'From the second you asked me to go to that wedding with you, you've done nothing but use me.'

'No. That's not it.'

'You know what, you make a terrible boyfriend.'

'What?'

I raised my voice. 'Consider this our break up. And just so you know, I'm not leaving you because I'm cheating on you, I'm leaving you because I deserve way better.'

Jake looked absolutely gobsmacked. I stomped away from him and returned to Nicholas.

'Can we get out of here?' I said to him. I actually expected Nicholas to tell me to do one after he'd clearly seen me kissing another man, but to my grateful surprise he looked at the tears building up in my eyes and nodded at me sympathetically.

'Of course we can,' he said. He stood up, grabbed my hand and led me out onto the street.

I didn't turn back once. I couldn't. The man I loved was a manipulative bastard. If I thought my heart was broken before, it now felt shattered in several billion pieces.

The street was heaving. People were strolling up and down, some admiring the marina, others enjoying drinks at their tables. All I could do was walk. I looked ahead and dragged Nicholas with me. I needed to get away.

I kept walking for a few minutes, right to the end of the waterfront. When it became darker and quieter, I finally stopped, and I grasped on to every bit of strength I had so that I wouldn't fall apart.

'Come here,' Nicholas said, shuffling me to rest against a wall so we had some privacy. I'd almost forgotten he was there.

'What happened?' he said, stroking away my tears with his thumb and curling my hair behind my ears. How on earth could he be so lovely after the way I'd just treated him?

'I'm so sorry about that,' I sniffled.

'Was he the boyfriend?'

'Ex-boyfriend,' I corrected sharply. Then I leaned forward. I couldn't look at Nicholas. 'Truthfully, he's not even that. He asked me to act as his girlfriend because he didn't want to go to a wedding on his own. I got a bit carried away maybe thinking there was more to it. But it turns out all he wanted was a plus one when his mates were watching. We barely spoke otherwise.'

'He used you?'

I nodded.

'What a bastard. You deserve far better than that. You're such a beautiful, talented and interesting person. You deserve someone who's going to love and admire all those things about you. He sounds like he was only ever out for himself.'

Just as I was processing Nicholas's words, he moved right in to kiss me. It was just a soft touch, before he edged back to gauge my reaction.

I didn't know how to react. My lips were still throbbing from the incredible kiss with Jake. Part of me never wanted to kiss anyone else ever again.

Nicholas took my lack of a reaction as a positive sign, and he placed his lips on mine once more.

It was nice. But that was it. Just nice. There was no fizz, no trembling, and not one single sign of a firework.

I pulled away and Nicholas smiled.

'Sorry. I shouldn't have done that,' he said.

'No. It's fine.'

'You're just pretty irresistible.'

'Thank you.'

I looked into Nicholas's sparkling blue eyes. They were hypnotic. He was everything I should be looking for in a man. I might have not been totally comfortable on this date, but I certainly wasn't ashamed to be with him. That was something, right? And maybe none of what I was feeling was about him and all of my confusion was totally related to Jake.

'It's not quite how I saw this night going,' I said. 'Perhaps we could try again sometime? I think I should go home now and pull myself together. I promise I'll be fully focused on our next date.'

'You'd like to go out again?' he asked, not hiding his joy.

'Yes. Of course. I owe you a proper date. Whenever you want.'

'Maybe dinner next time?'

'Of course. And maybe somewhere out of Ipswich, so there won't be any ex-boyfriends hanging around.'

'There aren't any more that I need to be aware of, are there?' he asked with a smirk.

'No. Just the one pretend one. Other than that, you're quite safe.'

'Good. How about next weekend, then? Maybe Friday night?'

'Sounds perfect. You pick a place. Anywhere you want to go.'

'I'm looking forward to it already.'

Nicholas took my hand and led me to the road. Within minutes we'd flagged down a taxi and not ten minutes after that we'd pulled up outside my house.

I quickly grabbed a ten pound note from my purse and handed it to the driver. Too many men had been paying for me lately and I was starting to get twitchy. Getting back some independence was a must.

'I was going to pay,' Nicholas said.

'And I did.'

We got out of the taxi and Nicholas followed me to my front door.

'Thank you for a lovely evening,' he said.

'Don't lie,' I replied as I opened up.

He laughed. 'A first date to remember no less. Although maybe not one to tell the grandkids.'

This made my stomach churn.

'Well, goodnight then,' he said and then he kissed me again. He pulled away quickly to check my response.

Truthfully, I was far too tired, upset and angry to decipher what the best response should be, so instead I decided just to stop thinking.

He moved in again and this time his lips met mine with more vigour. He wrapped his arms around me and I gave up.

I wrapped my arms around him in return and I let him devour me.

Sod it. I was broken hearted, horny as hell (albeit because of another man), fed up with being single, and feeling a huge need to move on and get Jake out of my system. Suddenly having sex with Nicholas seemed like the perfect solution.

Was it a good idea? Absolutely not.

Did I care? Absolutely not.

He pushed me into the living room, kicking the front door closed with his foot, and we started to explore each other more fervently. Hands were everywhere, and his lips began edging down my neck.

'Shall we move this to the bedroom?' he whispered.

I stopped. His urgency snapped me back to reality. 'No,' I said. 'This isn't a good idea. We barely know each other.'

'You like to get to know somewhere first?' he asked, as if he didn't understand.

'I think that's better.'

Neither of us moved for a second.

'I was kissing another man less than an hour ago,' I reasoned.

'He kissed you,' Nicholas corrected.

Those words brought tears to my eyes. Jake had kissed me. A kiss I'd been longing for. The best kiss I'd ever had. And it turned out it meant nothing to him at all.

'Shh, don't cry,' Nicholas said. 'He's not worth your tears.'

Nicholas brushed my tears away, firstly with his fingers, then with his lips, and before I knew it he was kissing me again.

He whispered softly, 'I feel like I've known you forever,' and once again it snapped me back to the present.

I pushed him away. 'You barely know me at all.'

'I probably know you better than you think. We have a lot in common.'

I could see he really meant this. But we'd probably spent less than two hours together in total.

He moved in for another kiss when my doorbell went.

He stood back, almost nervously.

'Who's that?' he asked.

'I don't know,' I replied, straightening my dress.

I opened the door and nearly fell apart completely.

It was Jake.

THIRTEEN

'Can we talk?' Jake asked. He seemed very sorrowful. There was a taxi waiting on the road, its engine still running.

'What are you doing here?' I asked.

'I couldn't leave things like that. You've got it all-'

'Hello again,' Nicholas interrupted, joining me at the door and carefully wrapping his arm around my waist. What was it with these men marking their territory?

Jake's face went pale. 'Sorry, I didn't realise...'

'Can we help you?' Nicholas asked.

My instinct was to push Nicholas into the street, grab Jake and drag him inside. Where the men were standing felt totally wrong. But I had to acknowledge that maybe it was for the best. Jake being here would no doubt add to my misery. None of this could end well.

'I came to speak to Izzy,' Jake said.

'Then speak,' Nicholas replied.

I would normally have hated anyone else answering for me, but I was so upset and exhausted, I was happy to let the conversation just happen without me. I had nothing left to give.

'It looks like you're busy right now,' Jake said to me. 'Perhaps another time.'

'Perhaps not,' Nicholas said.

'Izzy?' Jake asked.

I took a breath. My whole body was trembling and I was still fighting tears.

'I think that says it all, don't you?' Nicholas said. 'Perhaps it's time you left. And perhaps it's time you left Isobel alone. You've caused her enough hurt. She doesn't deserve that.'

'No, she doesn't,' Jake said with obvious regret. He looked right into my eyes. 'Do you want me to leave, Izz?'

The word 'no' was teetering on my lips, but I knew I'd regret uttering it. This had to be the turning point. If I could get him to leave now, it would be one step nearer to that closure I so desperately needed. This was it.

'Perhaps it is best you leave,' I said, struggling against my sorrow.

Jake seemed absolutely gutted. He glanced at Nicholas then back at me. Then he nodded. 'If that's what you want.'

I nodded back and Nicholas pulled me in closer.

'Take care, Izz. And for what it's worth, I really am sorry.'

I nodded again, tensing every muscle I had to contain the anguish within me.

Jake turned around and got back in the taxi. I wanted to watch until he was out of sight, but Nicholas closed the door.

'Are you okay?' Nicholas asked, pulling me against him.

I cried a little on his shoulder and he soothed me. Then I looked up at his face.

'I think we'd better call it a night,' I said. 'Sorry.'

'Of course. I completely understand. You need to get your rest.'

I nodded.

'I'm only over the road if you need me. If you need anything at all you come knocking. And I'm sure Smokey's lurking around somewhere. He'll keep an eye on you too.'

I smirked. 'That cat has always got his eyes on me.'

'He probably feels protective of you. He's certainly taken a shine to you. And I can see exactly why.'

He kissed me tenderly. It was very sweet.

'Goodnight, Isobel. Sleep well.'

'You too. Goodnight.'

Nicholas let himself out and I immediately staggered upstairs.

I sat at my dressing table and studied my face. I was so made-up. Far more than I ever usually was. None of this felt like me. I liked to wear make-up but this was heavy and slutty.

I took out my face wipes and quickly erased any trace of it. I needed to put this night to the back of my mind. I'd just made a huge step in moving on from Jake. I should have felt proud.

So why was it I just felt rotten?

I spent Sunday flopped on the sofa in my pyjamas feeling thoroughly sorry for myself, but by Monday I was determined to get a grip. As always, I threw myself into my work. I was at my desk raring to go by seven a.m. and I worked solidly with barely a break all day. It was good for me, forcing me not to think about anything else.

But by Tuesday afternoon I began to feel frazzled. I needed a break from my computer. I needed some fresh air.

I popped my sandals on and I stepped out into the sun. I didn't really know what to do or where to go, so I walked aimlessly down a few streets. I couldn't be long. I had deadlines to meet. But stretching my legs and feeling the sun warm my skin was tremendous.

Twenty-five minutes later I returned home to find Smokey sitting patiently on my door step. He'd spent most of Sunday lazing with me, but I'd not seen much of him since.

'Hello Smokey,' I said. Acknowledging him made me turn around to look at Nicholas's house. I'd not seen him or spoken to him since he'd left on Saturday night. We'd not even swapped numbers. Was our date still on for Friday night?

I wanted to go out with him again. It felt like the right thing to do. The right thing to do morally, that is. The right thing in my heart was to get in my car and drive over to Henstone to declare my undying love for Jake. But I knew that was ridiculous. So morally sound decisions were taking over. It was the new me.

'Shall we go and see if your daddy's in?' I said to Smokey, picking him up.

As I did, Vivian appeared. She stepped outside, her hands full of empty shopping bags, and she locked her front door.

'Surely you're past this stage now,' she said, nodding her head towards Smokey.

I chose not to decipher her meaning.

'Cats will be cats,' I said with a smile, before heading over the road.

I rang the bell at Nicholas's door and stood patiently. Smokey wriggled, desperate to get free. I bent down to place him on the ground, and he leapt from my arms and disappeared around the side of the house.

I rang again. The car was there on the driveway. Nicholas had to be in.

I looked up to the first floor window to see if Nicholas was on the phone again waving at me, but no one was in sight. Why was he always so busy when I called?

I poked my head to the side to peek through his living room window, curious to see why he was so tied up all the time.

I saw Smokey run across the room from the back of the house, no doubt where the cat flap was.

Then Smokey stopped dead still. Like weirdly still.

I watched, hoping that he was okay, when something utterly mad happened.

He expanded in size.

His fur ruffled, and then flesh pushed its way through

until Smokey was six foot tall and not Smokey anymore.

I stared in horror as Smokey's brilliant blue eyes caught mine. But they weren't Smokey's. They looked exactly like Smokey's – in a way I'd only realised.

Standing completely naked in the middle of the living room was Nicholas.

Smokey had turned into Nicholas!

FOURTEEN

Nicholas and I just stared at each other for a second. I could barely compute the physically perfect body standing before me, and I couldn't take my glare away from those blue eyes. Smokey's sparkling blue eyes.

He quickly left the room and I knew I needed to get out of there. I darted back over the road. I didn't know what else to do. I was terrified. Terrified of what I thought had just happened, and terrified that maybe I was going insane. Maybe my brain was more frazzled than I'd thought.

I fumbled with my lock, my hands shaking, and swiftly entered my house. I was breathing erratically as I paced around my living room, trying to make sense of things. Had I really seen that?

Suddenly my bell rang and I froze.

It had to be Nicholas. It had to be.

Taking a deep breath, I edged towards the door and opened it slightly.

'Can we talk?' Nicholas said, standing tall, now fully dressed in jeans and a shirt.

'I... I don't know what I just saw.'

'Please come over to my house so we can talk.'

'Can't we talk here?'

'I don't think that's wise.'

I was keen to know what the hell had just happened, but I was far too scared to be alone with him.

'No one's about. Tell me what I just saw,' I said. 'Why were you standing naked in your living room?'

'You know very well what you just saw.'

'I really don't.'

'I've been meaning to tell you for a while. The last thing I wanted was for you to find out this way. But you know now. And we need to talk about it. Please come over to my house.'

I hesitated, still trying to grasp onto anything that made sense.

'Did I really see that then?' I mumbled. 'Did you really just...? Did that really happen?'

'Whatever you thought you saw, it really happened. Yes.'

I dropped my voice. 'You're a cat?'

His head fell forward and I could tell he was getting irritated.

'Yes,' he replied. I couldn't move. That was the most ridiculous and terrifying thing I'd ever heard.

'You're Smokey?'

'I'm Nicholas. You named my cat form Smokey.'

'But he's been in my house. For months. He's been sitting by my side. He's seen me naked!'

'I think we're square on that now.'

I couldn't speak. All the compromising positions I'd let that cat see me in whipped through my head. Things I'd done and words I'd said that I wouldn't want another person to know or hear. Yet all the time a man had been by my side. A man in disguise.

I wanted to throw up.

'How could you do that?' I gasped. 'You've been letting yourself into my home. No! This can't be true.'

Panic joined the nausea.

'Please, I need to explain,' he replied. 'It's more complicated than you know. You need to come over to my house so that I can take you through it all.'

'I'm not going anywhere with you.'

I tried to close my door but Nicholas pushed it back. He was very strong.

'I'm asking politely, but my patience is wearing thin,' he said. 'You need to come over to my house so we can talk about this.'

'No. I don't want to know. Please leave me alone.'

'Right.'

With one gush of energy, he pushed the door completely open and knocked me back against the stairs. He slammed the door shut before I could scramble to my feet and he pinned me to the spot with his glare.

Those eyes. They now had the same venom in them that I'd seen in Smokey when he'd been attacking Jake. It really had been jealousy.

He loomed over me as I lay awkwardly on the stairs.

'I'm going to ask you one more time. Will you come to my house so we can talk about this? It's going to happen one way or another, so which is it going to be? The easy way where we walk over together hand in hand, quite civilly. Or the hard way.'

I had never been so frightened. I was stiff with it.

'What's the hard way?' I mumbled.

'Are you coming with me or not?'

'Please just leave. Please.'

'You had your chance. Don't ever say I didn't give you ample opportunity to do this nicely.'

He rummaged around in his pocket and pulled out a white cloth. He quickly smothered my mouth.

My levels of panic shot through the roof. I started to scream, but it was far too muffled. I fought back at him, throwing my legs and arms this way and that; in any way I could to struggle free. But he was using all of his force against me, pushing me down with both hands. He was so very, very strong.

The struggling got harder and harder as everything

turned darker and darker. Finally it all went black.

I opened my eyes. Before I could even decipher where I was, I felt the pulsating in my head. What was happening?

There was a small window to the side of me blasting light through. I didn't recognise anything. I sat up, which made me very woozy, and I tried to take in my surroundings.

My whole body throbbed as I realised I had no clue where I was.

It was a pretty pink room with floral wallpaper, and I was tucked up under a floral pink duvet. To my right was a small desk, and to the left there was a small wardrobe and a little open door that led to what seemed like a bathroom. That was it as far as decoration went.

I shakily stood up, feeling very uneasy and definitely scared, and I looked out of the window to get some bearings. The first thing I noticed was my house. I was opposite my house.

I was in Nicholas's house!

The memories came flooding back and the panic rose in me.

I fumbled over to the door but it was locked.

'Nicholas! Let me out! You can't do this to me!' The screaming did nothing for my headache, but the need for escape was far greater.

'Nicholas!' I shouted.

I struggled down to my knees and looked through the keyhole. It was a mortice lock, and from how shiny the handle seemed, it must have been brand new.

All I could make out was a dark shaded carpet and the edge of a bannister. That was it.

I heard footsteps and then I saw a figure approach.

I stood backwards as a key unlocked the door.

'Welcome back,' Nicholas said with a smile. He came into the room, closing the door behind him. He then made sure that he stayed close to the door, preventing me from escaping. I remembered very well how strong he was.

'What are you doing? You can't keep me here.'

'I just need you to calm down,' he said. 'Once you're calm, we can have a proper conversation. Then I can tell you everything you need to know.'

'I am calm,' I said, shaking with anger.

'There's nothing to be afraid of. I'm not going to hurt you. Quite the opposite in fact. We need each other. You couldn't be safer anywhere else in the world than here.'

'I find that hard to believe. Did you drug me?'

His face became stern. 'I told you I didn't want to do that. You left me no choice.'

'Not kidnapping me would be a choice.'

He shook his head. 'When I've had the chance to fill you in on everything, you'll realise why it was so important. I'm sure you'll forgive me. You'll probably even feel a bit silly for being so afraid.'

'I doubt it. Go on then. What do you need to tell me?'

'Not now. I don't think you're ready for all the details just yet. This is going to be quite a lot for you to take in. You're about to learn about a life-changing opportunity. Wonderfully life-changing. Things are about to get far better for you.'

'Are you trying to recruit me into a cult or something?'

Nicholas laughed. 'Of course not. Nothing as sinister as that. Opportunity probably wasn't the right word. But I think for now you need to get some rest. You need to get used to your new surroundings and settle in. Then I can tell you all.'

'I'm not going to settle in.'

'Isobel, you don't have any choice. Very soon you'll learn why and I know you'll appreciate it then. But what I have to tell you is big news. I don't think it's fair to spring so much on you in one day. You've only just learnt that I'm a cat person.'

'A cat person? Is that a real thing?'

'It certainly is. We're called Felivires. It's a great honour for you to be involved with us. Very few people have ever known of our existence. You should see this as a blessing.'

'Being scared half to death and being kept against my will is not a blessing.'

'I know I'm keeping you here against your will for the time being. It won't be forever-'

'I should hope not!'

'But it is necessary for now. Our futures depend on it.'

'You can't do this. This is illegal!'

'Please stop being so dramatic. You need to trust me. Sometimes things are taken out of our control for the greater good. We just don't see it at the time. This is very much one of those instances. Have faith. I promise you you'll look back and realise that this is the right decision.'

'You have to let me go.'

'I can't do that.'

'You need to let me go!'

I lurched forward and tried to shove him out of the way, but with one arm he pushed me back and pinned me to the bed.

'I don't want you to get hurt, Isobel. But if you're going to be hysterical then you'll end up hurting yourself. You need to think logically here and be reasonable. The sooner you calm down, the sooner I can share my news with you, and the sooner you'll get out of here. Fighting me will only delay things. You're a clever girl. Use your common sense and calm down.'

I relaxed under his hold. I hated capitulating, but if playing along would get me out of there faster, then that's exactly what I was going to do.

'Good,' he said backing away. 'Now what can I get you for dinner? I'm quite the chef, you know. Mexican? Italian? Or perhaps just a take-away curry for tonight to help you settle in?'

'I'm not hungry,' I said. I really wasn't.

'No, Isobel. You need to keep your strength up. It's really important that you look after yourself. I'll tell you what, I'll get us a pizza for tonight. What's your favourite toppings?'

I shook my head. 'I don't know.' The last thing I could process was pizza toppings.

'Very well. I understand. It's been a big day. I'll just get you a cheese and tomato for now. You can't go wrong with that. Is that okay?'

I wanted to scream that of course it wasn't okay, but I could see that playing happy families was calming him down and making him more amenable. I needed to keep that up.

'That sounds lovely. Thank you.'

'Good. I have a spare TV if you want it?' he said. 'I didn't want to just presume in case you wanted some time alone tonight to think on things. But I don't want you to feel bored.'

So many things were zooming around my head as he said this. Bored suggested that I was going to be here for a while. That notion petrified me. But I still played along.

'That would be very kind of you, thank you.'

'Good. I'll sort it out for you when the pizza has been ordered. See, we're having fun already.'

I nodded. He had a strange idea of fun.

'Oh, and what do you want to drink? I don't have alcohol. We both need to stay off the alcohol. But what about fresh orange juice? We both know that's your favourite.'

A chill spiked through me. Was he really a cat? Had he really been spying on me? It all seemed too bizarre to be true. But seeing him turn from Smokey to Nicholas played over and over in my mind. I felt violated. It was far too much for me to process.

'Again, very kind of you,' I muttered, praying for this nightmare to end.

'Great. I'll be waiting on you hand and foot, so just shout if you need anything. See you in a bit.'

With that he closed the door and locked it firmly shut.

I sat up and within seconds all I could do was sob.

FIFTEEN

As promised, once the pizza was on order, Nicholas set me up a little TV in the corner of the room, which he balanced on a coffee table. He laughed at how awful it looked and said that he would get me a proper TV unit in due course.

If those words weren't alarming enough, he then added that there was a selection of my clothes in the wardrobe, and my toiletries in the en suite. I nearly passed out with terror. He had packed up a whole bunch of my belongings while I was unconscious. It went beyond creepy.

Whilst he seemed to be promising freedom if I cooperated, all of these things suggested a much longer term engagement. I didn't know what to think.

That night I sat alone and picked at my pizza in between bouts of crying and staring at my very empty house across the road. I was so high up, so far away from the street below. So far away from anyone who could help.

It had been dark for quite a while and I was feeling very tired, but I knew I wouldn't sleep. I brushed my teeth with my own toothbrush and toothpaste from home, and I got into my pink satin pyjamas. I wasn't sure whether it was a comfort or not that I had my own pyjamas.

I tossed and turned all night, and the hours seemed to drag on forever. I was so glad when Nicholas knocked on my door at seven a.m. with a full English breakfast. Despite not feeling even remotely hungry, I thanked him and gushed at how lovely it looked, hoping it might speed up him talking to me.

I tried to eat as much as I could and I washed it down with my orange juice and coffee, made exactly how I like it. This man knew so much about me. I'd been letting him study me for months without knowing it.

I got dressed and put morning television on, and I prayed that Nicholas would be back soon.

By ten o'clock he reappeared.

'Good breakfast?' he said.

'Yes. Lovely, thank you. You were right, you are quite the chef. I wouldn't know where to start with poached eggs.'

'I know. You never have a good breakfast. But all that can change now.'

My stomach knotted, but I kept smiling. 'I think I feel better today. I needed a good night's sleep. Although, can I be honest with you?' I said this as calmly as I could.

'Of course. I want you to be.'

'I am a bit concerned that it's a working day and I'll be getting calls and emails that I can't respond to. I have client deadlines to meet.'

He looked at me softly. 'I understand that. I do. And I'm sorry for taking you away from that. But, truthfully, I think this break will be good for you. Do you realise that you sit at your computer for several hours straight every single day?'

'I run my own business. It takes dedication. Surely you know that being a finance director?'

He laughed. It was a proper laugh as if I'd said something very amusing. 'I'm not a finance director. I don't know anything about finance.'

'Then why did you tell me you were?'

'I came to realise that you're the sort of girl who is

impressed by men who sound important and busy. I wanted to get close to you. Don't judge me for lying. I had to contend with that ridiculous man you obsess over. Getting you to notice me wasn't easy.'

'Obsess?' I asked as my stomach knotted tighter. 'You mean Jake?' I suddenly felt terribly small and embarrassed.

'You talk about him constantly. Even to a cat. Jake Masters: the gorgeous God of your networking meetings. It was quite cringeworthy.'

I didn't know what to say. I wanted the world to eat me up.

'I knew I needed to find a way to make you listen,' Nicholas continued. 'I could tell he was breaking your heart. Besides, I didn't travel all this way to get pushed aside by some selfish moron.'

'Travel all what way?'

'My family lives about a hundred and twenty five miles away from here. It was hard tracking you down.'

A chill swept over me. 'Why were you tracking me down?'

'I've said too much. Let me go and get the dishwasher on, make us another cuppa, and then we can sit down properly and I can explain everything.'

'The dishwasher can bloody wait. I want to know! Why were you tracking me down?'

'Come on now, Isobel. We were getting along. I can't talk to you if you're going to be moody, can I?'

I took a few breaths to help alleviate the fire burning through me.

'Of course not. I'm just eager to know.'

'And you will. You'll know everything very soon.'

'Can you at least tell me what you really do for a living before you go?'

He paused before smiling. 'I work in retail.'

'Like a shop assistant?'

'No. More like management.'

'Why wouldn't you tell me that?'

He smiled proudly. 'My family owns a chain of pet stores. It's kind of what we know best. When my brother died, the whole business got handed to me.'

'I'm sorry to hear your brother died.'

'Don't be. I've lost many siblings. It's just the way it is being a Felivire. But now I'm CEO of the whole chain.'

'You didn't think I'd be impressed with that?'

'I'm not really actively involved. I have to sign the odd cheque and turn up to board meetings, but I leave everyone else to do the hard work. Why not? That's what I pay them forIsobel, I'm lazy. Really lazy. I was handed a hugely successful national chain to look after, but I just take the money and let other people worry about it. I know you despise that. I know you think hard work is vital to success. I prove that theory wrong. So that's why I never told you. I hope we can get over this. I really hope it won't come between us. I'm being honest with you now. I won't tell you another lie, I promise. But you have to not judge me. Can you do that?'

After a beat I said, 'Of course.' I was lying. I completely judged him. I was starting to hate everything about him. But I made sure to put on my sweetest smile. 'We all have to live the lives we want. I would never judge you for anything you do.'

'Thank you. That makes me feel so much better. Right, I'll be back in a few. Then I'll reveal all.'

He collected my plate, glass and mug and left the room. I heard the lock click behind him. I raced to the door and watched through the keyhole as his figure disappeared downstairs.

I needed some sort of idea as to what the house looked like. Even if I could get out of the room, I didn't know where I was in the house or how quickly I could get to the front door. It was all so frightful.

I sat back on the bed and pretended to watch television, ready for his return.

About fifteen minutes later the lock clicked again and he

entered with a tray holding two mugs. He handed me one and then sat down on the bed holding the other.

'Right then. Are you ready?' he said.

'Yes,' I replied, nervously.

'I know this is going to be a lot to take in. You might be fearful as well as excited. I don't know. But however you react, I understand. It's going to take some time to adjust. And there are lots of decisions we need to make. So I'll tell you everything now, and then you'll probably need some time on your own to process it. That's absolutely fine.'

'Time alone at home?' I asked with hope.

He smirked and shook his head. 'Let me tell you and you'll understand why.'

'Okay.'

'So, as you found out yesterday – albeit in far from the most ideal of ways – I am a Felivire. A cat person. We used to be fairly large in number, but we've had a bad run of things over the past fifty years or so and we're now very close to extinction.'

'I'm sorry to hear that,' I said, playing nice.

'I'm pleased you said that. You see, I'm actually the last male Felivire alive. There are plenty of she-Felivires. I, myself, have two sisters. But it's the men who are important.'

He spotted the annoyance on my face.

He laughed. 'I'm not saying that males are better than females. They're just more important for the continuation of our species. Let me explain. For every male Felivire that's ever been born, there is a bearer that is also born at around the same time. It could be anyone and they could be anywhere. We have never found out how they're chosen, but we know from the moment we're born that a female has been conceived to be our match.'

'What do you mean by bearer?'

'You're thirty-one, yes? Born in April?'

I hesitated. 'Yes.' I was now resigned to the fact that this man seemed to know everything about me.

'The same as me. We were born to be together.'

'Are you saying we're related?'

'Of course not. That would be sickening. We're not related, we're matched.'

'How are we matched?'

'In order for my species to continue, we need to obviously have offspring born with the cat gene. For reasons we don't understand, females can't pass it on. She-Felivires always have normal human children. It's only the men who can carry on the line. Hence why my brothers dying is so bad for us.'

'Surely it would make more sense for females to carry on the line?'

'I agree. But it doesn't work that way. This is nature. We can't change it. Then to add to the difficulties, a man can't just find any woman to bear his offspring either. It has to be a special someone. A strong woman who has been born to do just that.'

My heart stopped. A horrible notion prickled at my skin as I saw where he was going.

'If the man doesn't find his match and he impregnates someone else, she will inevitably die. It will be too much for her body to take. It needs to be the bearer who has the gift to carry his children.'

'You think I'm your match, don't you,' I muttered, cautiously.

He smiled warmly. 'I know you are. It took me quite a while to find you. I've been searching since I was eighteen. We're given clues along the way, as if the universe wants us to meet. I felt your essence one day in London and that's when I got my first look at you. I thought that was it, but then you moved, much to my frustration. Finally I tracked you down to Ipswich, and on that first day that I rubbed myself against you in my cat form, I knew for sure.'

I didn't know whether to laugh at how ridiculous this was or scream with terror.

'Don't tell me you don't feel it too. You say you're like

catnip to cats. Did you say your sweat must smell of it?' He chuckled, as if it were terribly enjoyable. 'I like that. It's almost true. You share some features with cats that other humans don't.'

'No I don't.'

'You know, we've never had a scientist within our people to really explore why or how. It would be great if one day we had a Felivire scientist who had the skills to examine our kind. We can't very well have any old person examining us. If the general public found out about us, we'd be locked up and experimented on before you could say whiskers. We need to have the skill set within our own kind to do more research. I really hope it could be one of our children.'

'Woah, hang on. I'm not having your children. Cat children or normal children. Let's just be clear about that.'

He studied me, not at all thrown. 'I understand how out of the blue this is.'

'You can say that again.'

'But you need to consider everything. If you don't meet your destiny and bear my children, you'll be killing off a whole species. Do you really want that on your conscience? You were, after all, born to do this.'

'But I don't want this. I didn't ask for this. You can't honestly expect me just to give up my life to have your children.'

This seemed to sadden him. 'I'm not going to lie. For many years I had dreams of meeting my bearer and falling in love. How ideal would it be for us to get married, live here and bring up our children together?'

'What?'

'You have to know, Isobel, I'd marry you in a second. I'm totally in love with you. You say the word, at any time, and I'm yours forever. But I know that you being my bearer doesn't necessarily mean you'll love me in return. You'd think it would work that way, but it doesn't. And you only owe me children. You don't owe me your life.'

'I don't owe you anything.'

'You were born to be a bearer. My bearer. You do in fact owe me that. But how we choose to arrange it is our business and our business alone. That's why I decorated this room for you. I even had that wall knocked in so you could have the upstairs bathroom as your own.'

'You decorated this room for me?' My skin prickled again.

'In the early days you're probably going to want to be near your children. It's inevitable. But I wanted to show you that I wasn't expecting you to share a bed with me. I'd love it if you did. And maybe in time, who knows. But I wanted to show you how open minded I am about you having a choice. If you just want to be the mother of my children and nothing more, then this is your space in this house and totally yours alone.'

My body began quivering with fear. This was crazy. There was something wrong with him.

'Well, you've certainly given me a lot to ponder on,' I said, trying to control my shaky voice. 'The future of the Fee-whatever-they're-called. The cat people. That's something I need to take very seriously.'

'Thank you.' He seemed relieved. 'I'm so pleased you understand.'

'Perhaps if I could sleep in my own bed tonight-'

'No.'

'I do need some time to let this all settle in. Make my decisions about our future.'

'Of course you do. But you'll do it here.'

'But you said I could go home when you'd explained it all.'

'And you can. When you've had my babies.'

Shards of fear cut through me. 'What?'

'I'm willing to be very flexible here, Isobel. I know that it's going to take some time for you to adjust. I appreciate that having sex with me with all this pressure on your shoulders is going to make things very difficult.'

'Sex?'

'You do understand how reproduction works?' he asked in a rather patronising tone.

The walls in the room started getting smaller and smaller as I felt everything I'd ever known fade away.

'I'm willing to give you all the time you need to get used to this and adjust,' he said. 'We have time. If it takes a few months, or even a year or two, so be it.'

I could barely breathe. 'Years?'

'Even when we start trying to conceive, there's no guarantee how quickly it will happen. We have to be honest about how long this could take.'

'You're going to keep me here for years?' The tears began blurring my eyes.

'I'm going to keep you here for as long as it takes until you've given birth to my offspring.'

'I have to stay here all through the pregnancy too?' I was properly weeping now.

'Of course you will. I'll need to look after you. Even for a bearer, carrying a litter is a toll on the body.'

'A litter?' The panic jolted me to my feet, so much so I forgot that I was still holding a mug of coffee. Brown liquid was thrown everywhere, and it quickly started soaking into the ugly pink carpet.

'Look what you've done now!' he moaned.

'I don't care!' I screeched, throwing the empty mug onto the bed. 'I want to know what you mean by litter. How many babies do you want me to have?'

'I don't know for sure. On average bearers have about five or six. Although there are stories of a bearer who once gave birth to twelve. How amazing is that!'

'Twelve babies?' I gasped. I could feel my windpipe getting tighter and tighter. 'You want me to have twelve babies? I don't fucking think so!'

'I realise this seems a lot to you. But you have to know that your body can handle it.'

'It might be able to, but I won't be! Let me out of here!'

I raced for the door but he grabbed me. He picked me

up and threw me on the bed.

'You need to stop over-reacting. This isn't the end of the world. You don't have to be with me if you don't want to. I'm only asking for you to give me what is rightfully mine. What you were born to do.'

'It's too much!'

His face became visibly irritated. 'I've had enough of these theatrics now. You need to calm down. Or do I have to make you?'

I stopped still. I lay under his glare, fearful of what he'd do next.

'Now I'm going to get a cloth to wipe up this coffee. You take a few minutes to compose yourself and then we'll finish this discussion.'

He disappeared off, locking the door behind him, and I curled myself up into a tight ball. I couldn't stop the tears. I began crying so deeply, full of such fear and despair, that I started to choke on my own distress. This had to be a nightmare. This was far too horrendous to be really happening.

I was so utterly bewildered. I know I saw him turn from a cat into a man, but surely this all couldn't be true. Yet that didn't seem to matter. Whether the story was true or not, Nicolas definitely seemed to believe it, and that was unbearably terrifying.

The door opened and he brought in a bucket and sponge. He locked the door again and slipped the key into his pocket, then he knelt down and started scrubbing up the coffee stains.

I sat up. I had to get him to see reason.

'What if I refuse?' I said. 'You can't keep me here forever. People will notice I'm gone.'

'Eventually. But this is the last place they'll look, I'm sure.'

'But Jake saw me with you. He'll tell the police. You were the last person I was with. They'll question you.'

'Of course they will.' He stopped what he was doing and

stared at me. 'I don't want to do it this way. I'd planned for us to go on a few more dates. I thought we'd start to fall in love, and then you'd be more willing to do this with me. It never once occurred to me that I'd have to lock you up in here. It's so far from what I want. I hate that I'm hurting you. But I can't risk making my people extinct. This literally is life or death. You must understand that. I will do everything in my power to ensure my species continues. And that means you have to give birth to my offspring.'

'I don't think you've fully appreciated just how stubborn I am,' I argued back, trying to be strong. 'I won't do this. I won't. I'm very sorry for you, but this isn't my problem. I deserve the right to have a family when I want and with the person I want. This is wrong. What you're doing is wrong. I simply won't do it.'

'Of course that's how you feel right now. You're in shock. That's why I'm more than happy to give you time.'

'I won't change my mind. I do not want this. I do not want you.'

'You can't say how you're going to feel in a few months.'

'I think I can.'

'No Isobel.'

'Yes.'

He stood up and leaned over me. Those glimmering eyes bore right down into me.

'I want you to do this willingly. I want you to enjoy this experience. I want you to love me and for us to bring up our children together. But you must understand, what I want more than any of that is the continuation of my species. And I will do everything in my power to make that a reality. So whilst I'm happy to give you time to adjust, I will not wait forever. You can't just keep me hanging on in the hope that I'll cave in first. You will be having my children, Isobel, whether I come in here to make love to you or I come in here and force you. It's happening either way. You need to decide what way it's going to be.'

I froze to the spot. Everything went a bit numb. The

walls closed in even tighter around me and I cracked inside as my reality seemed to vanish.

Nicholas knelt back down to finish sponging out the coffee and I slowly straightened myself up. My face was aching with the tears that I was trying to control. I wanted to get a grip; find a logical way out of this mess. There had to be a way out of this. This could not be my life. But the more I thought about it, the more upset I got. I couldn't stop crying.

He totally ignored me as he finished up. He didn't even look at me as he poured the water down the toilet. Finally he came to my side and stroked my hair.

'I love you, Isobel,' he said. 'This is hurting me more than it's hurting you. I'll leave you to it now. You take some time to think things over. Give me a shout when you're hungry or you need something and I'll be right back up. I'm not far away. Just take some time. Maybe have a little sleep. You'll see it's not as bad as you think. Just take some time.'

He kissed me on the head and walked away.

As the lock clicked again, I curled up back on the bed and screamed. I almost choked on my tears I was so shook up. It felt like my life had just ended and there was nothing I could do about it.

SIXTEEN

I spent most of the day curled up and crying. I kept going over and over how this had happened to me. Sometimes I stopped believing it and I even tried to convince myself that I could just get up and walk out. It was so difficult to get my head around the fact that I was being locked in this room and at some point in the future I was going to have to have sex with that awful man. And probably time and time again until I got pregnant. After witnessing Nicholas's determination, it felt unbearably inevitable.

I had flashes of thinking that I should just get it over with. The sooner I gave him what he wanted, the sooner I could attempt to get my life back on track. But then my innate stubbornness would kick in. I couldn't give in to this man. It was horrendous and he shouldn't be doing this.

I felt very thirsty by the time I heard a knock at the door much later that day.

'How are you feeling?' Nicholas asked as he let himself in, tray in hand. 'Any better?'

I just glared at him.

'I've brought you some pasta. It's my own special tomato sauce. It's got a bit of a kick to it so I hope you like it.'

He placed the tray on the desk. There was a glass of

water and a glass of orange juice next to it. I got the feeling I was going to get very sick of orange juice.

'You've been very quiet,' he said. 'I suppose you've got a lot of thinking to do. Do you have any questions for me at present?'

'When can I go home?' I asked.

He sat on the bed. 'I've told you that. When you've had my children. Although you may not want to leave then. And that's fine. You may want to be around them. A litter is always a lot to look after, so I could use the help. But once you've given me what is rightfully mine, I won't keep you any longer. I'm only keeping you now because you forced my hand. Seeing me in my cat form before we had a chance to connect was not part of the plan.'

'So it's my fault you've kidnapped me?'

He shook his head, annoyed. 'You make it sound so dramatic. So criminal.'

'This is a crime!'

'You sacrificing a whole species because you're too stubborn - that would be a crime. This is merely tactics.'

I wanted to slap him. The anger charged up inside of me.

He stood up. 'I'll leave you to eat. The second you've got any questions, just knock on the door and I'll race upstairs. Okay?'

I couldn't look at him. I heard him leave and lock the door again.

I moved over to grab the glass of water. At least now having a glass meant I could refill it from the tap. My mouth was so dry.

I looked down at the pasta. Part of me wanted to throw it at the door in a fit of rage, but I knew I had to eat. I hadn't had a thing since breakfast and I couldn't get weak. I couldn't be any more vulnerable than I already was.

As much as I hated to admit it, the food was absolutely delicious. He really was an amazing cook. Not that I'd be telling him that. I wolfed it down in minutes.

I sat back, feeling a bit better with food inside of me, and

I stared at the door.

I wasn't a person who moped. I never let things happen to me. I'd always been very proactive. I needed to adopt that mindset now. I was clever. Surely he couldn't keep me here forever against my will. There had to be a way out.

I tried to devise a plan.

Smashing the door down seemed like an option. I looked around the room for items to use. But there simply wasn't anything. Then my shoulders slumped as I realised even if I could get my hands on an axe or the equivalent, I'd make far too much noise. He'd been up here like a shot, and he was very strong. I knew he'd be able to overpower me.

Although I would have an axe...

I shuddered. I didn't know if I had it in me to kill him. That was a whole other thing. I definitely needed a far calmer exit.

I stood up to scan the street through the tiny window. Maybe I could catch the attention of someone I knew?

Straight away I spotted Vivian. She was there, needlessly attending to her more than perfect garden as always.

I banged on the window, but she couldn't hear me.

Another woman was walking down the road. I threw my arms in the air, hoping someone would see. This second person stopped at Vivian's garden and the two of them had a good chat. They weren't looking around. I was too high up. They weren't going to notice me.

I felt punched in the stomach as I realised no one was going to notice. In fact, it was going to take quite a long time before anyone would realise that I was missing. I was always forgetting to call my family and friends. I was terrible at replying to emails. It was the curse of being such a workaholic, and now it was going to cost me dearly.

I dropped down to the bed again when I realised what a waste of time my life had been. I thought I'd been on the verge of building an empire and my life of solidly working had made it all possible. But I was surely going to lose my clients now, my reputation would be in shatters, and I wouldn't be able to start again because everyone would think of me as that loose cannon who just randomly disappeared.

How could things have been going so well only for them to fall apart in an instant? It was so frustrating that there was nothing I could do.

I studied my house, suddenly realising that I'd left my laptop on. And it was plugged in. It had probably gone into sleep mode by now, but there was still electricity charging through my house.

What about my bills? I could be in this room for years. How was I going to pay my mortgage?

This was ridiculous. He had to see that.

I stood up and banged on the door.

'Nicholas!' I shouted. I knelt down to look through the keyhole. 'Nicholas!'

'I'm coming,' he shouted back. I saw him appear and I stepped backwards.

The door unlocked and he opened up.

'Can I help? Did you want something?'

'I've just realised a huge gaping hole in your plan. How am I going to pay my bills? I've got a mortgage, responsibilities. There is food in my fridge. My laptop is still on. You can't just keep me here. Things needs to be sorted.'

He shushed me and smiled. 'I love how practical you are. You're going to make a great mum.' Him just saying that made me freak.

'Here, sit down,' he said. He grabbed my hand and pulled me to the bed. I didn't refuse. I wanted to hear his response.

'I've thought about all of this already. I don't want you to lose your home. I also don't want to cause panic with your relatives. You haven't disappeared off the face of the planet. You're still here. You're just tied up for a while with a life-saving project. I understand that I'm asking a lot of you. You didn't know you were a bearer, and it's even harder for us as we're the last chance of keeping this species alive.

Therefore, I'm going to support you in every way I can.'

He squeezed my hand. I think I was supposed to feel grateful.

'For starters,' he continued, 'I'm going to pay your mortgage and bills. We'll have a sit down together in a few days when you've got your head sorted and you can let me know what needs to be paid and when. I could easily just do a bank transfer to your account each month. It's all very simple.'

'How are you going to afford that?' I asked, cynically.

'I'm the CEO of a national chain. I make loads of money. And if I can't share it with the mother of my children, then who can I share it with?'

'I am not the mother of your children.'

'Not yet, no. There's no need to worry about your house, either. I've got the key. I can go over and sort things out. I can collect your post. You can still keep in touch with the world.'

'You've got the key?' I asked with horror. I don't know why I was surprised. He had already violated just about every corner of my life, why should he stop now? But hearing it was still shocking.

'Yes. I thought you'd appreciate that.'

'Can I call my mum?' I asked.

He shook his head. 'I'm sorry. I don't think it's wise that you speak to anyone. Nor have internet access either. At least not until you're pregnant and have good news to share. But I will allow you to contact them through me. You write down what you want me to say and I'll type it out and send it.'

'Excuse me?'

'I'll check your emails and messages to make sure you're not out of the loop on anything. Together we can make this all smooth and easy.'

'What if I don't give you my passwords?'

He shook his head and smirked. 'I sat on your lap many times as a cat. I know just about everything there is to know.'

Terror spiked through me. This couldn't be true.

'You're going to set it up so no one knows I'm in danger?'

'You're not in danger.'

'I am. I'm in danger from you.'

'I'm going to look after you.'

'You said you'd rape me.'

'Don't use that word!'

'Force, rape: it's the same difference!'

'You know I don't want it to come to that.'

'Do you not have a conscience?'

He stood up, clearly irked. 'You're getting aggressive again, Isobel. You must remain calm. I will repeat this one more time and then I don't want to hear any more about it. My actions may seem harsh to you, but we are in the delicate position of losing the Felivires forever if we do not work together. We have to put our own needs aside and think of the greater good here. You know, for all the times I spent with you, I never once thought of you as selfish. But you really are.'

'You bastard!'

'You're really not the girl I thought you were.'

He moved to the desk to pick up the tray and I took my chance to race to the door. He quickly spotted me and before I could even get a grip on the handle he picked me up. He man handled me to the bed and pinned me down.

'You will not escape from here,' he warned. 'And even if you did by some miracle get by me, I will hunt you down. This is happening whether you like it or not. Mark my words: you are having my children if it's the last thing either of us do. Do you understand?'

I stared up at him. I had never believed anyone more.

'Do you understand?' he repeated, menacingly.

'Yes,' I uttered.

'Good. Now get some rest and I'll bring you breakfast at seven a.m. I thought muesli tomorrow. You need to get yourself as healthy as possible for the pregnancy. Agreed?'

I couldn't respond.

'Very well.' He picked up the tray and placed both glasses on it.

'Could I please keep a glass to fill up with water?' I asked.

His face softened. 'Of course. You can have anything you want. If you have any favourite meals, or any snacks you like, you just let me know. I want you to see this as your home. I want you to be comfortable here. I'm not a monster. I'm a desperate man who's doing all he can to survive.'

I think he actually wanted me to pity him.

I stood up to grab the glass from him and I sat back down on the bed.

'Goodnight then, Isobel. Sleep tight.'

'Goodnight,' I muttered as he left.

I heard the lock click, but this time it didn't sound the same as before. I left it for a minute, until he was well out of the way, and then I stood up full of hope. Maybe he hadn't locked it properly?

I carefully twisted the handle, but it didn't budge. It was locked tight.

I got on my knees to investigate outside when I blinked. I couldn't see anything.

He must have left the key in the lock.

He must have left the key in the lock!

I jumped up with excitement. The key was there. Right there for me to get!

I turned around to examine the contents of the room. But there was nothing that could help me. I'd need something small for starters to poke through and knock the key out, and then something thin that I could pass under the door to collect it.

That small burst of hope was getting smaller by the second. I checked through the wardrobe, the desk drawers and the bathroom just in case. But there was nothing of use. I had to find something.

Suddenly the key turned and he re-entered with another tray. On it was a slice of chocolate cake and a cup of tea.

'I thought this might cheer you up,' he said, placing the items on the desk. 'I made the cake myself. I hope you like it. I know chocolate cake is one of your weaknesses.'

I watched him leave, promising to myself that I would never talk to another cat for as long as I lived. He closed the door and the lock clicked properly this time.

I fell to my knees and locked through. I could see the carpet once more. That moment of hope was gone.

SEVENTEEN

Thursday passed by in much the same way. Nicholas dropped off food and drink, and I moped around, sometimes crying, sometimes watching telly, but mostly staring out of the window in the hope I'd find a way to escape.

The window was completely blocked in. There was no way to open it. I couldn't even yell for help. And even if I could somehow smash it, not only would I have to do it quietly so Nicholas wouldn't hear, I'd then have to drop down two floors unharmed. It was a no go.

By Friday morning I started to wonder if I'd lose track of the days. I was already struggling to remember what date it was. I think it was early August. The days were all so sunny and bright, and no doubt it was lovely and warm. But I was stuck in this prison.

After I'd eaten my boring yet healthy breakfast, I showered and got dressed. Then I leaned up against the window to torture myself some more. The sky was a perfect blue colour. How I longed to be outside. It terrified me that I might not breathe fresh air again for years. Surely that would be damaging to my health. So much for getting my body baby-ready!

Suddenly a car caught my attention. It stopped outside my house. I was pretty sure I recognised it, but I didn't want to get my hopes up.

A man got out. A sexy man in a gorgeous suit, fully finished with a tie. I knew exactly who that was. Even from a distance. It was Jake!

I knocked on the window. I called out his name. But he couldn't hear. I was too far up, too far away and too far behind double glazing.

He walked up to my front door. My car was parked right outside. It looked like I was at home.

He waited for a few minutes, trying the bell a couple of times. But of course there was no answer.

I banged and shouted again, throwing myself around in any way I could to catch his attention. But he couldn't see me.

'Are you calling?' Nicholas said, opening the door. 'What are you doing?' He joined me at the window and we watched together as Jake got back in his car and drove away.

'You were trying to get his attention?' Nicholas asked angrily. 'What is he doing here?'

'Probably wondering where I've got to!'

'He can't be that worried. You haven't had one call or text from him.'

'You're checking my phone?'

'We agreed that I would.'

'I never agreed to anything like that!' The anger was burning me. 'You are not permitted to look through my phone.'

'Then how am I supposed to help you?'

'By letting me go!'

'I'm getting tired of this now, Isobel. You really are trying my patience.'

He turned around and stomped out of the room.

I stood for a moment shaking with rage. Then it quickly flipped into desperate sadness and agonising frustration. I fell to the floor in tears.

Jake's appearance had been another crushed dash of hope. How was I ever going to get anyone's attention with Nicholas always in earshot? How was I ever going to get out of here? He was too strong, too much in control, and he knew too much about me. I was stuck. Completely stuck.

I felt the pain of loss strike me and I gasped for air. I had so many plans. So much ambition. It was all now not going to happen. It had been taken from me - ripped out of my hands just as things were starting to progress. And there was absolutely nothing I could do about it.

I'd never grow my business. Never become business person of the year.

I'd probably never even marry now. Who would want to be with a woman who had twelve children?

The walls became smaller and smaller as I saw my life shrinking before me. This was it. It would be me and Nicholas. I'd probably end up marrying him out of desperation.

My life as I knew it was over. All of my dreams were over. This was it.

I sobbed through the pain as I mourned my life and I mourned free choice. I would never see people again. I'd never be free to walk around on my own again.

How had this happened? I was completely trapped, under his evil control. My only hope of ending this was to bear several of his children. Then that would come with its own shackles.

I could barely breathe I was crying so much. I curled up on the floor and tried to soothe the deep pain that ached inside.

It was then that I realised how one thing more than anything else was breaking me.

I'd never see Jake again.

I'd lost him too.

I wouldn't even see him at networking meetings.

I sat up. It was Friday. The first Friday of a new month.

Jake must have been to the networking meeting that

morning. He must have noticed that I wasn't there and got worried.

He must think I'm avoiding him.

I'd certainly planned to avoid him. Although now his behaviour seemed so trivial. I'd do anything to sit in the pub with him again, watching him interact with others. Pretending to be his girlfriend.

The door clicked open.

'Isobel, what are you doing?' Nicholas said, running over to pick me up off the floor.

He placed me in bed and tucked me up. He then grabbed some toilet roll and wiped my cheeks.

'I can hear you crying from downstairs. What on earth is the matter?'

'You're keeping me here against my will.'

He sighed. 'You need to start dealing with this. You're torturing yourself. It's not good for you. You can't keep crying like this.'

I blew my nose, but the tears were like streams down my face.

'How about some more chocolate cake?' Nicholas said. 'A mid-morning treat?'

'No,' I said. As with everything Nicholas made, the cake had been to die for. But I wasn't in the mood for his treats.

'Is there anything else I can get for you?'

'No.'

'You really are making this unnecessarily difficult. Look, as it's Friday, I thought we'd put aside the soup and have a club sandwich. How does that sound?'

I rolled my eyes.

'Oh, Isobel. You need to find a way to start being more positive.'

'I'm so stupid, aren't I.'

'I'm trying. You can't say I'm not trying. You need to have a good look at yourself and stop being so pathetic.'

He glared at me before shaking his head in despair. Then he turned and left the room.

I waited for the lock to click, but it made that half sound again. Holding my breath, I gave it a few seconds and then I leapt out of bed. I knelt on the floor and peeked through.

Sure enough he'd left the key in the lock again.

I sat back with nervous excitement. This had to be the answer. It was the only mistake he was making and I had to find a way to make it work in my favour.

I stood up and focused my brain. It was time to conceive a plan for how this tiny error in judgement could be my escape.

EIGHTEEN

The first logical thing to consider was tools. I needed something long and thin to poke the key through, and then something flat and sturdy to push under the door to collect it. There was no way I could obtain anything myself. It needed to be something that Nicholas would willingly give to me without being suspicious.

Next I had to consider him hearing me. I was quite sure he had cat-like hearing. He was certainly strong and agile like a cat, and he seemed to miss nothing. While I wanted to believe that it was ludicrous to consider any of it to be true, the idea that he actually was a cat person made everything add up. I couldn't deny what I'd witnessed with my own eyes. And that meant one thing: I needed facts.

I needed to find out for sure what I was dealing with. Then I needed to find a way to overcome it.

The only thing I knew for sure at that moment was that he was far more likely to be sensitive to what I was up to with me being in such a state. He had concerns that I was trying to escape. Albeit well-founded concerns. So I needed to stop him thinking that I was. I had to get him to calm down; lure him into a false sense of security. Nothing I'd been trying so far was working. He was never going to willingly let me free. And battling with him was getting me nowhere. It was time to change my tactics.

Step one definitely had to be information gathering. In business, before you devise a strategy, you do a SWOT. It was time to find out about Nicholas's strengths and weaknesses, and I had to establish all the opportunities and threats.

Although I was eager to move forward with my new plan, it occurred to me that if I seemed too curious too soon, he'd become suspicious. I had to wait for him to come to me.

So I did. I sat with the TV on, not really watching it, polishing up the finer details of how to put step one into action, and waiting for Nicholas to make an appearance.

Just moments after the one o'clock news had started, the door lock clicked open and Nicholas entered with my club sandwich. He placed it down with my orange juice and looked at me.

'You seem to have calmed down. That's good.'

I didn't respond. I kept my cool and played my part.

He stared at me for a few moments and I kept my eyes firmly on the TV. Then he turned and walked towards the door. Just before he opened it, I spoke.

'I've been thinking about what you said.'

This caught his attention and he turned around to face me. 'What did I say?'

'That I am making this unnecessarily difficult. I suppose I am. I'm not happy with being trapped in this prison, but maybe it wouldn't hurt if I opened my mind up a bit to why I'm here and what you're trying to achieve.'

This seemed to please him. 'I think it would help you a lot if you did that.'

'Okay. Can I ask you some questions, then?'

He smiled. 'Of course. You can ask me anything.' He sat on the end of the bed and gave me his full attention.

'I think it might help if I learnt more about the... cat

people. I don't want to be responsible for the extinction of any species, but I suppose at the minute I've not really connected with your kind and therefore it's not really hit home just what's at stake. Could you tell me about yourself? Like what power do you have? Are you more human or cat, or is it a complete crossover? Do you have cat-like hearing and more sensitive vision, for example?'

'Great questions,' he said. 'Okay. As you saw, I can turn freely between human and cat form any time I like.'

I took a breath. I really had seen that. 'How do you manage it?' I asked.

'It's just a mindset. You learn it as a child and it becomes second nature.'

'Interesting.'

'When I'm a cat, I possess all the capabilities of any normal cat, but I also have a human brain. It's quite a powerful combination, as I'm sure you can imagine.'

'Is that how you managed to get into my house?'

'That was easy. Your cat flap is very old and it was simple to open up from the outside with a human hand.'

'You had to turn human to do that?'

'Very quickly.'

'That means you were naked in my garden?' I chuckled, as if it were all so fascinating.

'Only for a few seconds. Then I returned to my cat form and popped through. You understand that I needed to learn about you in order to create a bond.'

No! I screamed in my head, but I said, 'I think I can appreciate that. I'm not best pleased that you effectively broke into my house, but I can understand how desperate you've become to save your people.'

He smiled, as if relieved. If only he knew how I was going to make him pay. One way or another he'd pay for all he'd done to me.

'So what about when you're a human?' I asked.

'I have a few cat-like traits, as you say. I'm very quick and I have very acute senses. I can hear things happening quite some distance away. For example, I bet you can't hear that music playing two doors down.'

'What music?'

'Exactly.'

Shit, this is going to make popping the key out of the lock really hard. I thought. *It will definitely make a sound.* But I said, 'Amazing. Is it always the same? Like does your mood affect things?' I pretended to be considering what I meant. 'For example, are things heightened when you're stressed? Could a bad day at work make you more sensitive? That sort of thing.'

'Yes, but that's true of all mammals. All of our senses get heightened when we need them to be. I believe humans call it fight or flight.'

'Of course.' I nodded.

'Do you want to know more about being a bearer?'

I absolutely did not. The whole idea made me want to vomit. 'One thing at a time, maybe,' I said. 'I think part of the problem is that I've been so overwhelmed.'

He nodded. 'Of course. That's completely understandable. I should let you eat your sandwich. But you let me know whenever you're ready to ask more questions.'

'There is just one more thing I'd like to ask. If that's all right?'

'I've told you, anything.'

'Would it be possible for me to get a pen and paper?'

'For what purpose?' He seemed instantly suspicious.

'So that I can craft an email to my parents. You said if I write it, you'd type it.'

'I believe you normally WhatsApp your parents. You could just tell me what you want to say. You never share much with them anyway.'

That stabbing of how much my life was being violated struck through me, but I managed to keep my cool.

'Okay, look the email wasn't the truth. I was just a bit embarrassed. You see what I actually wanted the pen and paper for...' I paused, hoping he'd interpret my hesitancy for coyness, when I was actually desperately searching my brain for an idea. 'I want to write a journal. Writing things down has always helped me come to terms with my feelings. I've always had a diary.'

'I've never seen you write in a diary.'

Him and his bloody spying! 'Well I haven't recently. I've been happy. I haven't had any problems. But when I was a teenager I used to write in a diary all the time. It was such a useful way of me working through my issues and finding some logic. I think it will really help me clear my mind and find a way to be brave. Even if we'd connected as you originally wanted us to and we'd fallen in love, being a bearer and carrying a litter of cat babies is still a lot for anyone to get their head around. Being able to process my thoughts might really help me.'

He still didn't seem convinced.

'Perhaps when I'm feeling in a better place we could even go over my diary together and you can find out the process I've been through and what I've been feeling,' I added. Then just for good measure I said, 'It could help us both. It might bring us closer together.'

The firm glare broke into a warm smile. That did it! 'I think that sounds like a really good idea,' he said. 'You're right, this is a lot to deal with. I'm so pleased you're finding a way to work through it. I knew you were very clever.'

'Thank you.'

'Of course I'll find you a pen and paper. I'll bring something up later.'

'That's really kind of you. You've been very generous to me.'

'Nonsense. One way or another we're going to be a family. You look after family.'

Dread prickled through me. There was a long and terrifying road ahead of me being trapped in this man's world if I couldn't get my plan to work.

'Thank you,' I said.

'Right, enjoy your lunch and we'll catch up later.'

'Thank you, Nicholas.'

'Please, call me Nick.'

I nodded.

'That's what all my friends and family call me,' he added.

'Okay.'

I could see him waiting for me to return the sentiment and ask for him to call me Izzy, but that was never going to happen.

Instead, I stood up to grab my sandwich. 'This looks so delicious,' I said. 'You really are good in the kitchen. Lucky me!'

He chuckled. 'I hate cheap, nasty food. Only the best ingredients cooked in the best possible way.'

'Fussy like a cat!' I followed it with a fake giggle.

He joined in more sincerely. 'I guess so! Enjoy. See you later.'

He left the room and locked it up. This time he took the key with him, but I refused to be disheartened. He'd left they key twice in three days that I knew of. That was a mini trend. As soon as I got my pen poking device and paper to shove under the door I would be in a better position to access it. All I needed to figure out was how to do it so he wouldn't hear. It wasn't just the key, I also needed to get out of the house silently, in a house I knew nothing about.

There was still so much to work out, but I felt much better for having a plan. There was no way Nicholas was going to win this. He couldn't. My life was not over yet.

NINETEEN

The next morning Nicholas woke me up with a full cooked breakfast and a small gift. The second I saw it, my heart sank.

The pen he'd given me was fine. It was quite a thin one and I knew it would fit perfectly through the keyhole. But the paper was a little hardback notebook. It actually looked like a diary. How was I supposed to use that? Even if I pulled out the pages, they'd barely poke through the other side of the door, let alone catch a key.

But I had to seem grateful.

I used the morning to add in a few pages of notes, writing any old crap that seemed to suggest that I was working through the idea of being a bearer, just in case he insisted on reading what I'd put. Then I turned my mind to how I was going to get more appropriate paper.

Nicholas reappeared at lunchtime with some mushroom soup and more bloody orange juice that he'd squeezed himself. He might be lazy in the business world, but this man certainly put the hours in in the kitchen.

'This soup smells lovely,' I said. It was true, it did. But my words were also ensuring that I was keeping him happy and calm. 'I must tell you, I've certainly enjoyed writing this morning. It feels so liberating to have time back to do things.'

'I told you a break would be good for you.'

'Do you know what I used to love as a kid?' I said. This was another huge lie. 'I used to love to draw. I loved art. I wasn't very good at it, but it used to keep me entertained for hours. How would you feel about letting me explore that again? Before all my time has vanished looking after twenty-seven children.' I giggled to suggest that I was only joking, and he laughed in return.

'It would be an honour to help you explore your artistic side again. Do you want paints?'

'Pencils would be better. And paper. A3 paper. And A4. A whole selection. A whole selection of pencils, pens and paper and I'll be the happiest girl in Suffolk!'

'Now that's music to my ears.'

'Are you able to get me those things?'

'Of course.'

'Amazing! You have them in the house?'

'No, but I have money and contacts. Don't worry, I can get you anything you want.'

'Excellent. I'll leave it with you then.'

'Enjoy your soup and I'll be back up later.'

'Bye then.'

I could only manage a bit of the soup. My stomach was knotted with how nervous I was about executing this plan.

Things were going well so far. I had my poking device and I was getting a range of paper. I was sure some of it would be useful. All I needed now was noise to distract Nicholas from the sound of the key dropping to the floor. How could I create noise while keeping him happy? Things were well in motion, but I still had a lot of thinking to do.

It was early evening when I heard the doorbell go. I leapt off the bed with joy. Maybe it was someone who could rescue me? I looked through the window and saw a black car parked at the front. A few minutes later, a young man walked back to the car and drove off. I sighed. That wasn't my way out, but I still had a plan.

Seconds later, I heard Nicholas walk up the stairs and the door opened. He presented me with wads of paper and a few pens and pencils. They were all yellow and branded with a pet shop logo.

'You got these from your company?' I asked as he placed all the items on the bed.

'Yes. I asked one of my team to drop them off on his way home.'

'Did they wonder what you needed all this paper for?'

'They know not to question me.'

'Okay. Thank you.'

I was thrilled. The paper was good quality. It was thick enough to be sturdy, but thin enough to fit nicely under the door. Perfect.

Now to the final piece in the jigsaw.

'I've been doodling in my journal this afternoon, eager to get started. Then I realised I was missing some inspiration. Do you think I could have a radio, please? I do love music when I draw.'

'Of course you can. What a lovely idea.'

'Although I must warn you, I love music blasting out when I draw. I like it to fill the room.'

'How loud are you going to have it?' he said, not looking pleased.

'Loud enough so you can hear it too,' I replied. I'd already planned this bit. 'If we're both sharing the same music, it kind of feels like we're connecting. Don't you agree?'

'I suppose.'

'Perhaps I could choose the music sometimes, and you could choose it other times. Actually, do you know what! When you choose it, you could have it on loudly downstairs so that I can hear whatever you're listening to. It would be a great way for me to get to know you better.'

'You want to get to know me better?'

'I kind of think I have to get to know you better.'

He looked relieved. 'You do.'

'So one of us will play music really loudly so the other can hear. You live in a detached house. We won't be bothering the neighbours, I'm sure. Why don't you start tonight? Go downstairs now and put on whatever takes your fancy. I can't wait to hear what you're going to play. And I'll take inspiration and draw you something.'

'Oh, Isobel, I love this idea. We're connecting. Finally connecting.'

'Go on, Nick. Have a dance while you're cooking us dinner. And cook your favourite tonight too. I want to know what that is as well.'

His smile was beaming. Stupid man.

'I'm going to sort a play list out now, and I'll dig out a radio for you.'

'I'll get drawing!'

'I'll see you later.'

He disappeared, locking the door and this time taking the key with him. But I had everything in place now. All that was left was waiting for the opportune moment.

For the next three days, I had to endlessly endure his dreadful taste in music. Even the weather didn't like it - it had rained every day since he'd began playing it. He liked folk music, but it sounded like it was being played by tone deaf scarecrows. That's the image that came to mind every time he put on one of his stupid albums. So that's what I drew: fields, birds and scarecrows. Or at least what semi-resembled fields, birds and scarecrows.

I started to draw more abstract nonsense as the hours went by, and I kept calling him up to show off how I thought I was improving (which I wasn't). With each of my presentations he found something positive to say about the unbelievably terrible artwork, always being nothing but ridiculously polite. And each time I'd keep my fingers crossed that he'd forget to take the key with him when he left. But no luck.

It was now lunchtime on Tuesday and I was losing faith. I kept telling myself that it could be weeks before he next slipped up and I had to stay strong, but it was hard when boredom took over. I was also getting increasingly twitchy about being locked up in such a small space. Depression and irritation were creeping in. It was taking all my strength to not scream at Nicholas and bash him over the head with my TV.

I can't deny that I hadn't fully fleshed out the possibility of utilising my TV as a weapon. I'd also considered throwing my chair at him or overwhelming him with paper. But he wasn't an ordinary man. Whatever I wanted to believe, this man had got the reflexes of a cat. He could move so quickly and easily. By the time I'd even got the item in my hand, he would have knocked me down and then I'd be back to square one with my privileges revoked. I had to be smart and I had to be patient.

I was shading in a rather odd looking mouse when the door clicked open.

'How's my artist doing?' Nicholas said.

It amazed me how he could be so enthusiastic about the pile of crap that I was drawing. The kidnapping and cat-baby rape aside, he could have made a lovely partner. Somewhere below his evil criminal outer shell there seemed to be a caring man.

It was then that it dawned on me how different things might have been if I hadn't have fallen in love with Jake. I had been happy to go on a date with Nicholas. If Jake hadn't been in the picture, we might have gone on a few dates. I might have taken the time to get to know Nicholas better. I might have really fallen for him before I found out the awful truth.

What would have happened then? How would I have felt?

I shuddered at the thought.

'Are you okay?' Nicholas asked, a tray in his hand. 'Are

you cold?'

'No, just hungry I think. What have we got today?'

Nicholas placed down a delightful looking goat's cheese salad. It certainly looked tasty. Next to it was – you've guessed it – a glass of orange juice.

If I ever see orange juice again...

'Thank you. It looks delicious. Erm... perhaps I could have lemonade tomorrow?' I asked, bravely.

'You don't like my orange juice?'

'I love it. I just think variety is a wonderful thing.'

He chuckled.

'What's so funny?' I asked.

'You like variety?'

'Yes.'

'But you always ate the same things every week.'

It was another one of those insults about my life that I was getting very tired of hearing. I wasn't perfect. But who was?

'I made quick and convenient meals. I didn't have time for anything else. Unlike you.'

'You worked far too hard.'

'So now it's time for me to enjoy variety.'

'Well, there will be no shortage of that with me.'

'Good.'

'I'd better go and eat mine. Fancy some more of The Puffle Keys?' He was referring to one of the terrible bands that I had never heard of before and had no desire to ever hear again.

'Oh yes. Nice and loud. I'm loving their music!'

He grinned. 'Perfect!'

He turned around and shut the door and I looked at the orange juice before me, my heart sinking. That's when my ears pricked up.

A half lock. It was that half lock sound again that gave me such hope.

As I heard him walk away, I dropped to my knees.

Sure enough the key was still in the lock.

Seconds later the absolutely dreadful music of The Puffle Keys blasted through the house and I saw my escape finally open up before me.

At last. This was it.

TWENTY

I took a deep, calming breath. As much as I was desperate to burst out of there, I had to do this slowly and properly. I stood silently for a few moments, giving Nicholas time to get engrossed in something else and completely forget about the key that was no longer in his pocket.

I could hear him start to sing along with the terrible band and I knew he must be relaxed. It was time for action.

I stepped over to the desk and grabbed a pen. My hand was shaking as I picked it up. I had never been more scared in my life.

I moved back over to the door. The first stage was to knock the key through. That was all. If I took it step by step then it wasn't so overwhelming. It would be easy to do.

I knelt down by the door and lifted the pen. I knew that fate had to be on my side. If the key wasn't fully straight, it simply wouldn't budge. I had to hope that the universe wanted me to break free.

I unconsciously held my breath as I tried to line the pen up with the keyhole, but my trembling hands were making it so hard to tackle.

I sat back and took a few deep breaths. I could do this.

My nerves would not ruin this for me.

I gave myself a mini pep-talk and I re-focused on the keyhole. Once again I lined the pen up in front of the door.

A quick poke. Simple and easy. Not too soft so it will just hang out, not too hard so I end up shooting it across the landing.

Nice and easy. This was it.

I pulled my hand back, ready to give it a budge, when my heart leapt into my throat. The paper! I hadn't pushed the paper under the door.

I was a wreck now. I could barely stand. What a stupid mistake. How close was that! If I'd poked the key and it had landed on the carpet, this opportunity would have been lost forever. Nicholas would have surely become suspicious.

It was fine. I'd remembered. I could curse myself later.

I grabbed two sheets of A3 paper. I thought two would make it a bit sturdier. I placed them on the floor and, to my great relief, with a little bit of fiddling they slid easily underneath.

I left about five centimetres of paper my side, just enough to grab on to and pull back. I hoped there was enough the other side. I had absolutely no way of knowing. This really wasn't a foolproof plan, but it was the best I'd got. I needed a lot of luck on my side now. And I certainly deserved it after all I'd been through.

I grabbed the pen again, and for the third time I lined it up with the key.

My heart was pounding in my ears as I concentrated. This was it. It had to work. Please work!

I jabbed the key with the pen and it shot out in one swoop. I could see completely through the hole now. No key. How I prayed it was safely on the paper.

Carefully, I slid the paper backwards.

It definitely felt heavier. That was a good sign.

I slowly edged the paper back towards me, when suddenly I heard a faint sound against the door. I pulled the paper in completely and there was nothing on it.

No!

I looked under the doorframe. It was there! It was just a tad too big.

Damn it!

Not losing faith, I stood up. There had to be something narrow in this room that I could use as a fishing device.

I searched across my desk. Nothing.

Then I looked at the wardrobe. Of course!

I flung open the wardrobe door and I grabbed a coat hanger. They were stupid metal ones that were useless for keeping clothes in shape, but perfect for sliding under doors.

I knelt down and carefully manoeuvred the coat hanger, just to the side of where I could see the key.

It worked! Seconds later the key's head popped into sight. It took a lot of cajoling, but with my sheer determination I managed to get enough of the key under the door so that I could pull it through from my side.

I wanted to faint with relief. But that was only stage one. Now I had to get out of a house that I was completely unfamiliar with. And I had to do it making no sound at all.

Wasting no more time, I slid the key in the lock as quietly as I could. I very slowly turned it. It was easy. Then I pulled down the handle and the door clicked open.

Slowly and carefully, I pulled back the door allowing the music to pour through far louder. As much as I couldn't stand any of these songs, I had never been more grateful for any band. The Puffle Keys were legends to me now.

I stepped out onto the landing, wary of squeaky floorboards. I hadn't heard anything obvious squeak when Nicholas had walked around, but that didn't mean I wouldn't make unwanted noise. I had to be very careful.

I edged out to the top of the stairs and across the plush carpet, in only my socks.

Nicholas hadn't given me shoes. I apparently didn't need them. But that was the least of my worries right now. Besides, shoes would only be noisier, so I was seeing it as a positive.

I stood at the top of the stairs and looked down. There was a window at the bottom and what looked like another landing. I was definitely on the third floor. But where was Nicholas? He'd now stopped singing and could be anywhere.

Taking one step at a time, I moved down the stairs on my tiptoes, determined to make as little contact with any surface as possible. I was terrified, but the adrenaline that charged through my body was giving me a fierce drive forward. Absolute fear was not going to stand in my way.

I crept down step by step, the short flight feeling like a mountain. I was unintentionally holding my breath, but that was probably a good thing. Every breath could make a sound that his superior hearing might detect. Silence had never been more important.

I finally reached the bottom of the first staircase. To my right there was just a wall and to my left there was the landing. Peeking my head around, I saw that I had to walk past two more rooms - both with their doors ajar - to get to the next staircase.

Where was Nicholas?

I was finding it difficult to move now against the fear that was stiffening me, but I couldn't stop. I had to take this chance.

Holding my breath again, I edged slowly onwards. Every movement was gentle and deliberate as I made my way across his powder blue carpet.

I reached the side of the first door and I arched my neck forward to check if there was any sign of life inside. I couldn't hear anything except for the wails of the Puffle Keys. As much as it drowned out my movements, it also drowned out Nicholas's, which left me incredibly vulnerable.

I took a huge step past the first door and then I stopped again to check out any potential threats within the second room.

There was nothing obvious to halt my progress, so I carefully took another giant step. Flashes of Nicholas seeing me and dragging me back to that prison were helping to spur me on.

I took a few more gentle steps and I reached the top of the next staircase. I peered over the bannister to check out what was down there, and that's when I saw my first major problem.

The steps had a bend at the bottom. It was essentially a blind corner. I could only hope that they led straight into the hallway and this would be the last thing for me to contend with. But I still had no idea where Nicholas was, and there was every chance these stairs would lead me right towards him.

But I had no choice. I had to take the risk.

I tiptoed down, my own hearing now tuned in to just about everything. Why was he so silent? Wherever he was, he couldn't be far away, so why couldn't I hear him?

For every step I took, it felt as if twenty more appeared. I wanted to be out of there, but I still had such a long way to go.

Finally, I reached the penultimate step before the bend. I don't remember the last time I took a breath, and I was still holding onto everything so tightly as I cautiously inched my head forward to look around the corner.

Straight away I saw a line of coats hanging up. I almost gasped with relief. It had to be the hallway. I was so desperately close now.

I could now tell that the music was pumping out from a room towards the left. That was maybe the kitchen where Nicholas was happily eating? Or maybe he was reading a recipe book, engrossed in ideas, and therefore not moving at all?

Whatever room it was, the door was open. But it didn't matter. I had to get out of there.

I slowly stepped forward. I was soon to be at my most exposed. If he decided to move around at all, I would most likely be spotted and I had nowhere else to hide.

That meant I couldn't hesitate now. I reached the bottom step and I glanced to the right. Sure enough, just as I'd hoped, I saw the front door. It was right opposite the room where all the music was pumping from.

I closed my eyes for a split second to ready myself for action, and then I ran.

I didn't look back as I raced to the front door. I opened it as quietly as I could and I stepped out, enjoying the fresh air against my face for the first time in what seemed like forever, and feeling the relief wash through me.

I knew I'd have to shut the door behind me so that Nicholas wouldn't question anything. I grabbed the handle to pull it closed, when I heard a voice.

'What the...?' It was Nicholas.

Terror zipped through me. I left the door and just ran.

I didn't have time to look at my house. There was no point going there. I didn't even have a key. I had to just run and hope for the best.

'Isobel! Come back!' Nicholas shouted it like an order, as if he expected me to comply and return to his side.

I knew in reality that Nicholas could catch up with me in seconds. He was fast. Very fast. But from everything he'd told me, I couldn't believe that he'd want to draw attention to any special skills he had. We were out in the open now, in a very built up area. I had to have faith that he would err on the side of caution.

I had no doubt that he was chasing me, and I could barely breathe. But despite the fact that my legs were trembling and my feet were hitting gravel with no protection, I was finding some incredible strength. My legs were moving without me even thinking about it; the fear driving them forward in a way I was so very grateful for.

I didn't know where I was heading. I had been so focused on leaving the house, it hadn't occurred to me to have a plan of what to do next. The rain spitting down also made it somehow harder to think straight. Everything felt so gloomy.

Should I go to the police station? That was a mile away.

I heard Nicholas shouting my name, and I could tell he was getting nearer.

I decided that being around people was probably my best chance of survival. The more witnesses there were, the less likely he would be to kidnap me again. Or at least I hoped.

I raced around the end of the street and onto the main road.

My feet were getting soggy as I splashed through puddles, and I had no doubt they were being ripped to shreds as the ground wore away at my socks. But I couldn't feel it. I had never been more focused.

Thankfully, the road was busy. My mind told me to flag down cars; to wave my arms around and plead for help. But I was too afraid to bring attention to myself.

All I could think was that I'd have to explain who I was. Stopping for even a second would allow Nicholas to catch me up. What if he convinced the car driver that I was just a mad woman? I could be back in that room within minutes. He was so very charming, I couldn't take the risk.

My best bet was to lose him. If I could find somewhere to hide, or find a busy place with lots of people around, then I could surely buy myself some time to think.

I dared to turn around.

I screamed without meaning to as I saw Nicholas just a couple of metres behind me. He was gaining fast. Any second he would grab me and that would be it.

I had to get away.

I scanned the road. The traffic was so busy. Surely someone nice could stop. I was clearly running in fear away from this man. Why was no one stopping to help?

Why was I too scared to ask for help?

I spotted a tiny break in the traffic and, with no warning at all, I legged it across the road. I turned back to see Nicholas, now opposite me, trying to do the same, but the cars were in a stream. I had been lucky. I knew it wouldn't last.

I wanted to cry. I wanted to sit down and for all of this to be over with. But it wasn't and I had to keep moving.

I looked around, desperate for inspiration on how I could find safety.

Should I knock on a house door?

What if no one was in? I knew the second I stopped, Nicholas would grab me. And even if I screamed and struggled, he'd probably just drug me again and say I was his drunk girlfriend that he was looking after. He was so slick and confident, and I looked like a weird girl running in my socks. I couldn't take any risks. I had to stay in control.

A light up ahead caught my attention. A taxi. A taxi!

I threw my hands in the air to signal it to stop. But it just drove on past.

Nicholas was running alongside me on the opposite side of the road. As soon as he could find a space between the cars, it was going to end.

My breathing was erratic and my legs were throbbing as I tried to pick up the pace. Why was no one stopping?

Another light. This never happened.

Nicholas saw his chance to cross as I waved my hands in a frenzy.

The taxi driver saw me and pulled in. He hadn't even fully halted when I tried to grab the door handle. I could barely use my hands, I was so terrified. Nicholas was now stepping back onto the pavement. He was just in front of the taxi as I got my fingers to work and I yanked open the door.

I leapt in. 'Drive on. Please, please, please. That man is coming to get me. Please, drive on.'

I don't know whether it was my words or the terror in my voice, but the kind driver did exactly as I asked. Just as Nicholas placed his hand on the door handle, the car pulled away.

He'd managed to open my door slightly, but I was free.

I slammed the door shut again and turned around. Nicholas was standing there on the pavement, watching the taxi drive away, and all I could focus on were those terrifying blue eyes.

169

TWENTY-ONE

'Where do you want to go?' the taxi driver asked. He had an Eastern European accent, mousy hair and large muscles. I wanted to feel safe with him, but suddenly nowhere in the world felt safe.

'Erm... I'm not sure yet. Please just drive for a second and I'll let you know.'

'Are you okay?'

'Yes. I'm fine. Just a...'

'Do you want to go to the police station?'

I knew the answer should have been yes. But the second I imagined telling the police what had happened, I felt ridiculous. How could I explain what Nicholas wanted from me and why he'd locked me up? I could barely understand it myself. And if the police laughed at me, or just brushed me off as a nutter and left me to it, I'd be back stranded on the streets. I couldn't go home and I knew no one else in Ipswich. Well, not where anyone lived. I just saw people at networking meetings. That was the extent of my social interaction.

My heart stopped beating when I realised that I did know the address of one person. There was just one person in the whole of Suffolk who could offer me a safe place and who could help me. Just one person.

Could I go there?

Jake had driven to my house. He had noticed that I was missing. Perhaps he was the only person in the world to notice that I was missing. Nicholas had probably been messaging my whole family with happy updates, leaving them completely unaware of the horror I had been through.

I had to give it a try.

'Could we go to Henstone, please?' I asked.

'Henstone?'

'Yes please. If you get to The White Lion pub then I can direct you from there.'

'No problem.'

I saw the meter at the front roll up by another few pence. This wasn't going to be a cheap taxi ride. I could only cross my fingers that Jake would be there and would lend me some money. He was my only hope. I was now homeless, penniless and completely cut off from everyone. I couldn't let myself think what might happen if Jake was out. Or, worse, if he wouldn't talk to me.

I couldn't worry about that until and if it happened. At least I'd be far away from Nicholas.

A fear shot through me. Would Nicholas know that Jake lived in Henstone? He knew so much else about me.

I tried to think back to any point when I might have let it slip. But it was impossible to know. I had wittered on to that cat so much. I'd certainly moaned about Jake. Probably minutes before declaring my undying love.

The whole thing was absolutely mortifying.

All I could do was pray that I had not mentioned that one minor detail. Nicholas would certainly guess that I'd be on my way to Jake's house. I had very few options. And even if Nicholas didn't know the exact address, if I had said Henstone, it really wasn't a big place.

No. I couldn't think like that. I'd be safe with Jake. What could Nicholas do if I was with someone else? Drug us both?

An icy spike cut through me and I shivered at the notion.

'Where now?' the driver asked as I saw us approaching The White Lion pub. How had we got here so quickly? My dark and worrisome thoughts had consumed me so much, I could barely remember the journey.

'Just carry on straight for another couple of minutes,' I said, feeling sick at the prospect of seeing Jake. I hoped he wouldn't be mad with me. 'You should see a single track road on your left in just under a mile. You need to go down there.'

The driver continued on, far too fast for my liking considering we were looking out for a road, but I didn't want to say anything.

'Just here,' I said as we quickly approached the road I recognised. 'Left here, please.'

The driver turned and we travelled more slowly down the dusty road until we arrived at Jake's gate. The gate was open and I instructed the driver to go through it and park on the expansive driveway.

When he stopped, he turned to me. 'That will be thirty-six pounds.'

My heart was throbbing.

'My friend's going to pay for this. Just wait here while I knock on his door. Is that okay?'

'Sure.'

I stepped out of the taxi and very nervously headed to Jake's front door. I'd been shaking now continuously for quite a long time and it was starting to make me feel unwell.

I rang on the doorbell and waited, keeping everything crossed that Jake would answer.

After a few moments, the door opened.

Jake's natural smile fell off his face when he saw me. It wasn't disappointment - more like complete surprise.

'Hi.' That's all I could manage.

'Hi. What are you doing here?'

'I'm... I need to explain... I've been...' The tears I'd been keeping in control for far too long finally started to fall.

Seeing Jake - and knowing that he was in - seemed to mark the end of the horrible nightmare that I'd been so worried I might never escape from. I felt the tension release and I could no longer keep it together.

'Izz, are you okay? What's the matter? What's happened?'

'I... I...' I took a breath. 'I need to pay for the taxi. I don't have any money. Could you lend me some? It's thirty-six pounds. I'm so sorry. That's such a lot of money. I'll pay you back.'

The confusion on Jake's face only increased as he looked behind me to see a taxi on his drive.

'You got a taxi here?' he asked.

'I had no choice.' I was properly blubbering now.

'Okay. No problem. Come inside and I'll sort this out. Just go and sit down and take a breath. Okay?'

I nodded. 'Thank you. Thank you so much.'

I didn't move as Jake stepped out onto his drive. I watched him as he approached the taxi. It didn't feel right to just enter his house out of the blue like this.

He turned around to me. 'Go inside. Go and sit down.'

I nodded again, took a breath, and I headed in.

I made my way straight to the living room and I perched myself on the edge of his settee.

A few minutes later he joined me. The look of concern on his face had now tripled in intensity.

'Izz, what the hell happened to you? That driver just told me you jumped in on the street and claimed that someone was chasing you.'

All I could manage was a nod. How could I begin to explain this?

'I'm sorry just to turn up like this,' I finally mumbled.

'I'm glad you did. If you need help, I'm here for you. You need to tell me what happened.'

The tears started streaming again as I contemplated where to begin. I didn't have a tissue so my cardigan sleeve was having to suffice. I was exhibiting a new level of attractiveness.

'Let me get you a tissue,' Jake said. 'And can I get you a drink? A strong cup of tea? Glass of wine? Vodka?'

'Wine,' I said. I knew instantly it wasn't just about calming my nerves. That bastard had banned me from having alcohol to ensure my body was "baby ready", so wine was now all I craved.

'No problem. Red or white?'

'Both,' I said, before conjuring up a smile. 'You choose.'

He stroked away some of my tears before leaving the room. I tried to dry my face with my sleeve. I couldn't imagine what I looked like. But whatever state physically I was in, my brain was a greater mess.

He returned a few moments later with a whole toilet roll. I gratefully pulled off quite a few sheets and tried to calm my face down a bit. He disappeared again for another few moments, before returning, very kindly, with a glass of red and a glass of white wine. He placed both before me with a smile.

'I think you need both.'

'Thank you,' I said, picking up the glass of red to take my first gulp. It was then that I noticed just how much I was shaking. I was in far more of a mess than I'd realised.

'I'm getting myself a drink. I'll be back in a second.'

Jake returned with a bottle of beer and took a seat on one of the armchairs to give me space. He sat quietly and watched me for a few moments, and then in the gentlest of voices he said, 'Tell me what happened, Izz.'

I took a deep breath as my brain tried to process exactly what I should say. Could I tell him the truth?

I knew I had to. It was crazy but it really had happened. I had to tell somebody.

'It was Nicholas,' I uttered before taking another gulp of wine.

Jake shook his head. 'Who's Nicholas?'

'My neighbour. The man you saw me with that night.'

'The bloke you had the date with?' He said this quite

sternly and it made me fall silent.

'Sorry,' he said, his calmness returning. 'Please tell me.'

'I didn't go out with him because I really liked him or anything. I just couldn't think of a reason not to go out with him. I thought what harm could a date do?'

Jake opened his mouth to say something, but nothing came out.

'Anyway, I went over to his house... I don't know, a week ago? I don't know.' The tears were rolling down my cheeks again and I paused to blow my nose. Jake sat very patiently.

'He lives right opposite me in that big three-storey house,' I continued. 'I just popped over on the off chance to talk to him. He wasn't expecting me. There wasn't any real reason. Anyway, there was no answer. So I looked through the window. I don't know why. They're big windows and I just wanted to see if he was in. That's when I saw Smokey. You know, the horrible cat?'

'Yes. And I have the scars to prove it.'

'Well... I saw the cat. In the living room. And then it wasn't a cat anymore.'

'What do you mean?'

'It grew. The cat grew into Nicholas. Suddenly Nicholas was standing naked in his living room and there was no Smokey. But those blue eyes. He has the same blue eyes.'

'What?'

'I ran straight back home. I didn't know what else to do. That was a really weird thing to see, right? Then Nicholas knocked on my door, like a few minutes later. He was dressed and he said he wanted me to come to his house so he could explain. I was so scared.'

'You went over to his house?'

'I told him to go away. I tried to close the door. That's when he pushed me back and told me that I was going to his house, and I could either go the easy way or the hard way.' I took a breath to control myself. My mouth was now dry and I had another shaky sip of wine. 'I had never been so scared. I tried to get away from him, but he's really strong. Then he smothered my mouth with something and I passed out.'

'What?' Jake was sitting so far on the edge of his seat, I thought he might fall off.

'I woke up locked in a room. I was trapped on the top floor of his house. I've been trapped there for the last week. I saw you. I saw you arrive last Friday. I was screaming at you from the top floor. But you couldn't hear me.'

'What?' Jake looked utterly baffled. 'He kidnapped you... because... you thought he was a cat?'

'He is a cat. At least I think he is. He has to be! He's Smokey. Every time that cat entered my house, it was actually my neighbour coming in to spy on me. He knows everything about me.'

'How can your neighbour be a cat?'

'It explains why he was so vicious towards you. He was jealous. Seriously jealous.'

'This is...' Jake stood up. He took a few breaths as he looked around the room, his head clearly struggling to process all he'd heard. 'I'm going to kill him.'

I took a moment. If this was overwhelming Jake so far, I couldn't imagine what the next bit would do. I could barely believe it myself.

'That isn't the worst bit,' I said. This caught Jake's attention and he turned to me. He was angry and fearful, and it strangely made me feel safe.

'Nicholas told me that I'd been born to be with him. He said he'd been looking for me. Apparently, the cat people... whatever they're called. Erm... Felivires or something? Whatever. He said he's the last of a species that's dying out. They're on the verge of extinction. Then he said something about how only male cats can continue the line and they do that with female humans who are literally born to mate with them. Apparently our bodies our built to withstand carrying a litter.'

'*Our* bodies?' Jake said as he looked at me intently. 'You mean you? He thinks you're his mate?'

'Yes.' My lip began to wobble as another wave of sobbing hit me. I took a few breaths to keep it at bay. I needed to tell Jake this. 'He was going to keep me in that room until I was pregnant. I was to have sex with him until we'd conceived our litter, and then when I'd done my duty, only then would he let me go.'

'What the fuck?' Jake was horrified. 'Are you serious?'

I started to cry again. Not just through the reality of recent events, but now because I feared a man that I did love was going to think I was mad.

'That is the single most fucked up thing I have ever heard,' Jake stated, his voice cold and hard.

'I'm sorry.'

'What are you sorry for? *I'm* sorry. I can't believe that happened to you. I'm going to fucking kill him.'

Jake sat down next to me and handed me more toilet roll.

'First things first, you have to go to the police,' he said.

'What? I can't.'

'He locked you up to have sex with you. He talked about you carrying a litter. Exactly how many babies did he think you were going to have?'

'I don't know.'

'He's a deluded maniac. We can't let him get away with this.'

I looked up at Jake. 'Deluded?'

'He's not sane.'

'Whilst I agree that Nicholas has issues, I'm not so sure he's lying about this. I saw him – with my own eyes - turn from a cat into a man. He has abnormal strength and speed. He's not your average human.'

'You've been through a lot. You might not be thinking straight.'

'Believe me, I've toiled with this. But as horrifying as it is, I think Nicholas is telling the truth.'

'You want to have sex with him?'

'No! Of course not! I never want to see him again. But

if he isn't mad and it is all true, then...'

'What are you saying?'

'This is far from over with.'

Jake exhaled. He necked back some of his beer and then looked directly at me.

'Okay, if you believe it, that's enough for me. That cat certainly wasn't normal. But whether it's true or not, it doesn't stop it being any less dangerous. You have to go to the police.'

'No. You might be willing to believe me, but the police probably won't. I'll be sectioned.'

'You don't have to tell them about the cat stuff. You only need to say that he kept you against your will. It's not for you to say why. The crime is that he kidnapped you. Motive is their problem.'

'He also gave himself access to my phone, my house and my laptop. He was emailing people so no one would know I was gone.'

'What the fuck, Izz? I can't believe you've been through all of this.' Jake put his arm around me and hugged me tightly. It made me feel so much better.

'You need to tell the police,' he said, so incredibly softly.

I nodded as I looked deep into his gorgeous brown eyes. He seemed so genuinely worried about me.

'All you have to say,' he told me, 'is that your neighbour knocked on your door, knocked you out and then kept you against your will. You don't have to declare why.'

'I can do that.'

'You can't live across the road from someone capable of this. We don't know who else he might hurt.'

I hesitated, realising that Jake clearly didn't fully believe me, but he was there for me and that was the most important thing. 'You're right,' I said.

I had another gulp of wine to secure my confidence.

'Would you drop me down to the police station?' I asked.

'Absolutely not. After all you've been through, you're

staying put. The last thing we want is this weirdo keeping an eye out and then following us back here. I'm going to call the police and ask them to come round.'

'You'd do that?'

'Of course.'

Something popped into my head. 'I have to tell you something.'

'What is it?' Jake said, sweeping my hair away from my face.

'I can't say for sure that Nicholas doesn't know where you live.'

'How would he know where I live?'

I hesitated. 'I talk a lot.'

'You talked to him about me?'

'No, not to Nicholas. Well, not that I realised. I told Smokey about you when he was in my house.'

Jake seemed unsure of what to say for a few moments, but then he finally said, 'I have a state of the art security system. I'm sure we'll be fine.'

'Does it stop cats?'

'Cats can't kidnap people.'

I nodded. Jake was right. If Nicholas did turn up, the security system would keep the man out, and the cat was easily controllable. Of course it would be fine.

'Can I pop to your loo?' I asked, feeling the effects of the wine I'd necked back.

'Of course. You know where it is.'

I nodded and rose to my feet, and that's when I felt the pain.

'Ow,' I hissed. The burn in my feet from where I'd run in just my socks was finally making itself known.

'Are you okay? What's the matter?' Jake said, standing up to help me out.

'It's just my feet. I wasn't allowed shoes. I had to run from him in just my socks.'

Rage flashed across Jake's face again, but he controlled it well.

'Your feet must be cut to shreds. Right, you're going to have a bath. Come on.'

'I don't have anything else to wear. I don't even have access to my own house.'

'We can sort all that. That's just logistics. Go and have a bath, then you can put my dressing gown on. I'll wash your clothes. They'll dry in like an hour. All that matters for now is that you soak those feet.'

'I can't ask you to do all that.'

'You're not asking, I'm telling you.'

Jake helped me hobble up the stairs to the main bathroom. He sorted me out a towel and a cuddly dressing gown, and I waited for the hot water to fill the tub.

'You take your time, and when you're ready we'll call the police,' he said by the door, ready to leave me to it. 'Okay?'

'I can't thank you enough.'

'After everything you did for me,' he said, 'it's the least I can do.'

I knew he meant well, but those words were like a sharp blow to my stomach.

'You're safe now,' he added. 'I'm not going to let anything else happen to you.'

'Thank you,' I replied, hating how disappointed I suddenly felt.

'Take your time and I'll see you in a bit.' With that he shut the bathroom door and I felt the tears pour down my cheeks all over again.

TWENTY-TWO

Having a bath had been a great idea. I spent a good hour soaking, and it really helped to calm me down and relax me. It also soothed the sores on my feet.

By the time I arrived back downstairs in Jake's blue dressing gown, he was hanging my clothes on the line. I couldn't believe he was so domesticated.

'How are you feeling?' he asked me as I stepped out onto the decking.

'Much better, thanks. Do you need help?'

'No, it's fine.'

It wasn't easy seeing the man you're secretly in love with hang up your smalls on the line, but he didn't seem to bat an eyelid. I was very impressed.

'Right,' he said when he'd finished. 'How about a soothing chamomile tea, then I'll call the police and we can get this over with?'

'You have chamomile tea?'

'I have everything.'

'I can make it.'

'You can, but you're not going to. I want you to sit out here and enjoy the sun now that it's finally stopped raining. I told you, I'm going to look after you.'

'Thank you.'

After being locked inside a tiny room for a week, I couldn't deny how wonderful it was to feel the sun warm my skin again. I was more than happy to stay put.

After Jake had made the tea and he'd called the police, we both sat outside. I relished in the serene peace and quiet. I never wanted to move.

It took about an hour and a half for the police to arrive, and that's when I began to tense up again.

The two police officers couldn't have been nicer, though. They spoke to me with sympathy and allowed me to take my time explaining things. They asked a million questions, not all of which I felt comfortable answering, but Jake had been right: it wasn't my place to explain why Nicholas had behaved as he had. It was only my job to report the crimes committed against me. And that's all I focused on.

They seemed to take it very seriously and promised me that they'd be following up with Nicholas very soon. I imagined he'd be arrested, and before I knew it I'd be able to get back on with my life. Even if he didn't go to prison, I could legitimately get a restraining order, and the people around me would be more aware of the threat I faced.

When the police had left, Jake ordered in a take-away curry, and we watched some crappy comedies from the 1980s to take my mind off things. It helped. A bit.

At around ten p.m. I retired to bed and Jake tucked me in. He promised me he wouldn't be far, and for the first time in days I slept more peacefully. It wasn't just because I was away from Nicholas and with someone I trusted, but I felt peace knowing that the police were on the case too. The end of this nightmare was now surely in sight.

When I rose the next morning, I had an immediate urge to get on with my life. Jake had very kindly offered to let me stay at his house until the police had dealt with Nicholas and I could more confidently return home. I was so grateful for that. That meant today had to be about getting me some belongings.

Most of my clothes and toiletries were at Nicholas' house. So even if I felt brave enough to venture back home, it would be futile. Jake had instead insisted that he take me shopping.

At least the perk of having no social life meant I had a lot of savings. It was time to put them to good use.

Too afraid to go into Ipswich as it was too near Nicholas, Jake drove us to Norwich. He was also going to very kindly put all of the items on his credit card – as I had no way to pay for anything – and then I could do a bank transfer to him to cover the costs.

I'd never been to Norwich before. Being the main city in East Anglia, I had been keen to visit the place for quite some time, but I was always too busy working to ever do anything. For years, my shopping trips had consisted of me browsing online while at my desk. It actually felt good to be going out and about again.

We parked up at a small multi-storey car park, and we headed towards the main city centre.

'Where's first then?' Jake asked.

I hesitated. 'Is there a Primark?'

'Primark?' Jake spluttered, as if I'd said the most outrageous thing.

'What?'

'You don't wear clothes from Primark. You are perhaps the most stylish, glamorous woman that I have ever met. I know you wear designer clothes.'

It took me a beat to digest what he'd just said, but I told myself not to read too much into it. I had to stop setting myself up for a fall when it came to Jake.

'I have lovely expensive clothes at home,' I replied, 'but I can't get to them. I need to buy cheap interim replacements to get me by.'

'Well, let me buy you-'

'No.'

'It seems such a waste to buy clothes that you're never

going to wear again.'

'I don't have a lot of choice. I'll need quite a few things as we don't know how long I'm going to be trapped away from my home. It could be a week. Or longer.'

'But you're not going to be you if you don't wear the clothes you'd normally buy. After all you've been through, you need to feel comfortable right now.'

'It's going to be a long time before I feel comfortable again.'

'Can I please-'

'No.'

Jake stopped walking and I could see sheer determination in his eyes. 'Okay, why don't we meet half way. Let's go to a department store and get clothes that are closer to what you'd normally buy and I'll put in fifty percent.'

'That's very kind but-'

'Please, Izz. Let me help you.'

'It's too much.'

'I don't think so. I want to help.'

I walked on as I considered his proposal. It was more appealing to buy clothes that I'd probably keep. He was right, it was a terrible waste to buy clothes that I'd never wear again.

'I don't feel comfortable taking money from you,' I started. He went to say something and I held up my hand to shush him. 'However,' I continued, 'I do think you're right in your observations, and that buying clothes I'll never wear again is a waste. Therefore, how about I earn the money that you're going to be putting in. Like, I'll do cleaning for you.'

'I have a cleaner. She comes once a week.'

'There you go then! Give her a month off and I'll do the cleaning for a while.'

'That's too complicated.'

'It's not.'

'You're my friend. You're not cleaning for me.'

'What about typing? VA Services! Let me be your

assistant for a month.'

'All my needs are covered.'

'Come on, Jake. Help me out here. There must be something I can do to repay you.'

'All right. Okay, VA stuff. Let's say you owe me some time.'

'Good. That's settled then. I won't forget. I can do anything from social media and emailing, to market research or sourcing client Christmas gifts. Whatever you want, you name it.'

'Fine. I'm sure that will come in use.'

'Good. So what department stores are there?'

'I know where John Lewis is,' Jake said.

He led the way to John Lewis and I started to relax.

Jake was so kind to me, following me around as I explored the latest fashion and tried outfits on. He might have been a useless and ignorant boyfriend when his mates were around, but it was good to know he was attentive when it was just the two of us.

Not that he was my boyfriend. And not that I was enjoying letting everyone believe he was. I shouldn't have even been contemplating such things after the horrendous events I'd been through, but that electric charge I felt around him was making me giddy. I think I'd earnt the right to enjoy the buzz it gave me.

After three hours of shopping, with several bags in hand, Jake treated me to lunch. As I was perusing the menu at the lovely bistro, his phone rang.

'Sorry, I need to take this,' he said before answering. 'Jake Masters.'

He mostly just agreed with the person at the other end, although it didn't appear to be good things that he was agreeing to.

When he finally put down his phone, I said, 'Is everything all right?'

'Fine. Just clients. You know what they're like.'

My heart thudded.

'Clients. Shit, my clients! My business! It's been so long since any of them have heard from me. But I bet they've heard from Nicholas. What could he have told them?'

'Don't worry. You're back in control now. When we've had lunch, we can head home and you can get straight back into work.'

'How? I have no phone, no laptop. None of my notes. I don't even have a pen.'

'That's just material stuff. All of that can be easily sorted out. We're at the shops. We can buy whatever you need.'

'Easy for you to say, with your millions. I can't afford all that stuff. I've just spent a fortune on replenishing basic items like underwear and shampoo. I never thought about running my business. How could I be so stupid!'

'Millions?' he asked with surprise.

I shut my mouth. He stared at me, waiting for me to elaborate.

'Your friends told me that you'd sold your app for quite a lot of money. A few hundred million? Good for you.'

There was an awkward pause. 'Anything else my friends told you?'

Both Olivia and Kelly had asked me to keep the fact that they'd spilled the beans about Michelle a secret. I didn't feel now was the time to betray that trust. Besides, I had more important things to worry about than Jake's broken heart.

'They told me lots of things. I heard endless stories about your days at school and days at university. It wasn't that interesting if I'm honest.'

He watched me for a moment more.

'Going back to my emergency,' I said, needing this topic of conversation to end. 'I still have a phone and a laptop, I just don't have access to them right now. I'm sure as soon as the police arrest Nicholas I'll be able to get them back. I don't need new stuff.'

'You just need something to tide you over.'

'Exactly. Perhaps I could go to the library? Can you rent laptops?'

'Here's what we're going to do. I'm going to buy you everything you need to set up your temporary office-'

'No!'

'This is not a negotiation, Izz. I have money. As we've established, a lot of money. And, like you, I have very little to spend it on. Helping out a friend in dire need seems like a much better thing to do with my money than leaving it sitting in a bank account. So I am going to buy you whatever you need, and then when you're done with them you can sell the items and give me whatever money you get for them. Which should be a fair amount considering they'll be new.'

'But you'll make a loss. You won't get the same amount you paid for them. They'll be second hand.'

'It's money being used to help out a close friend who needs a lot of support right now. How is that a bad thing? What sort of man would it make me if I had the funds and I didn't help you out? If you were in my position, what would you do?'

He had me there. I wouldn't hesitate to do for Jake exactly what he wanted to do for me. How could I argue with that?

'Are you sure?' I asked.

'It's non-negotiable.'

'Then thank you very much.'

'Right, now order whatever you want for lunch and then we can get you all the supplies you need. Then this afternoon you can pick wherever you want in the house to be your office.'

'I'll just work wherever you want me to.'

'I want you to work wherever you'll be most comfortable. It's a huge house. I have an office set up. The rest is up for grabs.'

'You're being too kind. I feel like it's such an imposition.'

'That house is too big for one person. You're actually doing me the favour.'

I fell silent as I recalled just why he lived in that house. He was never meant to live in it alone. Maybe he needed some company just as much as I did. We might never be boyfriend and girlfriend, but that didn't mean we weren't right for each other.

'Can I get WI-FI in the garden?' I asked. After being stuck inside for a week, I was feeling the urge to get lots of fresh air.

He laughed. 'Yes. Of course you can. I've worked in the garden quite a lot. I know how to set things up just right.'

'Then that's where I'll be.'

'Perfect.'

In typical British weather form, it was raining by the time we got home, so I set myself up in the conservatory. It took a short while to kickstart the laptop and get it set up to my preferences, but before long I was back into my usual multi-tasking ways.

The first thing I did was cancel my old phone. I had to make sure I put a stop to whatever Nicholas could be up to. Then I got straight down to work. As my fingers brushed the keys of my new laptop, I started to feel like my old self again. I was in work mode and my brain was kicking back into gear. It felt good.

I had always saved everything in the Cloud. I was very grateful that such a thing existed as I typed in my password and gained access to my whole working life. It was as if I'd never been away.

That was until I saw my emails.

I screamed. Blue words were pummelling out of my mouth, almost cracking the warm atmosphere around me.

'What is it?' Jake said, running in to join me. 'Are you okay? What's happened? Is he here?'

I looked up at Jake. He turned pale the second he saw me, so horrified must my expression have been.

'He's ruined me!' I wailed.

'What?'

I couldn't speak it. It was too cruel to utter.

I turned my laptop round to show Jake. It took him a few moments to focus in on what he was seeing.

There were emails to every one of my clients. All of them. They said that I was closing my business with immediate effect. The emails were polite, thanking my clients for their time, but they were also to the point and incredibly final, eliminating any option for future work.

'Nicholas sent these?' Jake asked, anger creeping up over his face.

'Most of them have replied, and quite a few are pretty pissed off. Understandably. I was in the middle of helping one man organise a major event. I have all the details. He left it to me. This email says I'm happy to disappear and leave him high and dry. Nicholas didn't even bother to pass on work or have a discussion, or anything. Not that he would know the first thing about my work. Or care. How could anyone do that to another person?'

'Okay. Let's think logically. It's only been a week. I'm sure if you call all your clients and explain-'

'Explain that I was kidnapped by a cat man?'

'Explain that you were kidnapped. By your neighbour. Who stole your laptop and tried to ruin your business. It's the truth.'

'Who wants to work with someone who goes through that? I sound so unreliable.'

'Because you were kidnapped? Against your will?'

'That would be all very well if I worked as an employee. I could go back to the office to see my colleagues and I'm sure they'd be sympathetic and supportive. But it's different when you freelance. You should know that. Your reliability is the number one thing you have to offer. I disappeared for a week and sent them a weird message saying goodbye, with no handover and no explanation. It doesn't matter what the truth is or why this happened. They'll see me as unreliable.'

'It might be on the news. If Nicholas is prosecuted, it might be on the news. You should make sure it is. Make your story bigger. Make it hard for people to not understand.'

I shook my head. 'A major thing they had when working with me was trust. In one small email, Nicholas has taken that away. He's shattered my reputation.'

'You can't say that.'

'If someone can that easily infiltrate my life and take over my emails, I'm a threat.'

'Stop it. He had to turn into a cat to manage this. It wasn't easy.'

'They don't know that. How on earth can I explain that without sounding crazy? Face it, Jake, I'm ruined.'

'You're not. And I know that for a fact. This is what I do for a living. I help small businesses. We're going to spend tonight prepping our official story and then tomorrow I'm going to work with you every step of the way to build things back up. You'll come out of this stronger than ever. I promise.'

'I can't afford to pay for your services.'

'I don't want a penny from you.'

'Why are you doing this? Surely I'm a burden you could do without. You can't have time for all this.'

Jake paused. 'I don't have many friends, Izz.'

'You have dozens of friends. I've met them.'

'Mates from years ago. People to have a good time with. Yes, I have them. But people who know the real me. People I feel comfortable with. Someone I want to... I push people away. I don't want to push you away. That's a big deal. So let me help you.'

I didn't know what to say. Forget Nicholas and his cat baby nonsense, no one made my head spin like Jake. Sometimes it was good. Most of the time it left me wanting to puke. At that moment it could have gone either way.

Before I had the chance to utter a word of reply, though, the doorbell rang.

Jake walked away to answer it. I looked back at the emails again.

Truthfully, the emails didn't sound like me. They weren't

in my tone. I always tried to get the balance between professional and friendly just right. The emails he'd sent were monotone and clipped.

I sighed. Who would think that much about it? I was announcing my business closure out of the blue. I was hardly going to sound like myself.

'Izz, it's the police,' Jake said, coming back in to the conservatory.

'Oh, good.' I felt nervous, but there was also a sprinkle of joyful hope. Was this finally going to be the end? Maybe it would hit the news and I would have some context when I talked to my clients. I certainly needed help explaining everything.

I followed Jake towards the living room, but when we entered, my hope immediately died. The same two police officers were there – a man and a woman - but they looked far more serious than the day before.

TWENTY-THREE

'Hello. Did you speak to Nicholas?' I asked.

'We did, Miss Hargreaves,' the female officer replied. 'Maybe we should sit down.'

We all made ourselves comfortable as Jake asked, 'What did he say? Did you arrest him?'

The female officer took a breath. 'We had a very interesting conversation with Mr Jenkins. He seemed quite surprised by your accusations. Then he made his own accusations.'

'What does that mean?' I asked

'He made a complaint that you've been... stalking him.'

'Excuse me?' I spluttered.

'He said that you've been taking his cat from him, and even locking the cat up so that he's been forced to speak with you.'

'What? That's not true!'

'That cat hounded Isobel of its own free will,' Jake backed me up with. 'I saw it. It was always in her house.'

'Mr Jenkins also has camera footage of you repeatedly turning up at his door with the cat and spying through his window.'

I couldn't speak.

'Spying through his window?' Jake repeated.

'We saw you, Miss Hargreaves, on several occasions, hanging around his front door and then looking through his front window. He told us he's felt violated ever since he moved in.'

'I did that like twice when his cat wouldn't leave me alone and I needed to speak to him. Did you check the room? All my clothes are there. All my stuff.'

'Mr Jenkins happily showed us the room. There was no evidence that you'd been there.'

'The room was pink! Why would a man who lives on his own have such a feminine room?'

'Mr Jenkins explained that his mother stays in the room when she frequently visits. He decorated it so she'd feel at home.'

'His mother has never visited. He doesn't have visitors. No one ever goes to that house. Why don't you check the camera for that! And the camera will also show that I was dragged over the road unconscious last Tuesday. Did you ask to look at that?'

'Mr Jenkins was more than happy to show us anything. There was no evidence of any wrong-doing on his side. There was just a man who seemed quite concerned over your behaviour.'

'This is bullshit!'

'We also spoke to your neighbours to see if they've spotted anything out of the ordinary.'

'Good! The lady next door to me. She's seen how Smokey has hounded me.'

The female officer looked through her little notepad.

'Would that be Mrs Vivian Shuttleworth?'

'I just know her name's Vivian. I guess so. What did she tell you?'

Again, the officer paused before speaking. 'Unfortunately, she seemed to corroborate Mr Jenkins' version of events. She said she believed that you were luring the cat over to have an excuse to talk to Mr Jenkins. She said you even dressed up to go and speak to him.'

'That's not true!'

'She said as the two single young people on the street she didn't question your attraction to him-'

'He's creepy!' I insisted.

'She also said that you barely ever left your house except to go and speak to him. Other neighbours said similar things.'

'How would they know! I never see them.'

The officer made a small nod as if I'd just confirmed her point.

'So what does this mean? You just don't believe me?'

'Obviously, we take all accusations very seriously. But Mr Jenkins is a respectable business man with nothing but a glowing track record and seemingly no motive whatsoever to have kidnapped you. Could it be that you formed an infatuation with your attractive neighbour, and when he didn't reciprocate your feelings, you made up these lies in revenge?'

'No!' I shouted, not able to hide my shock and anger.

'He has decided not to press charges.'

'I should hope not. He kidnapped me. He kept me in that house for days. How can you see a few bits of footage of me dropping his cat back and then believe him over me?'

'She isn't lying,' Jake pushed. 'You can't seriously let this awful man get away with the things he did.'

'We'd love to believe you, Miss Hargreaves. But as it stands, it's his word against yours. And your neighbours seem to support what he is saying.'

'What about the taxi driver! He saw Nicholas chasing me. Loads of people must have seen that.'

'We asked Mr Jenkins about that. He claims you broke into his house and he was chasing you because he thought you'd stolen something.'

'This is ridiculous!'

My brain scanned for anything that could be evidence of what Nicholas had done. I considered mentioning the emails. I could show them how he'd been taking over my life. But it wasn't proof. None of it was proof.

'We'll get proof,' Jake said. 'If we get proof, can we contact you again?'

'Of course. If you have any evidence that could corroborate your accusations, then please do come forward with it. But for now, there's not much more we can do.'

My fists were clenched so tightly, I nearly cut my skin with my nails. Jake saw the officers out and it took all the strength I had not to punch the wall.

'I'm so sorry, Izz,' Jake said, returning.

'They're not going to do anything. He's literally got away with it.'

That was when my anger snapped into icy cold fear.

'That means it's not over,' I mumbled. 'He's still out there. He will still want his cat babies, and he still believes that I'm the only person who can bear them. He'll be coming for me.'

'You're safe here.'

'We don't know that. And even if I am, does that mean that I just live my life out here, with you? I can't live my life in fear that he'll find me, kidnap me, rape me. What am I going to do?'

Jake studied me. I couldn't tell what was going through his mind, but he seemed to be thinking hard.

We both stood in silence. There were no words possible that could help this situation.

Running away - hiding myself somewhere far away – seemed like the only option. But I didn't want that. Nicholas knew so much about me. I'd have to change everything to be invisible to him. I couldn't ruin my life like that. I shouldn't have to.

How could a man be so threatening and so evil, and not be a concern for the police? How could this be happening?

I began shaking I was so frightened. I had to sit down.

As I carefully placed myself down on Jake's sofa, he joined me and wrapped his arm around me.

'It will be okay,' he said.

'How?'

'Because it has to be. I don't know yet, but we're clever people. We'll figure it out. The police said they wanted evidence, so we'll get it. Think of it like this: if he does come round here looking for you, I've got cameras too. How will he explain being all the way over in Henstone?'

'He'll come disguised as a cat. Smokey the cat.'

Jake hesitated. 'He can't travel ten miles as a cat.'

'He'll park up at the pub then. He'll find a way.'

'The pub has CCTV.'

'He'll have thought it through. I know he will.'

'A cat won't be able to overpower you. Even a cat as viscous as Smokey. If he's a cat, it's no problem. And if he shows himself as a man, we'll have proof.'

I sat forward, frustrated. 'It won't be that easy. He's quick and smart and very capable. He won't take the risk of being caught, and his number one goal in life is to ensure I have his children.' I paused as one horrific option came to mind. 'Maybe I should try to negotiate with him.'

'What?'

'I'll have his babies if he leaves me alone. Like we agree to certain terms. He'll get what he wants but I'll have my freedom too.' I wanted to pretend that this was a good idea, but my erratic breathing and trembling hands were betraying me.

'Is that what you want?'

'No. I want nothing to do with him. But I can't see that I'll ever be free from him if I don't go through with this.'

'Even if he gets what he wants, you don't know that he'll leave you alone. What if he wants more children?'

'No. You could be the mediator. Set up contracts for us to sign. We could make it all a legal thing. This could work.'

'You think a man who is willing to kidnap and rape you is going to be honourable?'

'But there will be a contract. He'll have to.'

'He's already broken the law. He won't think twice about

breaking a contract. And what are you going to do if he does? Sue him?'

I stood up as the flare of fear shot through me. 'I don't know! I just want this to end. Ideally without ever having to see him again. But all I can see at the minute is that my choice is doing it freely or doing it being forced.'

'Just calm down.' Jake stood up and made me look at him. 'We don't have to make any decisions at this minute. For all we know, he's just a nutter and he's moved on to someone else.'

'He isn't a random nutter who likes to kidnap women. He's a cat man who believes I'm his only chance at prolonging his species. Shit, does this make me really selfish? If I don't do this, I'm ending a whole race. That can't be good.'

'Izz, you need to calm down. You need to take some time to get your head around everything before you can make a sound decision. Just take some time. Okay? Be kind to yourself.'

I took a breath. Maybe Jake was right. The last few days had been more than overwhelming. I needed some time to let things settle in my head before I could decide the best way forward.

'Okay,' I nodded. 'Perhaps I do need a breather. Are you sure it's all right if I stay here for a few days? Maybe a bit longer? I just don't know what else to do.'

'It's more than all right. It's fantastic. I'm pleased to have some company. It gets lonely in this massive house on my own. Seriously, you're doing me the favour.'

'Thank you.'

'How about a swim?'

'What?'

'It's stopped raining and the sun's come out again. I think a swim, followed by the hot tub and then a barbecue for dinner is the perfect antidote to stress. What do you think?'

'I don't know.'

'Doing something active will help your brain to switch off.'

'I don't have the luxury of switching off right now. My clients. I need to work.'

'Your clients think you've closed down the business. Whilst we need to rectify that, phoning them up in a panic with a different number to your usual one isn't going to help. You've dealt with more than enough for one day. Let's both take some time out to relax and we can explore all the options over a few beers later. Your brain always works better when it's not in a panic. Agreed?'

'I suppose.'

'Then it's settled.'

'Is that why you insisted I buy a swimming costume today? Did you have a swim and hot tub in mind anyway?'

Jake laughed. 'Hot tubs are always better shared. I barely use it. Come on, we need to start relaxing.'

TWENTY-FOUR

We didn't swim lengths in the pool, as I imagined we would. We had races instead, did handstands and generally played around. The laughter certainly helped to ease my worries. Although the fear of what Nicholas would do next never went far.

I was also suffering from a harsh confusion about a man who would barely speak to me when we were pretending to be dating, and now he was being kinder to me than I ever could have wished for. I couldn't figure him out.

But I tried my best to keep my thoughts at bay and I tried to focus on the enjoyment of splashing around.

After we'd spent about an hour in the pool and the tension had unwound, we climbed into the hot tub. Within minutes, all that hard work deleted itself. My stress levels twisted up beyond comprehension. The intimate nature of the situation didn't help, but that wasn't the main problem. It was that as we sat and chilled in silence, my mind was free to wander. And it wandered to very dark places.

It was the first time I'd really stopped to consider anything since I'd left that prison in Nicholas's house. The truth of what had happened and what might still happen seemed to crawl over me. Before long I could barely breathe

I was in such a panic.

'This is no time to relax,' Jake said, clearly sensing the tension mounting. 'We have a feast to eat. Shall I get the barbecue on?'

'Great idea.'

I got out of the hot tub and quickly headed up to the room I was staying in. I showered and changed, all the time trying hard not to dwell on the nightmare I was living in, and I returned to Jake and the barbecue as swiftly as I could.

The steaks were already sizzling away on the super quick and massively impressive barbecue that Jake owned.

Next to it I spotted sausages, chicken drumsticks, burgers, kebabs and corn on the cobs, all lined up ready to be cooked.

'Where have you got all this food from?' I asked, already feeling calmer now that I could tune my brain to something else.

'The fridge,' he replied with a smirk.

'That's a lot of food for just the two of us.'

He shrugged. 'It's nice to have someone to share a barbecue with. Do you want another drink?'

'Is there anything you haven't got?'

'I aim to please.'

'You are very pleasing.' I stopped at this, but he didn't seem to notice my sharp pause. He was too absorbed in tending to the steaks.

'Grab whatever you want from the fridge,' he said. 'I mean it. Anything you want is yours.'

'Thank you.'

I headed into the enormous kitchen and opened the rather intimidating fridge. I say intimidating because it had a TV screen on the outside that did things like manage the food. It even had internet access. Why a fridge needed internet access was beyond me, but there it was right before me, doing things that probably didn't really need doing.

I was quickly learning that Jake might not spend his money on going out with friends or having fancy holidays, but he wasn't short of any sort of gadget. He must have had the latest, most fancy everything in his house. It was all a bit too much for me. As far as I was concerned, a light should have two switches: on and off. This house gave me options I didn't even know existed.

I perused the robotic fridge. I hated helping myself to his things. It felt wrong, and I was contributing nothing in return. I would make it up to him. That was certain.

I saw a bottle of Budweiser, grabbed it quickly and then closed the fridge door before it started talking to me. I didn't know if it could talk, but I wasn't going to stick around to find out.

I made my way outside, used the bottle opener that Jake had placed on the table, and then I moved over to join him near the warmth of the barbecue.

As I glanced at Jake, though, he seemed startled.

'What is it?' I said. 'Something wrong with the food?'

'Look,' he mumbled.

I followed where he was pointing with his tongs and I saw two cats sitting on the grass, staring at us. One was a tabby cat, the other snowy white.

'You know I attract cats,' I said, for the first time feeling very uncomfortable about it.

'There are more over there,' he said, pointing to the far side of the garden where four more cats were watching us.

'This is why I can't help but believe Nicholas's story,' I said. 'I attract cats in the weirdest of ways. They are literally drawn to me. It isn't such a stretch to believe that I was born with a connection to cats.'

Jake poked at the steaks quite harshly. He threw the chicken legs onto the barbecue and then starting poking at them unnecessarily.

'Is everything all right?' I asked. 'You're not afraid of cats or anything are you?'

'No. I told you, I like them.'

He continued fiddling with the food.

'You look like something's bothering you.'

He poked the meat some more and then slowly said, 'Can I make an observation?'

'If you want.'

'I don't want to upset you. It just seems like we should explore all avenues.'

'I agree.'

'Perhaps... I was just thinking. Knowing that Smokey was drawn to you... and perhaps seeing other cats parade around your house... This Nicholas... Well... Could he have made up this cat story as a fucked up reason to get you into bed?'

'What? No!'

'I'm not saying it's normal. Or acceptable. But if he took... like a perverted interest in you... he might be willing to say anything to get you-'

'I saw him turn from Smokey into a man. I saw him turn from a cat into a man, right in front of my eyes.'

'But are you sure?'

'Why would I make that up?'

'You said you've been feeling stressed with work.'

'I thought you believed me.'

'I do. I do.'

'It doesn't sound like it.'

'I'm just trying to cover all bases. Make sure we've considered every angle.'

'The facts are that Nicholas can turn into a cat. I saw that plain and simple. He also has super human strength, speed and hearing. I have witnessed all that first hand too.'

'Okay.'

'Yes, we don't know for sure if I really have been born to bear his weird cat children, but considering this...' I pointed out at the cats and immediately halted. There were far more now. Perhaps forty cats were now sitting in Jake's garden watching me.

That was a lot of cats even for me.

Jake dropped the tongs on the ground and stepped back.

'Where have they all come from?'

'I don't know.'

'There are more cats here than there are people in this village.'

I shivered at the notion that these cats had travelled miles to be in my presence.

'You get this a lot?' Jake asked.

I shook my head, my eyes flitting around, watching the cats as they silently watched me. 'Not like this. Five or six cats is the most. This is... It's getting worse. It's got to be related to Nicholas.'

'You think he's sent out a message to all cats to find you?' Jake said.

'I don't know. How could he do that?'

'What is it called again? His species?'

'Erm... Something like Felivire.'

'Can we do anything to get rid of them?'

'The Felivires?'

'The cats. The millions of cats in my garden.'

'You got a water pistol?'

'That could make them angry. I don't want to anger them.'

'I think we should just ignore them. They might get bored and go away.'

'So we just carry on as normal?'

'Yeah.'

'Okay.'

Jake slowly picked up the tongs from the ground and he carried on tending to the food, but now everything felt tense. We barely said a word as he cooked, and we tried not to notice as more cats joined the party.

The second the food was ready, we quickly raced inside. There were now more cats than I could count, patiently watching us, and it seemed like the flow would never cease.

'We won't look again,' Jake said, locking the door and pulling across the blind. 'If they can't see us, they'll leave. Of course they will.'

'Definitely. Come on, we need to forget about them.

Look at all this food.' The table was filled with plates of juicy meat. Although I wasn't that hungry anymore – and it seemed neither was Jake. We just picked at it as best we could.

When we could eat no more, we hid in the living room, shutting out the last of the sun, too afraid to peek outside.

We had another beer, but neither of us could relax.

'I might just head off to bed,' I said.

'Sure. Get some rest and we'll start re-building your business first thing tomorrow. I promise.'

'Thank you. Night.'

'Goodnight.'

I made my way to the bedroom, my head spinning it had so much to compute. Thankfully, though, the sun and alcohol had done its job, and within five minutes I was fast asleep.

I woke the next morning at around six thirty. Once my head was realigned with reality and I remembered where I was, I quickly shot up and headed to the window. This room was at the back of the house and I had the perfect view of the garden.

I pulled back the curtains and instantly sighed with relief. There wasn't a cat in sight.

I headed out of the bedroom with coffee on my mind. I stepped past Jake's room and saw his door open.

He was sitting at his desk, still in his shorts and sweatshirt from the night before, typing away.

'Morning,' I said.

He jumped. He turned to me and I immediately noticed how red his eyes were. He looked exhausted.

'Have you been up all night?' I asked.

He yawned and nodded. 'What time is it?' He turned to his laptop. 'It's six thirty! Bloody hell.'

'What have you been doing?'

'After you went to bed, I thought I'd catch up on some work. I guess I must have got a bit engrossed. You know what it's like when you run your own business. It's hard to know when to stop.'

'I've never pulled an all-nighter before. You should get some sleep.'

'I'm all right.'

'You really should sleep. You look terrible.'

'Thank you.'

'You know what I mean.'

'I said I'd help you with work today.'

'You're not going to be much use to me if you can't stop yawning. Look, get a few hours in and we'll start later. There is plenty I can be getting on with.'

'Are you sure?'

'Yes. Right, I'm off to make coffee. I'll leave you to sleep.'

'Maybe putting my head down for an hour or so wouldn't hurt.'

Jake closed his laptop and headed over to his bed. I knew it would be just minutes before sleep grasped him.

I closed his door to and I crept downstairs to the kitchen, trying not to make too much noise.

I made myself some coffee and a bowl full of cereal, and I sat in the back garden enjoying the morning sun. It was so serenely peaceful. I was starting to really love this house.

After about half an hour, I decided to get myself ready for the day. I placed my dirty items in the dishwasher and I headed back up to my bedroom.

I crept passed Jake's room again before opening the door to my own room.

'Hello Isobel.' I jumped with fear.

Nicholas was sitting on my bed.

I couldn't move as my brain tried to catch up with how real this was.

I clocked that his feet were bare and he was dressed in track suit bottoms and a t-shirt that were a tad too small for him. I instantly knew he was wearing Jake's clothes. That meant he'd arrived here as a cat.

This was all really happening.

'I told you, one way or another you are going to have my children,' he said, quite plainly.

I turned and ran. I darted straight into Jake's room.

'Jake! Jake! He's here!' I rocked Jake but he was out cold.

'It's much easier to knock someone out when they're already asleep,' Nicholas said, standing in the doorway. 'I honestly thought he'd never go to bed. Thank you for the assistance.'

I was trapped.

With Nicholas standing guard at the door, there seemed to be only one option. I raced into Jake's en suite and locked the door shut.

Bang, bang, bang.

'A door is not going to stop me, Isobel.'

Bang, bang, bang.

Everything went silent for a second.

'I advise you to stand back,' he said.

I ran to the window. It was so small and we were one storey up. But I didn't have time for plans. There was an incredible thud and the door flew open.

'Jake!' I screamed. But it was futile.

Nicholas grabbed me around the waist and lifted me up over his shoulder. I tried to fight. I tried to wriggle free. But he was so strong, I could barely move against his force.

'Jake!' I screamed his name so loudly, but he didn't as much as flinch. He just lay in bed, oblivious to the horror around him.

Nicholas carried me to my bedroom and threw me down on the bed. I immediately jumped up, but he pinned me down with his hand. Just one of his hands could completely immobilise me.

'You know I'm a reasonable man,' he said. 'So you have a choice. You can come quietly with me now and we can resume our plans. Or we can once again do it the hard way.'

'The police are looking into you!' I shouted. 'If you knock me out and drag me back to your place, there will be evidence. Jake has cameras everywhere.'

This seemed to halt Nicholas. He took a second to consider his options.

'You're right. I'll need to disable the cameras. That could take time. So I guess for now we'll have to begin proceedings here.'

I gasped as the room around me drastically closed in.

'What does that mean?' I uttered.

'You know I didn't want to do it this way,' Nicholas said as he grabbed at the elastic of my pyjama bottoms. 'This could have been romantic. We could have made love. If this hurts, you will only have yourself to blame.'

Terror burned through me.

'Please. Please. I don't want this!'

'It's not about what you want,' Nicholas seethed. His anger was making his grip even tighter. 'It's about what you've been born to do. I don't like it either, but if we don't do this then my species will become extinct. You need to grow up and face facts. We have to do this. It's not a choice, it's a responsibility.'

'No!' I tried to fight him, but his limbs were like lead weights forcing me against the mattress.

He began struggling to pull down my pyjama bottoms and I screamed again. But my pleads were lost on him. His eyes were void of emotion.

A flash of a TV programme I'd once seen popped into my head. Cats hissed at each other. It was a sign of aggression, and they didn't like being hissed at in return.

I hissed up at Nicholas as violently as I could, willing to try anything. To my great surprise, he jolted back with alarm. He didn't move far, but it was just enough to lighten his hold. I took advantage of his momentary lapse, and I threw myself off the bed and ran.

I raced down the stairs. I didn't know where I was going to go. There was no one around here. Even if I tried to run into the village centre, he'd catch up with me. This time I knew he'd run at his full speed as there was no one around to see.

I burst into the living room and I looked around for a phone. My mobile was up in the bedroom, but surely Jake had a landline. He had just about everything else in this house. I had to call the police.

Nicholas kicked open the door and I shrieked.

I ran into the dining room, hoping there would be a phone in there, but Nicholas caught up with me in seconds.

He forced me down against the table, and my face banged hard against the wood.

'This is going to happen, no matter how much you resist,' he said, full of rage.

He pulled down my pyjama bottoms and I shrieked so loudly the walls almost vibrated. The only difference it made, however, was for Nicholas to push down on me even harder. I could barely breathe against the force of my body being squeezed against the table. My absolute fear was the only thing protecting me from the pain.

I could sense him preparing himself and the horror punched at me.

I tried to scream Jake's name again, but it was muffled as my cheek was so firmly jammed against the veneer.

Tears began streaming. I had never felt so scared and so utterly helpless. It was like the world instantly became dark and I knew I'd never see light again.

There was a loud thud and the weight pinning me immediately released. I shot up, ready to run.

'Izz, are you okay?'

It was Jake.

I turned around. He stood with a golf club in his hand and Nicholas lay on the floor next to us.

I scrambled to tidy myself up and then I nearly collapsed. Jake stepped forward and took me in his arms. All I could do was sob.

'Are you okay?' Jake asked again. 'Did he... hurt you?'

I didn't know how to answer that question. Nicholas had hurt me in so many ways.

'I'm fine,' I lied. I looked up at Jake. 'Thank you. How did you...? He drugged you.'

'Your screaming woke me up. What do you mean he drugged me?'

'I don't know. He made me inhale something and it knocked me out. He must have done the same to you.'

'What the fuck? No wonder I feel so woozy. But those screams. I could feel them.'

Jake's eyes looked black. They were virtually spinning.

'You want to sit down?' I said stepping back from Jake's hold.

Jake took a breath. He was fighting hard to stay alert. 'We need to deal with him first.'

We looked down to where Nicholas was.

'Where's he gone?' I screeched. All that was left were Jake's clothes.

I fell back onto a chair.

'This is never going to end,' I cried. 'He told me that one way or another I was going to have his children. I can't even begin to process how far he'll go.'

'They're my clothes,' Jake said. 'What...? How did he get in?'

'I told you, he's a cat. He must have snuck in last night. He said he'd been waiting for you to go to sleep so he could knock you out.'

'Are you saying he's turned into a cat now? To leave?'

'Do you believe me now?'

Jake wobbled down onto the chair next to me. He didn't look well at all.

'Are you okay?' I asked.

'We need to call the police. Now.'

'And say what?'

'We'll have him on camera. I have cameras all over the property.'

'Inside?'

'No, but all of the outside areas.'

'And they'll all show footage of a smoky grey cat walking

around. One of about a million cats that were here last night. What does that prove?'

'His fingerprints will be all over the house.'

'They're not going to come around to sweep for fingerprints if we can't show that he even turned up here. There is no way to beat him. Cats can go anywhere.' A chill swept through me. 'This is going to happen isn't it. He's going to get his way.'

'No. Absolutely not. I won't let it happen.'

'How are you going to stop him? It must be sheer luck that you woke up.'

'We need to be really careful moving forward. Check the whole house before we go to bed.'

I stood up in a panic. 'Do you think he's still here? Cats can hide in the smallest of places. He could still be here.'

'I gave him quite a whack,' Jake assured me. 'Believe me, he'll need time to recover.'

'Either way, this isn't over. He will come back and he will succeed. I know it. He wants this so badly, nothing will stop him. Maybe I just need to...'

'No! You're not giving in to him. Perhaps we're not safe here.'

'But where will we be safe?'

'I don't know. Somewhere with people. A hotel. Let's go to a hotel. At least for now. Until we can work out a plan.'

'I can't ask you to do that.'

'You're not doing this on your own. He was... He's going to hurt you. I have to help you.'

'This isn't your responsibility.'

'It isn't yours either. I'm your friend. You need a friend right now. Let me help you.'

'It's too much.'

'If I needed help and you were in a position to help me, would you?'

He had me again. I would do everything in my power to help him. Any time he needed it.

But I loved him.

'I'll find a way to pay you back,' I said.

'Just knowing that if I ever need help, I have a good friend to rely on, that's enough for me.'

'You do have that. Always. Right, I suppose we should pack.' My whole body was trembling, but I had to stay strong. 'Do you have a suitcase you could lend me?'

Jake smiled. 'Of course.'

TWENTY-FIVE

It didn't take us long to pack. Especially as I had very little to pack anyway. I put our cases in the car and Jake locked up. As he walked forward to join me, I grabbed the keys from his hand.

'There is no way you're driving,' I told him.

'Sorry?'

'You still seem really woozy.'

'And you've had a really nasty shock. You were just attacked.'

'But my head is free from chemicals. It's not safe for you to drive.'

He stopped and looked at me, clearly troubled. 'You're not insured on my car.' I could see him glancing at his precious Jaguar. He really didn't want me to drive.

'Well, we need to get away, and it's either me driving uninsured or you driving under the influence. Both are illegal, but at least one is unlikely to put other people at risk.'

Jake sighed. 'Take it slow.'

'I will.'

I sat in his luxurious car. It was so smooth, and everything gleaned with intense high quality.

'Where are we going?' I asked as I eagerly started the

engine.

'Left at the end of the road. I know a place in Norfolk. It's a nice hotel about five miles out of Norwich City Centre. It's far enough out to be isolated, but it's also a golf hotel, so there will be plenty of people around to notice if Nicholas tries anything. I'd say that's pretty perfect.'

'A golf hotel?' I said. 'Sounds expensive.'

'It's a four star hotel.'

'Do we need to stay at a four star hotel?'

'We need somewhere with a restaurant. And a bar if we're going to get through this.'

'But...'

'I'm covering the costs.'

'No chance.'

'We could be there for weeks.'

'This is stupid. We can't stay in a hotel for weeks.'

'We will do whatever it takes to make sure you're safe.'

'You can't pay for us to stay in a hotel for weeks.'

'And you can?'

'I have a credit card.'

'Not on you, you don't.'

Shit, he had me there.

'I know you said you have money just sitting in your bank account,' I argued, 'but it's your hard earned money. You shouldn't be frittering it away on my dramas.'

'I'm getting tired of this conversation now,' Jake said, becoming visibly irritated. 'I'm paying. End of.'

'I'll transfer some money to you,' I offered.

'I said end of.'

'But-'

'You have no income at the minute. You can't afford this and I most definitely can. Please can this conversation be over.'

His words were like a harsh blow in the pit of my stomach. I had no income. All of my clients had probably moved on by now, and I still wasn't in a position to sort things out. Until Nicholas was out of my life, I wasn't going to be stable enough to earn. It terrified me that my life was now ruined forever.

As good an idea as it seemed to run and hide, it felt like all we were doing was delaying the inevitable. I'd seen it in Nicholas's eyes: he would move the earth to make this happen. Nothing was going to stop him.

'Do you feel like you can drive?' Jake asked as my breathing became panicky.

'Just give me a minute.'

'I can drive.'

'No. No you can't. Now it's my turn to say the conversation's over.' I took a deep breath and pressed on the accelerator. 'Left at the end?' I asked.

We reached the hotel. It was almost like a castle it was so large and grand. This would not be cheap.

'You really want to stay here?' I asked.

'Do you not?' Jake replied.

I had to admit, it felt safe. We weren't close to anything of importance, we were miles from Suffolk, and there were golfers everywhere providing plenty of clubs to whack Nicholas with if he came near.

I went to open my mouth to mention money again when I thought better of it. Jake was being very kind and my whinging was starting to irritate him. It was time I just went with the flow.

'It looks lovely,' I said.

'Don't worry, I'll get us two rooms this time,' he said.

'No!' I immediately snapped. 'Please. No.' Forget about money, forget about my love of Jake. There was one very big reason why I didn't want a separate room. 'I don't want to be on my own. Please stay with me. Nicholas will try anything to get to me. It'll be all the harder for him if you're there with me.'

Jake smiled and then he kissed my cheek. 'Of course. That's fine by me. I said I'd look after you, and I will. I won't let him hurt you again. I promise.'

I knew that was a promise Jake couldn't keep, but I appreciated it anyway.

I let Jake check us in. I didn't want to hear what reason he gave for our long term stay. It was too much for me to bear.

We reached our room. It was on the ground floor, which I wasn't best pleased about, but it was all they had available. I opened the door and stepped in to what would be our home for the foreseeable future.

It was a nice room. The furniture was a bit dated, but the bathroom had a bath and was a good size, and the twin single beds were more like mini double beds, so I was very pleased with that.

'I think we'll be comfortable here,' Jake said, ever the optimist.

'Can I bagsy the bed near the window?' I asked, wanting to be as far away from the door as possible.

'Of course.'

I slumped down on the soft white duvet cover. It was cosy, but suddenly this room felt like another prison I was going to be trapped in.

Jake's phone rang. It made my heart pump wildly. Everything at that moment felt like a threat.

'Jake Masters,' he said answering it, before taking a seat on his bed. 'I don't know if you saw my email? Could we make it an online meeting? Would that be all right?'

I felt awful. This could ruin Jake's business too, being stuck here with me. Why was he being so nice to me? How long would it last?

I knew I'd be pushing my luck soon. I needed to find a way out of this mess fast.

Or I needed to give in to Nicholas before he hurt me badly trying to make it happen.

'If you speak to Georgette, she'll arrange it. No problem. Speak soon.'

'Who's Georgette?' I asked the second he hung up. I didn't want the burn of jealousy, but it was still there anyway.

'She's my PA. Don't worry, she doesn't know where I am, nor that I'm with you. I only tell people the things they need to know.'

I knew that was true.

He studied his phone and I let him carry on. He had work to do. I would have done the same, but I didn't know where to start picking up the pieces.

'Oh fuck,' Jake gasped.

'What is it?'

He looked pale. My skin prickled.

'Fucking hell, Izz.' He turned to me, his eyes wide.

'What is it?'

He stood up. 'Last night when I was working...' He paused and all of my body tensed up. 'I wasn't working.'

'What do you mean?'

'I was so freaked out by those cats, I decided to look it up. I thought if Nicholas was telling the truth and he really was one of these Felivire things, then there would be something about it on the internet. The whole world is online. If it really exists then there would be some mention of it somewhere.'

'That's what you were doing all night? What did you find out?'

'Honestly, not a lot. I couldn't find any useful search engine results. So I started to think around it. I started looking into cat people. You wouldn't believe the weird shit that's out there, but I kept going and I then found some forums. People asking questions about cat people. So I asked the question if anyone has ever heard of a Felivire. I said my friend has been approached by one. And I've just had a response.'

'From who? What does it say? Is it from Nicholas?' My body tremored.

'No. It's from a woman. Angela. She said she knows of the Felivires very well, and she's warned me that my friend could be in grave danger. She's suggested that we speak.'

'No. It could be a trap. It's probably Nicholas.'

'Or it could lead us to some serious answers. Look, let me find out some more. I'll connect with her and message her directly. Let me see what she has to say.'

'Make sure you don't tell her where we are. Tell her nothing!'

'Need to know, remember? Don't worry. I'm not going to say anything. But if this is real and she has information, this could be exactly what we need. The more we can learn about Nicholas, the more strength we have.'

I nodded. I wanted to believe this could be a good thing, but after so much horror, it was hard to feel optimistic.

'I'll connect with her now and I'll let you know as soon as she responds.'

'Thank you.'

'You never know, this could be the start of the end.'

TWENTY-SIX

By the time we were tucking into our room service dinner that night, the plan was all sorted. And I didn't like it one bit.

This Angela lived in Cambridgeshire. Despite the hour and a half distance between there and our hotel, she'd been very eager to come and meet us. It sounded far too much like a trap to me.

However, Jake had been wise and had insisted that we drive over to see her. We were meeting in a coffee shop in the town where she lived, and Jake had assured me that he was very confident that this was all legitimate and she was keen to share information. Information we desperately needed.

I knew I had to trust him.

The next morning we were on the road by quarter past nine, just after rush hour. It was Friday and far from the best day of the week to be travelling, but Jake didn't want to delay the possibility of getting more information and I was eager to get it over with.

Jake said he'd drive. I did suggest that he put me on his insurance, but that idea made a lead balloon look light and airy.

It was only seventy miles away, but as we were stuck mainly on A roads, it wasn't going to be a quick journey.

We talked about everything and anything to pass the time. I loved how easy it was to chat to Jake. The nerves I'd had in those networking meetings now seemed unreal. So much had happened since Jake had stood at my car window and had asked if I'd be his plus one at his friends' wedding. It felt like a lifetime ago.

I'd gone from adoring Jake across a room one Friday every month, to feeling in every way as if he were my best friend. No, scrap that. It felt more than that. Weirdly, I felt closer to him than I'd ever felt to anyone. I just dreaded to think how he viewed me in return. I knew I'd never have the courage to ask. Not that I wanted to know the answer.

'Tell me something about yourself that no one else knows,' Jake said, continuing our conversation.

'You mean other than the fact that a cat man is trying to kidnap me to ensure I'll have his cat babies?' I said with a smirk. Just saying it made me nauseous, but I thought if I made light of it, it might not be so scary. It was still ridiculously scary, but Jake seemed to enjoy my joke.

'I can't see you sharing that with many people, so thank you,' Jake said, smirking in return. 'I'm honoured you chose me to share it with.'

'Or you drew the short straw to have my ludicrous dramas bestowed upon you.'

Jake shook his head. 'No, I like that you came to me. I like that I can help.'

'Well, that's good, because I'd be lost without you right now.' I hesitated. 'You want to know something else about me that no one else knows?'

'Yes please.'

'It's something sad and pathetic, but it's true.'

'I'm sure it's not.'

'Oh it is. Here goes. I'm very lonely.' There, I'd said it.

'You're lonely?' he queried, no doubt checking that he'd heard correctly how pitiful I was.

'Very,' I confirmed.

Jake didn't say anything for a few moments. I wanted to follow up with something to make it sound better, but I couldn't think of what to add.

'Me too,' he finally uttered.

'You?' I asked incredulously. Then I recalled that he'd said something similar before.

'Yes. Me.'

'But you know so many people.'

'I have acquaintances. I certainly have work associates. But people that I'd call real friends... they're few and far between. My closest friend is probably Harrison, but he lives miles away.'

'What about your school friends?'

'They're mates to go drinking with. Maybe once we were good friends, but the more you grow up, the more you grow apart. I don't have a lot in common with many of them anymore. I'm now a bachelor, stuck on my own, hidden away in the sticks.'

I was dying to ask about Michelle. It was on the tip of my tongue. Maybe I could just nudge him in the right direction.

'What about ex-girlfriends?' I said. 'It couldn't have always been this way.'

'Of course not. But other people have settled down and I haven't. That's the way it is.'

I silently huffed. That had not answered my question.

'So why are you lonely?' he asked. 'Because you moved to somewhere new?'

'It's hardly new. I've lived here for years now. No, my loneliness comes very much from being too work focused. I left uni and all I could think about was reaching the top. I only socialised if I thought it would aid my career. I'd spend Friday nights mingling with the directors at after work drinks, listening to them harp on about their lives – their mostly very boring lives – and occasionally we'd throw in a bit of work talk when I'd try to squeeze in my latest ideas. I played the game very well. But now all I have to show for it are a lot of good work connections and very little else.'

'Do you still keep in touch with your uni friends?'

'I did. For a while. But when you haven't even got time for social media, you disappear very quickly. You know, when I sat in that room where Nicholas kept me, it was so horrifying to contemplate that no one would notice I was missing. I'm always too busy being busy. Not hearing from me for weeks is just the norm. I thought it was what I wanted. Now I'm not so sure.'

'The more I learn about you, the more I see how alike we are,' Jake said.

'I don't think so. You're cool, popular and sophisticated. And I might have had a good career, but you've knocked it out of the park. Look at you.'

'Look at you,' he echoed.

'I am not cool. And I'm certainly not popular.'

'Everyone in our networking group loves you. They hang on your every word when you do your one minute pitch. You speak with such passion and enthusiasm.'

'Don't be silly.'

'You can't see it, can you? I don't believe for one second that you've gained all your success just because you played the game well. You've been successful because you're amazing. You're talented and warm and anyone would be lucky to work with you. I mean, you're running your own business. That's not easy to do.'

A jab of sickness struck my stomach. 'It's hard to build up, but very easy to take down. I don't really have much of a business to speak of anymore.'

'You do. Of course you do. You've hit a glitch, but we're going to sort that out. Angela is going to give us loads of information so we can fight Nicholas, and then I'm going to help you build your business back up to be stronger than ever.'

'Maybe.'

'You know, Izz, your problem isn't your skill set. Your

problem is your confidence. If you could see you how I see you... I think you're incredible. Seeing you at those meetings was the highlight of my month. You're a true inspiration. You just need to see it for yourself.'

I fell silent. Had he really just said that? No words had ever meant more to me. I tried to calm the smile that was forcing itself onto my face. A huge smile that I needed very badly.

'Thank you,' I whispered.

'Right, what does Sat Nav say?' he asked, changing his tone completely. 'We can't be far now.'

We parked up in the tiny town centre car park. It was a beautiful market town, and getting busier by the second.

Jake brought up directions to the coffee shop on his phone. It was five to eleven and we were due to meet her at eleven. It couldn't have worked out much better.

We walked down a quaint little road, that must have been the high street. The shops were modern day outlets in gorgeous old buildings. It was like a mini twee version of Ipswich.

'Here it is,' Jake said as we approached *Tea For Two*.

'Is this the place?' I asked, glancing through the window of the very tiny cafe. 'Do you think there will be room for three of us?'

For a second Jake thought I was serious. But then I laughed and that stunning smile softened his face. It certainly helped with my nerves.

We opened the door and a little bell chimed. I loved it!

A woman instantly waved in our direction. She was much older than us. She looked about seventy, although she was dressed in business attire that seemed out of place with her age.

'Are you Jake?' she asked, gesturing for us to come over and sit down.

'Yes. Angela?'

'Yes. Thanks for coming. Thank you so much for

meeting me. You must be Isobel?'

'Yes.'

Jake and I sat opposite her on the small table at the back of the tiny place. It was surprisingly modern inside with very comfy chairs and snazzy menus.

'We have so much to talk about,' Angela said.

Now close up, I could see she couldn't be as old as I'd first assumed. She spoke with authority and was more animated than I'd expected.

Could I ask her age?

No. That would be very rude.

'First of all - tea? Coffee?' she said.

'It seems impolite to have coffee in a place called Tea for Two,' I said.

'Nonsense. They do the most fabulous cappuccinos here. Two, yes?'

'Sounds good to me,' I said.

'Do they come to the table?' Jake asked.

'Two cappuccinos!' Angela bellowed across at the busy waitress.

'Give me a few!' the waitress yelled back as she carried an overflowing tray behind the counter.

'They know you here?' Jake asked.

'I like it here. Nobody asks questions. We all just get on with our lives. I like that.'

'We're here to ask questions,' I noted.

'And you must. But you understand. Other people don't.'

'Understand what?' I said, although I knew the answer.

'Felivires.'

I took a beat. Just having it confirmed that such a thing really did exist was unexpectedly overwhelming.

'Tell me what happened to you. How did he find you?' Angela asked me.

'Find me?' I checked.

'Yes. The Felivire you know, how did he come to be in your life?'

'Erm...' My heart started to pump faster. Talking about this with someone clearly in the know made me weirdly nervous. I couldn't escape the idea that this was somehow a trap. 'He said he'd been looking for me for years. I lived in London for a while and apparently he... sensed me there. Then I moved to Ipswich and... He bought the house opposite me. He now lives opposite me.'

'Years?' she said, her eyes widening. 'Let me guess, suddenly you had a strange cat constantly visiting you? You couldn't get rid of him?'

'Yes. I... we called him Smokey.'

'You realise now it was him learning about you?'

A chill raced through me. 'Yes. I told that cat so much. I had no idea. How could I?'

'And how did he first approach you?' Angela asked.

'The cat?' I queried.

'No, the man.'

'Oh.' I hesitated. 'He asked me out on a date.'

'Of course.'

'I don't know if I liked him. I don't know why I agreed to it to be honest. It was all a bit strange.'

Angela seemed confused. 'What do you mean?'

'A charming as he was, he was also a bit creepy. I guess now I know why.'

'Creepy?' Angela said with surprise.

'Yes.'

Angela stared at me, clearly chewing something over in her mind. 'How many dates did you go on before he revealed his true self to you?'

'You mean the cat part of him?' I asked.

'Yes.'

'One, I suppose.'

'Just one?!' Angela asked, as if I'd said the most ludicrous thing in the world.

'But it wasn't really a big reveal. More that I saw him through the window.' I dropped my voice. 'I accidentally saw him change from a cat to a man.'

Angela shook her head. 'No. There is no way. They're so careful. They have to be.'

'I was being a bit nosey, I guess. I'd popped round to see him. We were supposed to go out on a second date and I-'

'You were going out on a second date with him?' Jake asked, sounding quite annoyed.

'I didn't know what I was going to do. I was confused. I mean he's handsome. He seemed great on paper. I thought maybe the creepy vibes were more my issue than his. I didn't know what to think.'

Angela was shaking her head again.

'What?' I asked her.

'You were literally born to mate with him. Biology alone dictates that you would find him attractive. You should have been very attracted to him.'

'Like I said, he's good looking. He seemed nice. I did go on a date with him.'

'But you weren't sure about a second date?'

'Why so many questions?'

'Something isn't adding up.'

'Like what?'

'This deviates from all normal patterns. Our increasingly busy world would explain why it took him so long to find you, but you should have been smitten.' She paused. 'What aren't you telling me?'

I turned to Jake awkwardly. I knew exactly why I wasn't smitten with Nicholas. I'd already met my perfect man, and I was head over heels in love.

Nicholas might have been able to look nice and say all the right things, but he was no Jake, and he never would be.

But I couldn't admit that now.

'I don't know,' I said.

Angela sat back, thinking.

The cappuccinos arrived and they were placed quite sloppily down in front of me and Jake.

'You want anything else?' the waitress asked.

'No. Thank you,' Angela said. Then she leaned forward.

'Are you two in a relationship?' she asked, pointing between me and Jake.

'No,' Jake replied quite firmly. Even though it was absolutely true, I couldn't help but feel upset by how quickly he'd answered the question.

'Really?' Angela said with surprise.

'We're just friends,' Jake confirmed. 'Good friends, but just friends.'

I smiled at Angela. I had no words.

'Did your Felivire believe that you two were in a relationship?' she asked.

'His name's Nicholas,' I said.

'Okay. What did Nicholas think?'

'He was jealous of me,' Jake said. 'He kept biting my leg. But that was his issue, not mine. As I said, Izz and I are just friends and we've never been anything more.'

I took a deep breath. I had to keep very quiet. I knew full well what Nicholas thought, and I had no desire to share it with Jake.

'Isobel?' Angela nudged, giving me a look that told me she was cottoning on to the truth.

'I talked to Smokey the cat all the time,' I replied. 'He would have been fully up to speed with the facts.'

'It still didn't stop him biting my leg, though,' Jake added.

This made Angela chuckle. She nodded at me but said nothing.

'Are you saying that I should have found Nicholas attractive and should have wanted to start a relationship with him?' I asked. 'Would that have meant I would have been more open to having his cat babies?'

'Absolutely not,' Angela replied quite abruptly.

'You seem certain.'

'I am. Because it's all lies. You would have dated him on the belief that he was perfect for you because he would have made himself perfect for you. Then they drop the bomb.'

'Do they ever accept no?' I asked.

'It's not a word they're familiar with.'

'What can we do to get him out of our lives?' Jake asked. 'He's convinced the police that Isobel is a stalker so they won't take us seriously. He turned up at my house and attacked her, but we only have proof of a cat having been there. Now we're living in a hotel trying to hide. It has to end.'

'He's going to make your life a misery,' Angela said, staring very directly into my eyes. 'He won't stop. He'll never stop. Even when you bear the first litter, they still want more. They're obsessed with continuing their species. Their horrible, evil species. They have power, influence and money. You can't beat them. I've tried, believe me I've tried.'

'There must be something we can do.'

'There is only one option you have. One single option.'

'What is it?' I asked. I wanted to feel hopeful but Angela's expression was deepening by the second.

'You have to kill him.'

TWENTY-SEVEN

'No!' I blurted out as the shock reverberated through me.

There was tense silence as both Angela's revelation and my reaction settled around the table.

'How do you know so much about these... cat people?' Jake finally asked, making the wise choice to change the subject.

Angela didn't take her eyes off me for quite some time. The silence became stifling. Then she turned to Jake to answer his question.

'I am a bearer too. Just like Isobel.'

'This all happened to you?' I asked. It was the most reasonable explanation for how she knew so much, but I still found this admission quite uncomfortable to hear. If she'd been through it, then it had to be real. Horrifyingly real.

'You managed to get away from him, then?' Jake asked.

'No.'

A chill shuddered me.

'I thought he was the most wonderful man in the world,' Angela explained. 'We dated for six months. I knew I was going to marry him. It never occurred to me at all that it might be too good to be true. How silly of me. A perfect love like that is always too good to be true.'

'Not necessarily,' I found myself arguing, although I knew she was right. I'd thought Jake was perfect for me, but it turned out he made a lousy boyfriend.

Angela smirked before she added, 'It was too perfect. He ticked every box and a little bit more. Then one weekend he whisked me away to a remote cottage. No one else was about for miles. I had no escape and that was when he told me the truth.'

'You must have been shit scared,' Jake said.

'The cat thing I could have dealt with. It's incredibly strange, but when you love someone, you deal with strange things. The real shock was the fact that everything about him seemed to change as he told me. His once soft and caring eyes became cold and determined. Whereas before he'd been so protective of me, suddenly I was like his toy to play with. His words said all the right things, like we were going to be a huge family and we'd get married and it would all be wonderful, but his whole body became stiff and desperate. I knew then and there I was going to have no choice.'

'You agreed to it all?' I asked.

'Of course I didn't. No woman would want that. A loveless marriage to a man who's obsessed with the continuation of his species. I also knew that if I had sons, they'd be the same. I'd be subjecting more girls to this horrible torment.'

'So what did you do?' I asked.

'I ran. Although I didn't get far. He quickly caught up with me. You must know how fast they are. He tied me to the bed, saying he'd free me when I'd calmed down and I'd had time to adjust. The only adjusting I did was to realise that until I appeared to comply, I was never going to have any freedom. So when our weekend was over with, I pretended to be excited by the prospect. I assumed if I played along he'd let me go home. I suggested a week of romantic baby making later that month, when I'd managed to clear my calendar a bit. I was sure if I seemed enthusiastic, he'd let me have that little bit of freedom, and then I could find my escape. But it wasn't to be. He locked me up and said we could have our romantic week right then and there.'

'Oh my God,' I gasped.

'I refused to have sex with him. Of course I did. But he... did it anyway. Over and over and over. Until I fell pregnant.'

Tears began burning my eyes.

'We had seven children the first time.'

'The first time?' Terror began shaking me as it all became far too real. 'How on earth did you cope with all those children?'

'You don't get to keep all your babies. His three sisters were given most of them. They have the choice of what they want from your litter and you get whatever is left. Of your own flesh and blood. I looked after my two daughters, trapped in his house, trying to work out how we could get our freedom. And his night visits would still continue. I was still fertile so I still had a use.

'How many children did you have?' Jake asked.

'Fifteen.'

Jake gasped but I was frozen with fear.

'Even fifteen wasn't enough for him. He wanted more. He knew my body could take it. I am physically very strong. There must be a truth to us being born as a bearer. But what he never factored in was that I am also emotionally strong. I had never once given up. Despite everything he put me through, I was far from broken.

'One night when he crawled on top of me, I was ready. As he tried to plant his seed in me yet again, I stabbed him. Right through the back. Over and over.'

I was instantly nauseous. Scrambling to my feet, I ran to the little toilet. The second the door was locked, I held my head over the bowl, expecting to gag and vomit. But instead I just sobbed.

I tried to breathe as the fear and upset grappled with me.

This was all coming my way. Nicholas would be just as relentless. I knew it. But I couldn't kill anyone. I couldn't.

'Izz, are you all right?' Jake said, tapping on the door.

'Yes,' I said as I wretched.

'Izz, can I come in?'

I took a breath and found the strength to stand. With trembling fingers, I released the lock and opened the door.

'Izz,' he said, coming into the small space and locking the door behind him.

He took me in his arms. I felt so safe and warm in his arms, but I knew they'd never be enough to stop the horror that was inevitably coming my way.

'She killed him,' I mumbled.

'She just told me she killed her sons too.'

I turned around, ready to vomit again, and Jake grabbed my hair. I wanted to throw up so badly, my stomach was churning wildly, but nothing appeared.

After a few moments, I turned back to Jake.

'Sorry,' I said.

'Don't you dare apologise.'

'She killed her own sons?' I asked. I had to sit down for fear of collapsing. I closed the toilet lid and perched on the edge.

'She said it was the only way to prevent any more pain.'

'There's something not right with her.'

'She's been tortured for years. We have no right to judge her.'

I heaved. That torture was coming my way. How bad would it have to get to drive you to the point where you wanted to kill someone? Kill your own sons?

'I'm not killing Nicholas,' I stated, trying to be strong, but the tears gave away my fear.

'Of course not. She was alone. You've got me. Two heads are always better than one. If he's going to get to you, he'll have to go through me first.'

'He managed it once.'

'And we've learnt from that.'

'There has to be another way. Killing people can never be a reasonable option for anything. It's wrong.'

'There is always another way. And we're two smart people. Together we will figure it out. Okay?'

'Thank you, Jake. I don't know why you're being so nice to me, but I couldn't be more grateful.'

He hesitated, then he hugged me and said, 'I owe you one, Izz. You were so good pretending to be my girlfriend. This is the least I can do.'

Something shifted inside of me. Something dark and painful. He owed me one?

As I pulled away from his embrace, Jake didn't seem like the electrifying man that I loved anymore. I suddenly felt irritated as I saw with clarity how he really was so far from perfect.

I stood up, eager to get away from him.

'Are you okay?' he asked as I budged past him towards the door.

'Yep. Come on. We should get back to Angela.'

I opened the door and stormed back over to the table.

'You killed your sons?' I said to Angela the second I sat back down. Jake was still making his way to his seat.

She studied me, working out how to respond. I could feel my eyes tingling. It must have been so obvious that I'd been crying. She must have thought of me as so weak when she had been such a fighter. But I was never going to give in. I would find another way. Death was not the answer.

'I didn't want to do it,' she said. 'You must know that. It certainly made it easier that I had no relationship with them. I'd been left with two daughters. My sons believed I was their aunt, and they were being brought up to believe that it was their right to trap and rape their future bearers. All that mattered was the continuation of their species.'

'Could you not have worked with them to make things better?'

'Excuse me?'

'Let's look at the facts. As bearers, our bodies are

stronger, making us the only ones capable of carrying...' my stomach churned, '...a large number of babies. So your sons wouldn't have the freedom to marry just anyone. They could fall in love with someone, have hopes of raising a family, and then effectively kill the mother of their children through the pressure of having so many... offspring. Meeting and forming a relationship with the bearer is the best way to go. Could you not have tried to make them honest and respectful? Why has it got to be so brutal?'

Angela laughed. It was a proper belly laugh. I didn't understand the joke.

'You think these are reasonable people? You think Nicholas is reasonable? Yes, they might have been nurtured to focus on nothing but the continuation of their species, but that's only part of the problem. They're not innately nice people. They're selfish and lazy. They come to you when they want something and then insist that you leave them alone when they're done. It could never be a two way relationship. They're fundamentally lone creatures. They're cats. They're not fully human. You know cats. You know cats well. When danger comes, a cat will never run to you. It won't look out for you. It will run away and look after itself. Every member of that family puts its own personal needs first. My daughters are just as selfish. Nothing I could say or do would make any difference. I hated them. A mother shouldn't hate her children, but they are in no way like me.'

'Many people like cats,' I argued. 'Despite what the stereotype says, cats aren't always self-serving. They can be lovely pets. They're sensitive and caring at times.'

'Felivires are not. It's the worst nature of a cat combined with the worst nature of a human. It's a species that must be eradicated.'

'That's not a judgement for you to make.'

'I thought I'd got them all. I found one more litter had been born a few years before my own. I tracked them down and killed them too. Is your Nicholas part of the pet shop owner family?'

'Yes,' I muttered.

'He must have slipped the net. He has to be the last one. I've not heard about another Felivire in years. He's the final step to make this nightmare end for good. You have to kill him.'

'No.'

'You are in more danger than any other bearer ever to exist. He must realise he's the last one. The future of his species now lies solely on your shoulders. All he will care about is getting you pregnant. Nothing else will matter to him and he will have no ethics at all about how he makes it happen.'

'I can protect her,' Jake said.

'I can protect myself,' I objected.

'He is strong and fast, he's able to sneak into places unseen, he has great night vision, no sense of morals at all, and everything in the world to lose if he's not successful. How are you a match? He will succeed.'

'The RSPCA!' I shouted out, excited by the idea that popped into my head.

'What?' Angela asked.

'We could call the RSPCA. Say there's a stray cat. They'll capture him.'

Angela shook her head. She seemed vexed. 'He's not a cat. He's a human cat hybrid. The second he sees a van, he'll know to hide.'

'We'll tell them to come in a car. We'll tell them it's a clever cat so they need to come in disguise.'

'They'll be locking you up. I've considered all of this. They're a horrible but incredibly smart species. They won't fall for traps. They're not going to wander into a cage. And if you try to pick them up, they could just change back and floor you. You couldn't come up with any idea that I haven't considered. I didn't want to kill him. I loved him once, remember? But it came down to him or me, and I wanted to survive.'

'Do you think he would have killed you?' I asked.

'What do you want to do with your life?' Angela asked, showing her growing frustration.

'What?'

'Do you want more than being a baby making machine that's trapped in a room for the rest of your life? I wanted more. So much more. He might have never physically killed me, but he took away my life, and I reckon that's pretty much the same thing. Killing him was self-defence.'

'Killing your sons wasn't.'

'It was for the girls out there who were soon to be baby-making slaves.'

I wanted to find the loophole. I needed to find the flaw in what she was saying. I could not believe that killing someone was the only option. It could not be true.

'He's not really a man,' Angela insisted. 'He's not. You aren't killing a human. You're killing an evil alien. If Martians came down to attack us, would you think twice about killing one of them?'

'Stop it,' I snapped. 'Stop making it sound like it doesn't matter. It is never acceptable to take another life. If I did do it then I'd be no better than him. I want to be better than him. I will not win by playing him at his own game. I will win by being better.'

'Oh, Isobel, I fear for you. Your life is about to get very dark and scary. When you're trapped away from everyone you love, six months pregnant and realising that you have no life of your own anymore, remember that I tried to warn you. You have an option now. But the window for you having a choice is getting smaller every day.'

'That's right. I have a choice.'

'A choice he will take away.'

'She also has me,' Jake said. 'You didn't have that.'

'I pity you both.'

'I think we'd better leave,' I said, standing up. 'Thank you for your time, Angela, but I pity you too. I'm sorry for what you went through, but the burden of having taken so many lives must be a prison all over again. I won't let that happen to me. I will be free. You mark my words.'

'You have that same determination I did. I wonder what you'll do with all that fight when you have no options left.'

'Goodbye, Angela. Nice to have met you.'

I turned around and didn't look back. I marched outside.

I was instantly halted by the sight of all the cats waiting patiently by the door. There were dozens of them. It was quite the spectacle.

People up and down the street were staring, but I couldn't deal with that. I marched straight down the road and back towards the car. The cats began following me, but I refused to acknowledge it. So many people were watching, fascinated by this Pied Piper display, but I couldn't let it get to me.

I was nearly at the end of the street when I realised that Jake wasn't behind me.

I turned and saw him just leaving the tea shop. He jogged to catch up with me, weaving through the cats, but not making a fuss about it.

'Sorry,' he said. 'I wanted to pay for the drinks.'

'Oh yeah. I forgot about that.'

'Seemed only right. Are you okay?'

'Not really.'

He glanced at the cats that surrounded us. 'We should get back to the hotel.'

I nodded but I didn't move.

'Am I going to be okay?' I asked.

'Absolutely. There are two of us. Nicholas might be determined to capture you, but I'm just as determined to keep you safe.'

Jake put his arm around me and I felt that irritation flare up again.

In so many ways he was just as bad as Nicholas. He kept secrets from me, he manipulated me, and now I was trapped with him. I didn't know how else I could survive at that moment. I couldn't access a penny of my money and I had

no independence at all.
    None of this was right and it had to stop.

TWENTY-EIGHT

I didn't say a word as we walked back to the car, and other than to agree with Jake periodically as he made comments about the music on the radio or the temperature in the car, I didn't make a sound during the journey back to the hotel either.

We stopped to grab a sandwich at a service station for lunch, but I struggled to contemplate anything other than the mess I found myself in. I had to find a way to get myself out of it.

For every idea I came up with, though, I found a million reasons why it would never work. It was seeming that I was to be at the mercy of a man, no matter which way forward I progressed.

Jake hadn't queried my weird silence at all. Maybe it wasn't so weird. Angela had given us more than a lot to think about. He was just letting me chew over it. Little did he know I was questioning his motives too.

The traffic had been pretty bad, and we finally got back to the hotel at about four p.m. We were immediately shocked to see how busy it was. There was barely a space free. We had to park right at the back of the overflow section. It was the golfers. The golfers who were here for just a few hours had parked right near the entrance, while we, as residents of the hotel, had to walk what felt like half a mile from the car to the front door. This was doing nothing for my bad mood.

We finally reached our hotel room door and I waited for Jake to open it. He started rummaging through his pockets looking for his key card, and then he gave me an uneasy smile.

'You've lost your card?' I snapped.

'Have you got yours?' he asked quietly, clearly assuming (quite correctly) that I was a time bomb seconds away from exploding.

'No! I told you when we left I was leaving it in the thing so the electricity would stay on and my watch would charge. You said you had yours.'

'Maybe it fell out in the car?' he offered.

'We have to walk all the way back there?'

'No, *I'll* go back to the car to look.'

'And I'll just, what, stand in the corridor for the next hour waiting for you?'

'I'll be ten minutes.'

'I'm going to the bar.'

'Yes. Good idea. You do that.'

I stomped off, not even looking back, leaving Jake to retrieve that stupid card.

I made a beeline straight for the bar and the pleasant young man dressed in the smart uniform (they had a waistcoat and everything!) smiled.

'What can I get for you?' he asked.

Vodka straight was coming to mind. I needed something short and sharp to calm my nerves. But it felt far too early for that. I was staying at the hotel long term. I didn't want a bad reputation.

'I'll have a small merlot, please,' I said instead. It would do.

Shit, I hadn't got any money. How could I not think about payment?

I knew that I could put it on the room. Jake had told me to order whatever I wanted, whenever I wanted.

At any other time I would have walked off, feeling far too uncomfortable about spending someone else's money. But I needed that drink badly. Sod it, I'd pay him back.

'Anything else?' the barman asked as he placed the glass of wine before me.

Should I order something for Jake? It seemed only polite. It was his money after all.

'A pint of lager. Whatever isn't too strong.'

He poured the pint and placed that in front of me too. 'Is that all?'

'Yes, thank you. Can you put in on room 107, please?'

'Of course.'

I was given a receipt to sign and then I grabbed the drinks. The bar was quiet. There was a separate bar for the golfers, and I had no doubt that bar was probably heaving, but the space I was in was luxuriously peaceful.

I took a seat next to the window and looked out across the beautiful gardens. I was relaxing already.

'Found it!' Jake's voice echoed across the space, disturbing my brief moment of something that resembled tranquillity. Irritation instantly surged through me again.

'That was quick,' I said, huffing.

'I felt bad leaving you.'

'I got you a pint. Hope that's okay.'

'Thank you.'

'Actually, thank yourself. You paid for it. But I'll pay you back.'

'Stop saying you'll pay me back. I told you, it's fine.'

We sat in silence and sipped at our drinks.

An hour later, after barely saying a word to each other, Jake bought us another drink.

He came back to the table with our second drinks in hand and took a seat. I could see in his eyes the silence was getting to him. I was still struggling to piece together everything that was happening. I needed time to switch off and process. But Jake clearly had other ideas.

'I think we should go out for dinner tonight,' he announced.

'As in out and about?'

'What is Nicholas going to do in the middle of a busy restaurant?'

'Watch us and then follow us back here.'

'We'll go to some restaurant in the middle of nowhere. How will he know?'

'He can practically sniff me out. The more we travel, the more chance there will be of him finding us. The golfers seem to be keeping the cats away here. I vote we use that to our advantage.'

'Okay, then let's at least get dressed up and have dinner in the hotel restaurant. I'm talking the full three courses, pre-dinner cocktails, two bottles of wine - the works.'

I loved the idea of that, but the concern of money once again churned in my stomach. I stared at him, contemplating my answer.

'Good idea,' I finally said. 'But whatever the cost, I'll transfer fifty percent into your account. I might not have my cards, but I can do a bank transfer.'

'Don't be ridiculous.'

'How is that ridiculous?'

'You're not earning money right now.'

'I still have money.'

'A finite amount, yes. But you're going to need that when all of this ends and you want to build your business back up. Don't fritter it away.'

'Fritter it away? Food is vital to survival.'

'You know what I mean.'

'So it's frittering it away if I spend it, but for you it's all right?'

'I have spare cash that is waiting to be frittered away. It's pleading for me to do something with it.'

'So I'm just some poor woman now who doesn't have a handle on her finances?'

'What? No! I never said that.'

'If we're going to have a lavish dinner, then I'm paying my half.'

'That's such a waste.'

'But only a waste of my money?'

Jake took a gulp of his beer. He was becoming annoyed.

'I have millions and millions of pounds, Izz. I literally have more money than I know what to do with. It just sits there in my bank account. Then I think: I know, I'll invest it. But rather than get rid of the money, I just end up making more of it. And then that just sits there, and... I don't know what to do with it.'

'Oh poor you. My heart bleeds. What a terrible life you must lead.'

'I'm lonely, Izz,' he insisted. 'Really lonely. I sold the business...' He stopped himself. I knew exactly why he'd sold his business. Why wouldn't he tell me? 'I sold the business, made a lot of money... and then I've been fortunate enough to keep making it.'

'That's not an accident. You're clever and savvy and you work really hard.'

'But that's all I have.'

'You have an incredible house, a deluxe car, every gadget under the sun-'

'And no one to enjoy any of it with! Without companionship, none of it's worth anything. It's just meaningless stuff.'

I sat back. Suddenly everything fell into place. I'd been wondering why he'd been so keen to help me. We barely knew each other, but he'd put his life on hold to support me through this crisis. Now I knew why. He was lonely and I'd become his play thing. I was a damsel in distress that he could throw money at, making him feel like the knight in shining armour. This was his chance to be the rich hero while easing the emptiness of his life.

Well I knew too well that you can't buy companionship. And he should have too after what had happened with

Michelle.

'Right, we'll play it your way then,' I said, unable to hide the edge to my voice. 'If you want to shower me with gifts and food and whatever else to help ease the pressure of your overflowing bank balance, then let's do it. I'm sick of feeling guilty. Let's burn a hole in your wallet.'

I knocked back my wine and stood up.

'I'm going to get dressed up. Are you coming?'

Jake looked up at me cautiously. He nodded, gulped down most of his pint, and followed me.

He let us into our room and I went straight to the wardrobe.

Instantly I felt deflated.

I had so few clothes. I only had whatever Jake had bought for me. All I had that was remotely smart was a skirt and blouse that we'd bought in case I had to go to and visit clients.

That would do.

I grabbed the items and shot into the bathroom.

I slammed the bathroom door shut and sat on the edge of the bath. I had to calm down. I took a few breaths and I tried to get a grip. But the tension was just too deep set now.

I stood up and looked at my face in the mirror. Although I wasn't one for spending ages on doing myself up day to day – there were just too many other things that were more important on my to-do list – when it came to a night out, I'd always made an effort. I had so little make-up, though. Again, I'd used Jake's money to buy just enough to satisfy client meetings. Just a bit of eye make-up to perk up my face. As I looked at myself now, though, I seemed so dowdy. I wanted to curl my hair and give my cheeks some pizzazz. I wanted to look attractive.

I wanted Jake to find me attractive. I hated that I was nothing more to him than some stupid girl who needed rescuing.

I stood back and decided just to get on with it. I threw my jeans and t-shirt on the floor and I put on my black pencil skirt and pink blouse.

I looked like I was going for a job interview.

With unintentionally slumped shoulders, I grabbed my clothes and headed out of the bathroom. I stepped into the main room and stopped.

Jake was doing the buttons up of his shirt. He was wearing a suit. He was making an incredible effort and he looked absolutely gorgeous.

I'd always had a weakness for men in suits. Growing up, my friends had talked about their fantasies of a man in uniform. There had been a fire at our school one day. It wasn't anything serious, but the girls in my class had talked for weeks about which of the firemen they'd found most attractive.

I'd never understood. For me, I liked a sharp tailored suit. It screamed success and I had always been attracted to ambition and success. Jake oozed that smart sophistication and it never failed to make my body tingle.

But not once, in all the years that I'd fantasised about my perfect suited man, had I ever imagined that he'd be spending money on me. In my fantasies we were suited, powerful and rich together, side by side and absolute equals.

'You look beautiful,' he said as he slipped his arms into his tailored black suit jacket. He wasn't opting for a tie tonight. It was only dinner at a restaurant. A tie was probably too much. How I loved him in a tie, though.

'You look like you're at work,' I snapped back.

This seemed to throw him. He stared down at his amazing suit.

Truthfully, I'd never seen Jake where a black suit to a meeting. He wore grey or blue and never looked anything but extremely professional. This was clearly his going out suit. It had a more casual feel to it and it fitted him exquisitely. I had the urge to be nasty, though.

'All you need is a briefcase and tie and they'll be thinking you're part of a conference,' I said.

'I'm never one to turn down the opportunity to

network,' he said, letting my bitterness bounce off him. 'You never know where the next big deal might be coming from.'

'The next big deal that earns you even more money that just sits there idly in your bank account.'

'Yes,' he said, refusing to engage with me.

'Good for you.'

'Shall we go?'

'I'll just put my plain black court shoes on and then we can both look like we're heading to the conference.'

'Is there even a conference on here tonight?' he asked. 'Might be fun to crash.'

'Fun is relative, I suppose. This day couldn't get much worse.'

I caught Jake sighing with frustration. Good.

'You lead the way,' I said when my boring black shoes were safely on my feet.

To me, shoes really mattered. I'd always spent far more on shoes than clothes. But I couldn't have asked Jake to buy me Jimmy Choos. That was too much. These boring, black, virtually-flat-at-just-three-inch heels had cost just forty pounds. They felt different to my normal dream shoes. I was going to have blisters in the morning.

Jake opened the door and I berated myself for how moody and self-pitying I was being. I was lucky to have anything at all.

'Thank you,' I said as I walked by him. He checked the door had properly closed behind us and we headed down the corridor to the restaurant.

It wasn't particularly busy and we were shown to a table to the side, thankfully away from other nosey guests.

'Do you have a cocktail menu?' Jake asked as we sat down.

'We have a drinks menu and there are a few cocktails on there,' the waiter said. 'I'll get that for you.'

'Thank you,' Jake nodded.

He caught me staring at him. I couldn't take my eyes off

him. I felt both lustful and bitter. It wasn't a good combination.

'I'm going for a rum cocktail,' I stated.

'You like rum?' he asked.

'No. I just think they're always stronger. I'm getting pissed tonight.'

'Glad to hear it. I might join you.'

The waiter returned, but before he could hand over the menus, Jake said, 'We'll have two rum cocktails. Doesn't matter what they are. Surprise us. And make them strong.'

'Of course.'

He left the menus on the edge of the table and trotted off to sort out our order.

While I had to admit that I was quite turned on by Jake's command of the situation, the control freak in me needed to know what I was going to drink. Not knowing was quite frustrating.

I stared at the menu for a few moments but didn't move.

When I'd made the decision that I would resist flicking through the selection of rum cocktails to ascertain what might be coming my way, I gazed back up at Jake. He was watching me in return. Might have been for a while.

I sat back, and silently we just glared at one another. There was this weird chemical charge between us and I didn't know whether I absolutely loved it or it made me extremely uncomfortable.

'Your drinks,' the waiter said, breaking the pressure. He placed a long, green tinted drink before us both. I took a sip.

'A mojito. How original,' I grumbled.

'What were you expecting?' Jake asked.

A beat. 'A bottle of Havana Club with one straw?'

'That's not really a cocktail, though, is it.'

I shrugged. 'They could have put a dash of lime in it. A sprig of mint, maybe.'

'We'll get that next then.'

'Of course. Because money's no object.'

'You know, it's cheaper to buy a bottle of rum in Cuba than it is to buy a bottle of water.'

'You've been to Cuba?'

'Once.'

'Of course you have. I bet you've been everywhere. You probably even have your own aeroplane.'

'I'm not that rich.'

'I'm sure it won't be long. What with all your incredible investments.'

I sucked up the sharp liquid through the straw, barely noticing the cool bitterness against my throat. Within seconds, I'd finished it all.

I can't deny, the head rush was lovely.

Jake did the same. He copied me exactly.

'Same again?' he asked.

'I thought we were having bottles of rum that are cheaper than water?'

He paused. 'Maybe after dinner.'

Jake looked across the room. He located the waiter, barely moved his hand, and the man came running over.

I loved the way people responded to Jake. He had an aura of magnificence and people seemed to flock around him in awe. I certainly found him irresistible. No matter how hard I tried to hate him.

How could he have said he's lonely?

He ordered two more cocktails and I found myself glaring at him again. He stared straight back at me and that delicious pressure increased for the second time.

Our eyes were locked in some sort of silent combat, but now the delightful rush from the drink was making it seem far more playful.

I don't know how or why, but I felt like he was getting the edge. In the unwritten rules that were forming in my head, he was beating me at this staring game.

He was good at this. So good at this. Whatever this was. I was becoming mesmerised by him, but I couldn't let him win. I would not let him win.

An idea came to me. I had a card up my sleeve and it was time to play it. This would secure my ultimate victory.

'Why have you never told me about Michelle?' I asked.

The look on his face made me instantly regret it.

TWENTY-NINE

'How do you know that name?' Jake said to me, a mixture of anger and shock shooting out of his eyes.

I wanted to recoil. I felt like I'd done something really wrong. But I remained still and composed.

'Your friends told me about her. Why didn't you?'

'Why would I?'

'Because she was a huge part of your life.'

'A huge part of a life that existed before I knew you. Besides, you weren't actually my girlfriend, so why would it be relevant?'

'Your friends certainly thought it was relevant. She broke your heart.'

'You don't know what you're talking about.'

'So she didn't break your heart?'

'Here are your cocktails,' the waiter said, placing down the green drinks before us. We didn't take our eyes off each other, though.

'Thank you,' we both said.

'Would you like to order now?' he asked.

'We're going to need a few more minutes,' Jake said, not breaking away from my glare.

'No problem. Let me know when you're ready.'

'What difference does it make to you whether she broke my heart or not?' Jake asked.

His clear aggravation with this topic was making me feel quite uncomfortable. I knew I shouldn't be pulling at this thread, but it seemed I could resist no more. I had to know.

'We've spent so much time together,' I said, far less assertively. 'Not just now, even before all this crap with Nicholas. We were supposed to be in a relationship, and you never once even so much as hinted that there had been this major previous relationship that had left you in a bad place.'

Jake sat back, clearly not expecting me to say that. 'Is that what my friends told you?'

'You know everything about me. And at this moment, far more about me than I'd be willing to share with anyone else. Didn't you feel as if you could open up to me in return?'

For a very small second I thought Jake was about to spill everything. He sat momentarily silent, conjuring up his response. But when he opened his mouth, all he said was, 'It's nothing to do with you. It was a long time ago and I don't want to talk about it.'

He looked away and sipped at his drink, signalling that the conversation was over with. It instantly sent a bolt of rage through me.

'You really are a crap boyfriend, aren't you?'

This seemed to jolt Jake. His head snapped back in my direction and he looked absolutely shocked.

'Is that why she broke up with you?' I challenged.

'How am I a crap boyfriend?' he asked, seeming genuinely hurt.

'Oh, come on. Are you serious?'

'Why would you say that?'

'Every time we went out you spent all night chatting to your friends and you completely blanked me. I was left all alone, having to entertain myself with people that I didn't know from Adam, while you had the time of your life catching up with your mates.'

The penny seemed to drop. Jake looked down at the drink in his hand. He knew exactly what I was talking about.

'Was that why Michelle broke up with you? Because you were just never there. Although in her case, from what I can tell, you were literally never there.'

'You have no right to comment on stuff you don't know about,' he warned.

'Then enlighten me.'

'I don't want to talk about her.'

'I thought we were friends. But we're not, are we.'

Jake shook his head, but he didn't say anything. It could only mean I was right.

'You're such a user.'

'A user?' he asked with surprise.

'Yes. A user. You used me to get your friends off your back, and you weren't even that nice to me in the process. And now you're using me as some kind of "stop being lonely" project.'

'What the hell is that supposed to mean?' he said, sharply.

'You admitted you were looking for companionship and some way to fritter away your many millions. I give you exactly that and you love it.'

Jake slammed down his drink. He was angry. Really angry now.

'I don't fucking believe this,' he hissed.

'What, that I've got you all sussed out?'

'No, that you can be so bloody thick!'

'Excuse me?' Now it was my turn to sit back in shock.

'Did it not occur to you once that there might be another reason why I kept my distance from you when we went out? Why I didn't tell you about my ex-girlfriend? Why I've done everything in my power to help you out over the past few days?'

'It's because you're pathetic, controlling and lonely.'

'It's because I'm in love with you!'

Absolute silence.

The words seemed to hang in the air, as if they hadn't quite reached me yet. I was struggling to believe he'd just said them.

How could I respond?

Jake seemed uncharacteristically emotional. I honestly thought he was about to cry. This was all far too much for me to process.

'You're in love with me?' It was all I could say. I had to get clarification.

He didn't respond.

Neither of us moved. That pressure appeared between us again, but this time it was more complex and confusing.

'It's good to know how you feel in return, though,' Jake said as all the strength on his face seemed to crumble.

I had to say something. Obviously, I didn't actually think any of the nasty things I'd said. I needed to verbalise that very thing, but I was still a little unsure that all of this was really happening.

Jake edged forward.

'For the record, I have been mesmerised by you since the very first moment I laid eyes on you. And I knew I'd fallen in love with you before we'd even got to that stupid wedding in Northampton.'

'If you're in love with me, why did you avoid me?'

'I avoided you *because* I'm in love with you.' He exhaled sharply. 'I should never have asked you to that wedding. I just... I was dreading it. Then you said you had no plans that weekend. I guess I thought if I asked you then we'd get to know each other better and I wouldn't have to face it alone. It seemed the perfect solution. But as we drove up there... it was like I felt myself... I'd never felt like that before. I saw a whole new side to you, and it took me from having a bit of a crush to being... Well... I knew I was in love.' He paused, his inner turmoil scrunching up his face. 'What a fucking mess. I didn't know what to do. So I didn't do anything. I was... I was scared that you'd...'

He sucked up most of his cocktail.

I still couldn't find any words. Was this a joke?

'Michelle was a bitch,' he said and I wanted to cheer. 'I loved her, but it wasn't equal. She loved my money and status. She didn't love me for me. Maybe no one ever will. My success always seems to be the gloss that people are drawn to. No one ever sees me for me. It's clear now neither do you.'

I wanted to shout that I did, but the words just wouldn't form. I couldn't get to grips with what he was telling me. It felt like a dream.

'I was an absolute mess when she left me,' he admitted. 'I bought that house because I thought it was what she wanted. I hate it. It's not me at all. And when she moaned about it and made those ungrateful comments like she always did, I knew I'd had enough. I was stuck with a house I didn't want, far away from anybody I knew, I didn't have a job, and I'd lost a ton of money on a company that I had worked so fucking hard to build up.'

My heart broke for him.

He looked at me very directly. 'I didn't tell you about any of this because I was ashamed. How could I admit to you – the most amazing woman that I've ever met – that I had been so easily duped by some money grabbing bitch?'

Everything was starting to slot into place and I felt dreadful for how wrong I had been.

'I did love Michelle,' he continued. 'At least for a while. It seemed like we had a lot in common at first. Then it became habit. Then it became pride. No one wants to admit they've made such a stupid mistake. It was someone to share my life with at least.' He looked at me. I'd never seen such sincerity in those beautiful brown eyes. 'You've made me see things differently, though.' He shook his head. 'Sorry, you don't need to know any of this. I don't expect anything in return. I'm not telling you... I'll still help you out. There is no expectation here. Just go easy on me, okay?'

'How have I made you see things differently?' I probed.

'What?'

'You said I've made you see things differently. Tell me how.'

Jake hesitated.

'Please,' I said softly.

He sighed. 'When I met Michelle, I fancied her, we grew close and it sort of developed. We sort of just evolved into a relationship.' He paused and his eyes seemed to deepen. 'But with you...'

'Yes?'

'You excite me. In a way she never did. I get this strange buzz of energy every time you're near me. It's like you charge me with electricity or something. You're fun and interesting, and you never fail to surprise me. You wear the most gorgeous clothes and ooze all this sexy sophistication – which I'm not ashamed to admit is my weak spot. Yet you're not even remotely vain, and you're so incredibly grounded. I think you dress nicely to feel empowered. You do it for you, not for anyone else. That's what I do. Michelle was my partner, but she was never my equal. Sorry.'

'What are you apologising for?' I said as the wow factor of his words radiated through me.

'Because-'

'I'm in love with you too, you idiot!'

This almost floored him.

'What? You don't have to-'

'And for like almost exactly the same reasons you seem to be in love with me,' I added, cutting him off. I felt like dancing around with excitement. 'You're *my* electricity. Since the moment I met you, my whole world has been flipped by some kind of crazy buzz. I've never felt like this before. I could barely speak to you in our Friday meetings, I was so in awe of you. Forget your money and status. You can keep all that. You know full well I'm not interested in your bank balance. What I love about you is that you make everything shine. You have charm and warmth and sparkle. The world is a much darker place when you're not around. And, just so you know, your suits are so fucking sexy. That's my weak spot too. Our Friday meetings were never good for my blood pressure.'

He burst out laughing, and that strange pressure instantly dissolved into something so lovely and warm. I couldn't help but laugh along with him.

'Really?' he asked.

'Really.'

'But you... what you said about me.'

'Yeah. I guess we both push people away when we're afraid of getting hurt. I had no idea you felt this way.'

'You're not joking?'

'Not one bit. I love you.'

'I can't believe this. You have to know it killed me staying away from you when we went out. I just didn't know what to do for the best. On the one hand I felt guilty for asking too much of you, and so I thought giving you space to enjoy yourself was the right thing to do. Then when we were together, I didn't trust myself not to kiss you. I thought you'd slap me or something if I tried it on and then I'd lose you forever. Do you know how much I want to kiss you?'

As he said those words, the pressure between us doubled in intensity. This time I recognised it most definitely as lust. Luscious lust.

All I wanted to do was kiss him too. We were at the exact moment where we should be kissing, but we were stuck on opposite sides of a table in an increasingly busy restaurant.

'Turns out I'm not really hungry right now,' Jake muttered, reading my mind.

I smiled. 'It is far too early for dinner. What were we thinking?'

'Yeah.'

Jake looked across the bar and the waiter (who appeared from nowhere) came running over.

'Are you ready to order?'

'We're going to get room service.'

'Those cocktails were strong,' I said, trying to justify our change of minds.

'Could we put the drinks on our room?' Jake asked.

'Of course.'

'I'll come to the bar to sign for it,' Jake said. Then he looked at me. 'Ready to go?'

'Hell yes.'

THIRTY

Jake signed for the drinks and then we swiftly made our way back to the hotel room. I was jittery with excitement. I couldn't control the smile that insisted on warming my face as we practically skipped our way back.

Jake opened the door and I walked in. I headed into the middle of the room, not really knowing what to do next. Jake controlled the closing of the door, very slowly, and then he rested against it, seemingly in the same "what the hell do we do now" mindset.

Our eyes were locked but we didn't move. We just stood, frozen by the lustful energy that was charging the atmosphere. I had never wanted anyone more. But that also made me ten times more nervous about this.

I edged a step forward, hoping that Jake would copy me, and that we'd soon make our way over to each other. But Jake did nothing. He just watched me.

I took another tiny step forward, and Jake stood up straight.

But he didn't edge forward as I had expected. He strode directly over to me, took my cheeks in his hands, and kissed me.

Wow. That electrical buzz that I so often felt in his

company went into overdrive. My skin fizzled with delight as his lips caressed mine. So carefully. So lovingly.

I wrapped my arms around him and we melted into one another. That was when the heat began to rise.

The tender kissing became more needy, and the loving touch turned into a lustful craving.

After quite a lot of very pleasurable time had passed and my lips were raw and pulsating, Jake pulled back.

His eyes looked hungry for me. It was extremely hot.

He knotted his fingers between mine and I caught him quickly glancing at the two single beds next to us.

'I say we make a mess of my bed first,' I uttered. 'Then yours.'

I was serious, but this made Jake laugh.

'Do you not like that idea?' I checked.

'I think it's the best idea I've ever heard.'

Now it was my turn to laugh.

'Shit, do we have any contraception?' I asked.

Jake looked sheepish. 'Would you judge me if I said yes? It wasn't like I was expecting anything. But when you share a room with the woman you're secretly in love with, you kind of make sure you're prepared for any eventuality. Just in case.'

'Judge you? You're my hero!'

I still couldn't believe that he felt for me the same as I felt for him. It was surreal. But I knew if I started to analyse it, I would ruin the moment. So instead I went against every one of my natural instincts and I decided to go with the flow.

I kissed him again and led him to my bed.

We stood for a moment, taking our time, enjoying every second of this fantastic build up.

Jake kissed my lips gently before moving down to my neck. Then he started to unbutton my blouse in between the most tender of brushes.

It had been a very long time since I'd spent the night with a man. And now I was about to have sex with the man of my dreams. I had to keep control and not embarrass myself. I was already beginning to tingle in ways I'd forgotten were possible.

Or maybe I'd just never felt like this before?

It was all quite overwhelming, but in a very pleasing way. I had to make this moment last for as long as humanly possible.

We savoured each other as we slowly removed each other's clothes, and the tension in me rose and rose. I was having to work extremely hard to keep myself in check.

Jake had the most beautiful body. His skin was soft and tanned, and his muscles firm and toned. He was everything I had imagined he would be.

When we were both fully naked, Jake gently lowered me down on the bed, and I finally got to feel all of him. Our rhythm together was so seamlessly comfortable, it was as if we'd been making love to each other all of our lives.

Slowly he found his way inside me and I could hold on no longer. Within seconds my body was sparking. It was the most powerful and pleasurable climax I'd ever experienced.

He seemed to very much like my reaction to him, and before I'd even had a chance to catch my breath, he relinquished all control himself and found his own climax.

As the exquisite intensity relaxed, Jake glanced into my eyes and we shared a look that I've never shared with anyone before. It was love. Real love. I had no idea it felt like this.

Jake shifted next to me and I snuggled up into his arms.

'So that's what sex is supposed to feel like,' I mused. I hadn't meant to say it out loud, but the words just couldn't be kept inside.

'I guess so,' Jake said, kissing my forehead. He seemed just as reflective as I was.

We held each other closely for a while. No words were needed. It was just perfect as it was.

Then Jake said he needed the toilet.

As he tottered off, I stretched out, that smile spreading

across my face again all of its own accord.

All of the horror that was ruining the rest of my life seemed a million miles away, and I was happy to let it stay there for the time being. My body felt relaxed and content and I suddenly realised how long it had been since I'd not felt stressed out about something.

The bathroom door opened and Jake came towards me, full of glee. He stood at the end of the bed watching me with a cheeky smile.

'Can I help you?' I said.

'Yes. We're only fifty percent done,' he replied.

I was confused.

'We have to make a mess of my bed now.'

I laughed. 'Of course. We must get right onto that.'

'Then I think we might have to mess up your bed some more. Just to be sure,' he added.

'It could be a long night,' I said.

'Oh, I do hope so.'

Jake picked me up and moved me from one bed to the other, and before I knew it we were wrapped up in each other's bodies all over again.

I have no idea how long we'd been enjoying each other for, but some while later my stomach began to grumble.

'I think I've built up quite the appetite,' I said, resting my head on Jake's stomach, back in my bed. 'Yep, your stomach is grumbling too.'

Jake laughed. 'We can't have that.'

'We did say we were going to order room service.'

'That was a while ago. I bet they've been waiting for our call.'

'That poor man! I bet he's been hovering over the phone, pen and pad in hand.'

'It's time to put him out of his misery.'

Jake got up and flicked the TV on where the room service menu could be found. Within about three seconds of looking at it, he nodded.

'Have you decided already?' I asked.

'Yep. I'm going to have the burger. You can't go wrong with a burger.'

'Chicken or beef? I know you're anything but a vegetarian.'

'What makes you say that?'

'Putting aside the barbecue that had a whole farm on it, you always stack your plate high with bacon and sausages at our breakfast meetings.' I looked at his gorgeous body. 'I don't know where you put it all.'

'Home gym,' he said, patting his stomach. 'Remember?'

I smiled. 'How could I forget. So, chicken or beef?'

'Beef. Always beef. I don't understand chicken burgers.'

I looked at him with mock confusion. 'It can be a hard one to fathom. You see, what they do is, where they normally put the beef inside the bun, they decide to put chicken instead. It's genius.'

'But it's not, is it,' he argued.

'How is it not?'

'They put like mayonnaise on it and stuff.'

I burst out laughing. 'How is that bad? I love mayonnaise! And to prove it, I'm going to have the chicken burger.'

Jake shook his head and tutted. 'You really are a wild one.'

I giggled. 'I think madcap is the word.'

'You'll be having pineapple on your pizza next,' he said as walked towards the bedside table.

I pulled a face. 'No. Sweet and savoury do not mix.'

'Yes!' he replied with great enthusiasm. 'I totally agree.'

He dialled the phone.

'Yes, hi, we'd like to order room service, please.' He spoke in a formal but friendly tone. 'One beef burger and one... chicken burger.' He pulled a face and shook his head. 'Can we also get a bottle of champagne and some strawberries, please. Two glasses. Thank you.'

'Champagne?' I checked as he put down the phone.

'Does that really go with a burger?'

'Maybe not a chicken burger, but that's your fault.' He headed to the wardrobe and grabbed the two fluffy white dressing gowns. He threw one over to me and unravelled the other one for himself.

'Are we celebrating?' I asked as I wrapped myself up in the lovely soft fabric.

'We certainly are. It turns out the woman I love feels the same way about me. And she's great in bed. That's definitely worth celebrating.'

I couldn't control my giggle. I felt like a school girl who was experiencing her first crush.

He sat down next to me on the bed and played with my hair. Jake Masters was playing with my hair! I couldn't see how I'd ever get used to him touching me. It was sensational.

'You're not so bad yourself,' I muttered through my smile.

My mind flashed back to all of the times when I'd been excited that he had just spoken to me. And now we'd spent some incredibly intimate time together. It was mind-blowing.

How had this happened? I suddenly felt very glad that I'd Googled local networking groups ten months ago and I'd taken the decision to visit Ipswich Connected. Imagine if I hadn't.

I sat upright.

'What is it?' Jake asked, seeing me tense up.

'Imagine if I hadn't.'

'Hadn't what?'

'Imagine if we'd never met.'

'I'd rather not.'

'No, no, no, no. I mean…' I stood up. My brain was getting a bit panicky. 'You saved me. Without realising it. And you're still saving me.'

'Saved you?' Jake looked quite confused.

'It's just dawned on me exactly what it means.'

'Could you be less vague, please?'

'Nicholas.' Jake's face dropped. 'He's been looking for me for years. He's been planning for years how to get me to be the mother of his children. As Angela said, his primary goal was to get me to fall in love with him, and he was going to manipulate me in any way possible to make that happen. But he couldn't do it. He was too late.'

'Too late?'

I looked straight into Jake's eyes. 'I am madly in love with you. You're like my dream man.' I instantly wished I hadn't said that and I felt my cheeks flush, but Jake seemed very pleased with my admission. Thankfully. I decided to plough on and shake the words away. Part of me still felt sure that if Jake knew how much I was really besotted with him, he'd run a mile. 'I thought Nicholas was attractive, but my head had already been turned by you. You - dazzling me in the way that you do. He didn't stand a chance. You literally stopped him from being able to manipulate me. He gave it a good go, but you were... like... shielding me from him.'

Jake threaded his fingers through mine and pulled me closer to him. 'You really do like me don't you?' He seemed thrilled.

I nodded shyly.

'You know, I would have been devastated if you'd decided to date that Nicholas. When I saw you out with him, I was... angry. Fuming. I've never felt jealousy like it. I wanted to rip his throat out.'

I loved it.

'I used to count down the days until the next networking meeting, when I knew I'd be seeing you,' he continued. 'I never for one second thought you felt the same way. You were so quiet around me.'

This made me laugh. I sat down next to him.

'I was a wreck around you,' I confessed. 'It's not like me at all. I was like a lovestruck teenager who couldn't string a sentence together. I'm so glad it didn't put you off.'

'Not at all. Although I'm not going to lie: when I found out just how bloody chatty you are, that's when I knew I loved you. I much prefer the Isobel that never shuts up.'

'Oi!' I hit him playfully with a pillow.

'That's a good thing! Believe me. I meant what I said before: you never fail to surprise me. Like the darts thing! You are so good at darts.'

'Yeah, I've always had a knack for throwing things accurately. So be warned.' I threatened him with the pillow again.

'Consider me officially warned,' he joked with his hands up in surrender.

'Darts have always just clicked with me. I played a lot at uni. The lads I used to beat then didn't much like it either.'

'It was more than just beating that bloke in the pub. You annihilated him.'

'No I didn't.'

'That's it!' Jake stood up with excitement, as if he'd just had the best idea ever.

'What's it?'

'Darts. I'm going to buy you some darts.'

'I already have some at home. Somewhere.'

'No, not to play with. Well, eventually maybe. But as a weapon.'

'What?'

'We don't know when or how, but we have to assume that Nicholas is going to find us eventually. And we don't have any clue yet how to beat him. But we need to be ready. If you had darts, it's something to hurt him with. I know you know how to handle a dart. I saw that.'

'This is starting to sound like an Angela idea.'

'I'm not saying you have to kill him. You could throw a dart at his leg. A dart in the thigh is far from fatal, but it will definitely slow him down a bit, and you have excellent aim.'

I sat back. I didn't like this.

'This is a brilliant idea,' Jake added.

'I don't think-'

'And it's non-negotiable. I'd rather you have them and not use them, than Nicholas attacks you and you have no way to defend yourself.'

'I really can't see myself stabbing anyone with a dart. No matter what they're doing.'

'Please. It will make me feel much better. And I promise, it's just so you can go for the arm or leg. It's about hurting him so he backs away.'

I felt a shiver. The horror was returning.

'A really dangerous man is coming for you,' Jake said. 'He has the advantage at the moment as we have no clue how we can defeat him. We need something in our arsenal to help us defend ourselves. Hiding won't last for long, and we both know it.'

I nodded. 'I suppose buying some darts doesn't mean anything. Like you said, I don't have to use them.'

'And you might feel very pleased you have them if the worst happens.'

A knock at the door came just at the right time. I needed this conversation to end. Jake opened up and our food and champagne were placed on the little coffee table near the window.

We both thanked the waiter and he left.

'It's burger time!' I said, trying to break the unpleasant tension that had manifested at the mention of that man's name.

Before Jake tucked into his beef, he popped open the cork of the champagne. He poured us a glass each and held his high.

'To love,' he said.

I joined in the toast. 'To love.'

Although now all I felt was scared.

THIRTY-ONE

Jake stirring to go to the toilet the next morning woke me up. Not that I had been asleep for long. In what had seemed like a romantic idea at the time, we had decided to sleep together in my bed.

It had been so nice slowly drifting off with his arms around me.

But that sweet notion soon wore off. I had drifted off for all of about ten minutes when Jake shifted and it jerked me wide awake again. Then I shifted and I could tell it disturbed him. I hadn't shared a bed with anyone for a long, long time (let alone a single bed!), and the romance was all too quickly replaced with irritation. Good hearted irritation, but irritation nevertheless.

After a good few hours of discomfort, I knew I needed to say something. As good as he smelt and as glorious as his embrace was, I was tired and I needed space.

I rolled over to find Jake wide awake and staring at the ceiling.

'This is so nice,' I said, starting off with a positive.

'I know,' he said.

'The thing is, though...' I hesitated. I drew circles on his chest, somehow believing that it would seem cute and it would soften the blow of what I was about to say.

But that was when Jake said, 'It's a bit of a squash, isn't it.'

I stopped my circling. As much as I completely agreed with him, there was a ridiculous part of me that was upset by his comment.

'Do you not like sleeping next to me?' I said, knowing full well that wasn't what he was saying at all.

'Of course I do. This is amazing. It's just... different. I've been single for so long, it's kind of weird sharing a bed with someone again.'

'I know what you mean.'

'You do?'

'It's lovely being next to you. But we've both gone from having big beds to ourselves to sharing this tiny single, and it's a bit...'

'Have you slept at all?' he asked, gently.

'A little bit.'

'So you won't be upset if I get out and move back to the other bed?'

I paused. 'Not at all.'

'I do like sharing with you.'

'Perhaps we could swap and get a double if we're going to be here for a while?'

'Great idea. Let's look at that tomorrow.'

Jake kissed me and then shuffled out of my bed and into his own.

The sudden space I felt was luxurious. I spread my limbs to every corner and then curled up into a ball.

I looked across at Jake who seemed to be doing the same thing, and I felt bad. I missed him. I didn't know how I was going to sleep, feeling like I'd turfed him out.

And that was the last thing I remembered before Jake's trip to the bathroom woke me up.

I glanced at my phone on the bedside table that sat between the beds. It was only quarter past seven. My eyes felt sore and heavy and I turned over in the hope that Jake wouldn't know I was awake and he'd creep back to bed and leave me alone.

But he was an early riser, just like me. Once we were awake, we were awake. The daylight was calling us to get moving, and I knew that my brain was too engaged now to switch off and let me get more rest.

I heard Jake come out of the bathroom and pick up the kettle. He filled it with water and switched it on. I could pretend no more.

'Morning,' I said. I rolled over to see Jake wrapping a dressing gown around himself.

'Morning, beautiful,' he said. He sat down on the bed next to me and kissed me. 'Ready for a coffee?'

'I'm ready for a full English. I'm absolutely starving.'

'It's all that exercise you were doing last night.' Jake smirked.

'I think you're right.'

'How about we go and empty the restaurant of food and then we head into Norwich to get you some darts?'

'You're still keen on that idea?' I asked.

'It isn't open for debate. It's happening. I need to keep you safe.'

'All right. If that's what you want.'

When our bellies were full and the breakfast buffet was properly dented, we made our way to Jake's car. It was around nine am and the golfers were already there in droves.

'I think that's why we haven't seen many cats,' I mused as we sat in the car.

Jake looked at me. 'I may need a bit more context there.'

'Sorry. The golfers. Everywhere I've been through my whole life, I've always attracted at least one or two cats. But there are none here at all. It must be a first, and it's just dawned on me why. With balls flying about and golfers walking everywhere, it's not exactly a cat's idea of paradise.'

'That's why I suggested this hotel. It's always rammed with golfers in the summer. Well it's pretty rammed all year round, but the summer is the worst.'

'Do you play golf?' I asked, picking up on his insight.

'I haven't in a while, but I used to be pretty good. What about you?'

'I always wanted to learn. You can make excellent business contacts on the golf course. But it was the learning part that got in the way. I just wanted to be good at it. I didn't have the patience for slow improvement.'

This made Jake laugh. 'Strangely, I know exactly what you mean. I used to go to the driving range all the time with the lads at uni. Harrison used to love it. That's how I got started. Maybe I could teach you?'

I smiled eagerly. 'Now that I would love. With you wrapping yourself around me to show me how to putt, I'd happily slow down my improvement.'

We both laughed.

'You're on,' Jake said. He could barely wipe the smile off his face. It was so lovely.

'Can we never come back here to play, though,' I said, looking around. It was a beautiful hotel, and clearly a popular golf course, but I knew it would always remind me of dark times.

'Of course,' Jake said, squeezing my hand.

It only took us about fifteen minutes to get to Norwich, and Jake parked in the same car park as before, right near the castle.

We began walking up towards the city centre, but after about thirty seconds Jake stopped. He pulled out his phone.

I looked over at what he was doing and saw that he was pulling up directions. There was a specialist darts shop about a fifteen minute walk away.

'Could we not have parked closer?' I asked.

'Possibly. But I know how to get to this car park.'

I couldn't argue with that.

We walked on and I rejoiced in how quiet everywhere seemed. That's one of the things I'd always loved about mornings. Especially a Saturday morning. People were slower to start their days and you could relish in space.

We carried on and reached some cobbled streets, and I took in the buildings around me. They all seemed old and full of character.

'Norwich really is lovely,' I said.

'It's all right,' Jake replied.

'Oh, of course,' I said, nodding. 'It's no Ipswich.'

Jake was Suffolk born and bred and I couldn't forget that. East Anglia often felt like a place on its own, outside of the rest of England, and the rivalry between Norfolk and Suffolk could be quite heated at times. Jake was one of the most open minded, inclusive people that I'd ever met, but as soon as someone talked about Norfolk, there seemed to be this subtle disliking about it, as if it had been drummed into him from birth that Suffolk was better and that was that.

Don't get me wrong, Jake would chat away quite happily to anyone from Norfolk, even to a Norwich City fan (except maybe on derby match days), but there was still always this underlying whiff of conflict (albeit mostly lighthearted) and I'd noticed it in most of the locals who had Suffolk in their heart.

I'd moved away from home at the age of eighteen and had never settled anywhere through my adult life, so this dedication to a place you called home seemed alien to me. But I also quite liked it. I wanted to feel so passionate about a place that the neighbouring town (or city) irked me quite irrationally. I felt jealous that Jake had that. It suddenly made me feel very empty.

'Ipswich might be smaller, but it's better for it,' Jake said, meaning every word. He wittered on about all the wonders of Suffolk as we carried on through the pretty little streets, but I couldn't concentrate on what he was saying.

I had believed for years that work was all that mattered. That my way to happiness was going to be through success and money. And, of course, I still wanted that. But something suddenly made me feel that wasn't enough anymore.

I was starting to see that I was ready for change. I was ready to settle down. I was ready for work to become number two in my life. I was ready for whatever was coming next, and I knew I was going to grab it with both hands.

'It's left up here and across the bridge,' Jake said, studying his phone.

'There's a bridge?' I asked.

We turned the corner to find the bridge, but it was only small and looked pretty much just like the rest of the pavement.

As we stepped across it, the clouds started to part, releasing the heat onto us. I was glad for my summer dress. I linked my arm with Jake's and stroked his beautiful soft skin.

'That tickles,' he said, twitching.

'Are you ticklish?' I asked.

A brief pause. 'No comment.'

'I'll take that as a yes.'

I could feel Jake tense up at the idea of me tickling him again, so I quickly changed the subject. That nugget of information would be stored up for later, though.

'What water are we crossing now?' I asked. 'Is this a canal?'

'It's a river.'

'Ooh, which river?'

'Erm... River Wensum.'

'Did you just look that up on your phone?'

'No! I just couldn't remember straight away.'

We both laughed and I felt weirdly happy.

A few minutes later we arrived at the small street where the darts shop could be found, and I noticed how everywhere was getting increasingly busier.

We entered the shop and very quickly made a decision. I wasn't too fussed. As much as I loved that Jake was buying me a gift, I also knew that he was only buying the darts for me because of Nicholas. It took all the romance out of it.

Jake paid for them and I stuffed them into my bag. I was hoping I wouldn't need to think about them again any time soon.

We thanked the helpful shop owner and we stepped out onto the pavement.

'Shall we grab a coffee while we're out?' Jake suggested.

'All right. Although we shouldn't-'

Too late.

I looked ahead and saw, right before me, a very familiar cat.

That smoky fur and those piercing blue eyes made me shudder.

'Is that...?' Jake uttered.

'It is,' I said as the horror burned through me.

'Smokey?' he finished.

'Nicholas,' I corrected.

I couldn't take my eyes off Smokey. My head said I should just keep moving. What could he do in cat form in the middle of a city on a Saturday morning?

His eyes were fixated on me, though, and it seemed to freeze me to the spot.

Slowly Smokey's attention turned to Jake, and I swear I saw anger rise on that cat's face.

He hissed loudly, screeched, and then leapt towards Jake.

Jake shouted out as Smokey bit his leg. I was so pleased that Jake had jeans on.

I tried to grab Smokey and pull him off, but Jake suddenly lurched forward with a yell.

There was another cat on his back. It was hanging there, its claws deeply dug into Jake's t-shirt.

Another cat appeared. This one jumped onto Jake's arm, scratching him viciously. Then another one. Then another one.

I tried to help. I tried to pull them off. But for every cat I yanked away, another five appeared.

Jake fell to the ground under the pressure of the cats, and all I could see was fur.

'Someone call the police!' I shouted, turning desperately to the faces that were gawping at us, bewildered by the most bizarre cat attack that played out before them.

I bent down with determination and tried to break Jake free. My hands were swiped at, but the stinging only spurred me on. I had to get him free.

Dozens of cats were now surrounding us, joining in with this cult of hatred towards the man I loved. How was Nicholas doing this?

Nicholas! If I could get Nicholas away then I was sure the other cats would relinquish their anger.

I looked through the swarm of fur - the hissing and biting and howling - and I located that smoky fur I'd know anywhere.

Jake had stopped screaming now and I was terrified. I grabbed at Smokey and yanked him. He held on tight, and I feared what damage it would do to Jake. Sod Smokey's claws. I hope it ripped his claws out. But I didn't want to cause Jake any more harm.

I pulled and pulled, and then Smokey turned around and went for me. He bit my hand, but my love for Jake was no match for him. I held on tight despite his efforts to fight me away.

Finally feeling him freed, I threw Smokey down the street, not caring if I hurt him or not.

He landed effortlessly on his feet and I glared at him, daring him to come back. I'd just about had enough. When he didn't move, I turned back to Jake. One by one, I yanked cats away, showing Nicholas that I was not going to give in.

The cats quickly started to calm down and finally leave Jake alone, and I could once again see his body.

As I knelt down to help him, Smokey hurtled towards us. He hissed at me wildly, knocking me backwards, and then he ran off down the street and out of sight.

I caught my breath before pushing away the few remaining creatures, but they seemed bored now and ready to move on.

Most of Jake's clothes were ripped to shreds, and blood was soaking through the fabric. He'd managed to protect his face with his arms, but the backs of his hands – in fact any flesh on show - was a bloody mess. Fierce red lines from the dozens of claws were everywhere.

'Someone call an ambulance,' I shouted to the onlookers, and I could see that one man was already on the case.

Jake was barely conscious, but he was still with us. Thankfully.

I held his hand and he moaned against the pain. There was blood trickling out onto the pavement and I knew we needed to get help fast.

'They're on their way,' the kind middle-aged man said.

'Thank you,' I replied.

Now all we could do was wait, and hope the ambulance arrived soon.

THIRTY-TWO

It took twenty minutes for the ambulance to arrive, in which time Jake had lost consciousness. He looked like he'd been shredded. I was so frightened. I couldn't lose him.

A nearby shop had given me a few towels to help ease some of the blood, but mostly people just gawped in shock. I couldn't blame them.

'Can you tell me what happened?' one of the two paramedics said as I stood back to let them do their job.

'He was attacked by cats.'

Both of the paramedics turned to me with surprise.

'Cats?'

'Yes,' I replied. 'Dozens of cats. They jumped up at him and started... attacking him.'

'I saw it all,' one helpful old man chipped in with. 'He was just minding his own business when this grey cat pounced on him, and then hundreds of other cats started joining in. It was the weirdest thing I've ever seen.'

I could tell that the paramedics had more questions, but they didn't say another word about it. They quickly got to work on saving Jake.

All I could do was stand there, trying to control my tears.

'It's the claws you've got to watch,' the old man

continued, to both me and the trained medical professionals. 'You don't know where those cats have been. Make sure you give him antiseptic.'

'Thank you for your help,' I said as firmly as I could, hoping he'd leave.

He didn't take the hint. He watched on as if the whole event were playing out for his personal entertainment.

Most of Jake's cuts were quickly bandaged up, just enough to get him to the hospital, and we were soon on our way with the siren blaring loudly.

The Paramedic sitting with us asked me more questions, but I could barely take them in. Too much had happened in a very short space of time.

We arrived at the hospital in what seemed like a flash. Jake was quickly whisked away and I was told to check him in at the reception desk.

The Emergency Department was unexpectedly quiet and I was able to walk straight up to the uniformed middle aged lady that sat behind a glass partition.

'How can I help?' she asked, sliding open the window.

'My frie... boyfriend has just been brought in by ambulance. I was told to report to you.'

'What's his name?'

'Jake Masters.' I paused. 'Although it might be Jacob. I think his friend said he was Jacob. Jacob Masters.'

'Date of birth?'

Shit.

Anything of use suddenly seemed to flush itself out of my brain. We had definitely shared birth dates. Why couldn't I remember what he said?

It was April. I knew that. I remembered him bringing cakes to our networking meeting. But when in April I had no idea.

'April,' I muttered.

'April the what?'

'I can't remember,' I replied. 'Sorry. It's been very traumatic. He's thirty-two if that helps?'

She looked at me, clearly doubting my status as girlfriend. Probably doubting that I knew Jake at all.

'Do you know his address?' she asked.

'Yes! He lives in Henstone. One Tabbington Road.'

'Postcode?'

I paused. 'I don't know. I just go there. I've never written to him.'

She refrained from rolling her eyes, but I knew she wanted to.

'Can you tell me why he's here?'

'He was attacked by cats.'

She stopped dead still and glared at me.

'Cats?' she repeated, incredulously.

'Yes.'

I could have elaborated. I could have explained that the cat/man hybrid that was trying to impregnate me was jealous that I'd fallen for Jake and so got his cat buddies to gang up on Jake and rip him to shreds. I wanted to elaborate so people would stop giving me that look as if I'd been imagining things. I was sure she was thinking it was probably a tiny dog that looked like a cat and I was so stupid I'd got it wrong.

The whole thing was so utterly ridiculous. I was sure one day I'd look back and laugh. But at that moment I wanted to throw up I was so scared.

'A whole bunch of cats came out of nowhere and attacked him,' I explained. 'Ripped his skin to shreds.'

She let my words sink in.

'What's your name?' she asked me.

'Isobel Hargreaves. Jake's girlfriend, as I said.'

If I were to tell you she looked at me sceptically at this point, it would be the world's biggest understatement. She definitely thought I was crazy. It made it even more alarming that everything I'd told her was absolutely true.

'We'll let you know when there's an update. Please take a seat,' she instructed, and then she turned away.

I looked around the brightly lit waiting area and headed

for a seat near the window, away from where most people were sitting. The second my bum hit that plastic chair, I lost all control of my emotions. Everything I'd been grabbing onto so tightly seemed to shatter, leaving me feeling like an uncontrollable wreck.

The first thing to hit me was guilt. If I had never met Jake then he wouldn't be in the hospital scratched to pieces.

A chill shook me.

If I had never met Jake then I might be carrying Nicholas's litter of cat babies.

That cycle of guilt and relief - mixed in with absolute fear that Jake wouldn't survive this - taunted me for the next couple of hours. I was too afraid to move from my seat for fear that I'd miss an update, but as the time rolled on I was getting more and more panicky and upset.

'Isobel Hargreaves,' a male voice finally called out. I looked up to see a man in blue scrubs.

'Yes,' I said, walking over to him.

'Follow me,' he said.

He led me into a tiny room with a bed and a desk in it. He sat at the desk and I sat next to him.

'Could you confirm who you're here with?'

'Jake Masters. Jacob. My boyfriend. Is he okay?'

'Could you tell me what happened?'

'He was attacked by cats. Dozens of cats. They came out of nowhere and just... pounced on him.'

His eyes flicked up with that same look of disbelief. 'Do you know why?' he asked.

I paused. Would someone ask why if it was a dog attack?

'No idea,' I lied. 'It was the strangest thing I've ever seen. We'd just come out of the darts shop. I like to play darts and Jake was treating me to some new ones, and then we stepped out onto the street and he was attacked. Maybe we'd stepped into the middle of a cat territory thing. You know how territorial they are. I don't know.'

'That's pretty much what Jake told us. In incidents such as these, we have to call the police. They'll be here shortly.

I think they'll probably want to talk to you too.'

'Jake's awake?' I asked, ignoring everything else the man had said. Nothing else seemed to matter.

'Yes. He's stable. He's lucky. There seemed to be a lot of blood loss, but I don't think he'll be left with any permanent scars. This whole thing is very strange.'

'Tell me about it. So he'll be okay?'

'Yes, I think he'll make a full recovery.'

The relief brought tears to my eyes. 'Can I see him?'

'We're moving him to a ward. We want to keep him overnight for observation, just in case. When he's settled we'll let you know. If you could just remain in the waiting area until the police arrive.'

'The police?' That detail finally began sinking in.

'Yes. As I said, they'll probably want to talk to you.'

'About what? It was a random cat attack.'

'That's not for me to say. It's normal procedure for us to involve the police in circumstances like these.'

'Cat attacks?'

'Any sort of attack. If you could just take a seat back in the waiting area.'

Was that it? I'd waited two hours for that?

'You'll let me know when I can see him?' I said, feeling the need for something more.

'Of course. Thank you.'

He stood up and I knew my time with him was over. I headed back to the waiting area.

The relief that Jake was going to be okay didn't last for long. As I took my seat once more, I was soon consumed with worry about what the police were going to ask me.

I was immediately pleased we were now in Norfolk. I certainly didn't want the same police officers that had come to Jake's house turning up. They already thought I was a weird stalker who kidnapped people's cats. I'm not sure what they'd make of this. But this was a different county, so I was sure they'd know nothing about my complaint against Nicholas.

Taking my chance that it wouldn't be instant that I'd be called by the police or in to see Jake, I quickly grabbed a coffee and a sandwich and had a short refreshment break before returning to watch the clock.

It was three hours before the police woman called my name.

She took me to another small room that looked pretty similar to the one before.

She sat on the bed while I took the chair.

'Do you want to tell me what happened to Mr Masters?' she said softly.

For what felt like the millionth time, I said, 'He was attacked by cats. I don't know why. They just appeared out of nowhere. There were witnesses on the street. Loads of people saw it. It was the strangest thing.'

She took down some notes and nodded sympathetically.

'Could you tell me what you were doing in Norwich?'

I paused. 'We were buying darts.'

'You came all the way to Norwich to buy darts?'

'No. We're in Norfolk for a weekend away. We're staying in...' All words escaped me. 'I can't remember the name of it. It's a big golf hotel about five miles away. Sorry, it's been a very stressful day.' I now wanted to cry so badly. I felt so tired and frightened, and all I wanted to do was see Jake. I didn't want to be in this room being questioned by this woman. A woman who should have been protecting me, but who would probably lock me up if I actually told her the truth.

'It's fine,' she said. 'So you left your hotel to go into Norwich to buy some darts?'

'Yes. I love to play darts and Jake, as my new boyfriend, decided he wanted to treat me to some new ones. How is this relevant?'

'I'm just trying to get a complete picture. I've never heard of a cat attack like this before. It's very unusual.'

I knew she was going to look into us. She was going to find out that I'd been accused of cat kidnapping by my neighbour. Somehow I could see this becoming a huge mess for me, when we were actually the innocent victims.

But I kept my mouth shut.

'I thought cats were cute, friendly animals,' I said. 'But this was vicious.'

'Is there anything else you can tell me?'

I wanted to tell her everything. I needed help badly. I wanted them to make sure that Nicholas never got within a mile of me or Jake ever again, either as a man or a cat. I wanted them to take me seriously and understand the threat that I was facing.

But I knew if I uttered one single word of the truth, it would be me that would end up under the spotlight.

It was so unfair.

'Not that I can think,' I replied. 'It was so random. So much for our romantic weekend away. We haven't even been together for that long. He will be okay, won't be?'

'You'll need to ask the doctors about that.'

'I hope I can see him soon. Is he in the ward yet?'

'Again, you're better speaking to the doctors.'

'Okay.'

'If you think of anything else, you will let us know?'

'Anything else, like what?' I asked.

'Anything that could explain why a few dozen cats decided to randomly attack your boyfriend. I've been around long enough to know nothing is ever random. There will be a reason.'

'Like Jake beckoned them on or something?' I said, far too aggressively. Probably because she was right.

'No. I'm not saying that. I'm sure you were just in the wrong place at the wrong time. But it will be good for us to find out why this happened. We need to make sure this sort of thing doesn't happen again.'

If only they knew.

'Right. I understand.'

'Thanks for your help, Miss Hargreaves. I appreciate it. We'll let you know if we need anything else.'

'No problem.'

She led me back to the waiting area where I took my seat once more.

Things were cooling down a bit by late afternoon and the waiting area was becoming busier and busier.

I was now extremely tired and fed up, and my worries seemed to be piling up at an incredible rate. I had to use all my energy to control my tears. I was too proud to sit sobbing in the packed waiting area, but I couldn't take the risk of going to the toilet in case my name was finally called.

The seconds dragged, making every minute feel like an hour, and every hour feel like a week. People were being called in, and the faces around me were constantly changing, but all I could do was watch the time and keep my tears in check.

Eventually, at around seven p.m., my name was called. I practically ran over to the woman behind the desk. I was given instructions to go to a different part of the hospital and I was told that I could now see Jake.

Shakily, I headed over there. Maybe it was because I was scared. Maybe because I was hungry. I didn't know, but I felt quite peculiar.

I finally found him. He was sitting upright in bed and his eyes lit up when he saw me.

He was bandaged up with just his face on show. The small cuts on and around his ears were the only visible evidence of the onslaught.

'Hi,' he said. I leaned in to kiss him and he winced as he moved to meet my lips.

'Are you okay?' I asked, gently. There were four other occupied beds around him. I knew we'd have to talk quietly.

'Stings a bit,' he said as he tried to flash me his beautiful smile, but I could see how much pain it caused him.

'I'm so sorry.'

'It's not your fault.'

'We both know what happened.'

'It's not your fault. Don't go thinking it is. You were

honest with me, so I knew what was going on. I knew the threat. I stood by - and I still stand by you. Maybe you should stay at the hospital tonight.'

'Where? In the waiting room?'

'I could ask if they have a spare bed?'

'No.' I dropped my voice. 'Nicholas must know we're here, and it's a hospital. Anyone can walk in or out.'

'It's a busy, public place.'

'I'll be safer at the hotel. At least I can lock the door. He can't know what hotel we're staying in. Hell, I can barely remember it. We have that advantage.'

'I can come back with you.'

'No! You need to stay here. There was so much blood.'

'They said I'll be fine.'

'They want to keep an eye on you.'

Jake paused. 'Did everyone look at you like you were mad when you said I'd been attacked by cats?'

'Yes,' I said quietly.

'Maybe I'll make the news,' Jake grinned.

'That's all we need.'

'I can discharge myself-'

'No way. You need to get some rest and have proper medical support. You'll be better in no time, but you need to look after yourself.'

'I'm worried about you.'

'It's not up for debate. Now, can I get you anything? A magazine? Puzzles? I'll bring you some clothes and toiletries tomorrow. Shit, your car is still in Norwich!'

'Leave it there!' Jake ordered.

'Don't you trust me driving your fancy car?' I joked.

'No. I mean yes, of course I do. It's not that.' Jake took a breath. I loved how precious he was about his car. 'What I meant to say was that Nicholas must know my car,' he clarified. 'I drove to your house. If he locates it then he might be able to follow you back. It can stay there for days if needs be. I don't care. You're all I care about.'

My heart throbbed. It sounded stupid in my head, but I

was so touched that Jake placed me well above his car. I really felt loved.

'Are you sure?' I said. 'If nothing else, it'll cost a fortune leaving your car in the car park for days. It might even get towed.'

'None of that matters. Your safety does.'

'It's your precious Jaguar.'

'I can always get another car. There is only one you.'

I took his hand in mind and held it ever so gently. I think I'd experienced every possible emotion that day, but it was nice to now feel nothing but love.

'Thank you, Jake. Is it Jake? Jacob? I got all flummoxed checking you in.'

'Jacob. I'm Jacob Harold Masters. Don't ask.'

'That's a good name. Well, thank you for everything Jacob Harold Masters.'

'You don't need to thank me. I'm always going to look out for you. Saying that, in the cupboard next to me you'll find my bank card. Use it for whatever you need.'

'I can't do that.'

'How else are you going to get on? How else are you even going to get a taxi back to the hotel? We're working as a team on this, so do as you're told.'

I looked at Jake as the fear trembled me once more.

'What is it?' he asked, ever so softly squeezing my hand.

'I can't even remember the name of the hotel we're staying in. I'm a complete mess.'

'Oh, sweetheart. I can come back with you.'

'No. I'm an independent woman. I've been on my own for years. I don't want to be reliant upon anyone else. I'm just scared.'

'You have every reason to be. Are you sure you don't want to stay here?'

'I need to be in a place where I can lock the door. Besides, the hotel is busy, and it will be overrun with golfers tonight. Maybe I'll sit in the bar with them all night!'

'You have the key card, don't you?'

'Yes,' I nodded. 'It's in my bag.'

'The name of the hotel is on that. If you forget, just look at that.'

I shook my head at how obvious that was.

'I guess I really do need you,' I said.

'You do at the minute. And there's nothing wrong with that. We all need someone to rely on at times.'

'You're the one in the hospital bed. You shouldn't be looking after me, it should be the other way around.'

'I have no doubt you're going to look after me. Now do as you're told and get my bank card.'

'Thank you.'

I sighed and opened the cupboard.

'Visiting time is over,' a voice called.

'Already?' I said. 'I've only just got to see you.'

'Come here, I'll whisper my PIN,' Jake said.

'You really trust me?' I asked, full of sincerity.

'More than anyone I've ever met. Now come here.'

I leaned in and Jake whispered the four magic digits.

'Thank you,' I said.

'Now bring me some nice looking clothes tomorrow,' he said. 'I've got to look good for these nurses.'

'Oi!' I joked. I went to hit his arm but quickly thought against it. I dreaded the think what his skin looked like. I hoped he wouldn't be scarred.

'I'll see you tomorrow,' I said, kissing him gently.

'You look after yourself. You promise?'

'I promise.'

'I love you.'

'I love you too.'

I slowly turned away and headed out of the hospital. As I walked down the corridor, grasping Jake's credit card tightly in my hand, tears poured down my cheeks.

I was now completely alone, just as Nicholas no doubt wanted. And I was absolutely terrified.

THIRTY-THREE

I headed back to the main hospital entrance. I remembered there was a special phone in the lobby where you could order taxis from. It was easy enough to request one, and within ten minutes I was on my way back to the hotel.

I paid for it with Jake's credit card, feeling terribly guilty about spending his money, and I thanked the driver. I grabbed my bag tightly, now very pleased I had the darts inside as some sort of protection, and I stepped out of the taxi. Without looking back, I swiftly headed in to the hotel reception, eager to be around people. As I walked through the doors, I scanned my eyes everywhere. I couldn't think how Nicholas would know where we were staying, but he'd tracked us down to Norwich, so anything seemed possible.

Other than the receptionist behind the desk, there was no one about. It was very quiet.

I made my way through the corridors, eager to get into the safety of my room as quickly as I could. I knew I would be locking the door and not moving until I went back to the hospital the next day. I'd already decided to order breakfast in bed, just in case. The less I moved, the less chance there was of Nicholas finding me.

I made it to the door. I swiftly opened it and I shut it firmly behind me. I threw my bag to the floor and felt around for the slot in the pitch black, looking for where to put the key card in so I could switch the lights on.

'You took your time.'

I turned in shock, my body trembling. I knew that voice all too well.

Before my brain could even process that Nicholas was there, let alone make a run for it, he had darted across from wherever he'd been waiting and he'd pinned me against the door.

It was very dark, but this clearly wasn't an issue for him.

'Hello, Isobel. This was certainly a good hiding place. I never would have found you here. Well done.'

Words failed me. I was too terrified.

He slipped the key card from my fingers and popped it in the slot. A few lights pinged into life, but all I could see were those glistening blue eyes staring down at me.

'I'm not angry,' he said. 'Don't worry. You could say I like a cat and mouse game.' He paused to smirk. 'But enough is enough. It's time you stopped putting off the inevitable. You will be having my children. And we'll be starting tonight.'

I gasped, but it was barely audible.

He picked me up and threw me on the bed.

'No,' I whimpered as my brain started to click into action. I tried to stand up, but he knocked me down.

'There's something I need to make very clear,' he warned, his voice cold and firm. 'You *will* be doing this with me. You *will* stop messing me around. Because if you don't start fulfilling your destiny, then I *will* make sure that the next time my cat friends see your precious Jake Masters, they won't be holding back.'

'What?' My eyes began to burn as his words became chillingly real.

'It wasn't an accident that your Jake survived. It wasn't because you pulled me off him. It was because I allowed him to live. It was a warning. But if you continue to fight me, then I will make sure my friends go all the way. Do I make myself clear?'

I couldn't speak.

'We will stay here tonight as it's late now, but first thing tomorrow you'll be coming back with me to my house, where we'll live together until you've given birth to my children. Do you understand?'

Still no words would form.

'The second I even suspect you trying to escape, I will make sure that Jake is visited by some friends of mine. Cats can get everywhere. We're very good at not being seen. Even in a hospital.'

'You can't do that! How are you even doing that? Cats don't follow orders.'

'When you think like a cat, it's very easy to know how to manipulate them. Cats worship Felivires. Just as they worship bearers. That's why they're always hanging around you. If you knew how to communicate, you could get them to do anything. It's good, isn't it.'

'No.'

'I'll teach you.'

'I don't want to know. I want you to leave.'

'You need to stop fighting this. It's your destiny. It's literally what you were born to do. You never know, you might enjoy it.'

'Are you serious?'

He shrugged. 'We'll see.'

I needed to get away. I needed to get back to Jake.

My darts!

I looked over and saw my bag near the door, where I'd stupidly thrown it down earlier.

'I was going to suggest we relax with a drink first,' Nicholas said, 'but I think it's probably best we get started. Don't you?'

'Started?' I asked.

'Yes. We have a long night of love making ahead.'

Nicholas stood up as my chest tightened, and suddenly my brain became weirdly focused. I began scanning through options in my head, like I was flipping through a Rolodex at superspeed.

I thought of running, but he was far too strong and quick for me to overpower him. If I shouted for help, he might gag me. And if anyone did hear, he was clearly good at charming people. I also couldn't take the risk of him drugging me again. I had to stay lucid.

My darts were the only thing that could work. Thank you Jake!

I just needed to get to my bag.

Nicholas took his shirt off, his eyes not leaving me as he did. I think I was supposed to be swooning. He had an impeccable body, but there was no way I could ever find him attractive.

He bent over right in front of my bag and took off his shoes.

'Am I allowed a few moments to freshen up?' I asked, sitting up. 'I can see very well I'm not going to have any choice. But you could at least allow me the dignity of feeling my best if I'm going to be... forced against my will.'

'Don't say it like that!' he snapped.

I stared at him. How could he think this was anything other than rape?

'I think you smell divine just as you are,' he said. 'But if you want to freshen up, that's completely understandable.'

I stood up and grabbed my bag. 'I'll be five minutes. Am I allowed five minutes on my own in the bathroom? It's not like there are any windows in there. I won't run off.'

'Give me your phone.'

'What?'

'Give me your phone.'

I happily obliged. I had no one to call anyway.

'You have five minutes,' he said. 'I'll be waiting.'

I stomped off and slammed the bathroom door behind me.

I quickly opened my bag and grabbed my darts. My fingers were sweaty and trembling as I took them out of their little case. As they were new, the flights weren't even on them, and I knew I needed to add them if I was going to have any chance of throwing them at Nicholas accurately.

I couldn't stab him. I'd have to be close and he was so strong and quick. He'd no doubt sense something was up and overpower me before I even had a chance to raise my arm. The best option I had was to throw a couple of darts in his back, and when he was doubled over in pain, I'd make a run for it.

I tried to delicately thread the flight onto the end of the dart, but in my wobbly state, I dropped it on the floor. My hands were practically useless.

I picked it up and sat on the toilet to help compose myself.

I tried again to slide the flight into the slits. I'd never even hesitated over this before, but suddenly it was like sliding a notebook through a keyhole. It wasn't happening.

I could hear myself breathing heavily, and I realised I was being far too quiet. Nicholas would wonder how I could so silently freshen myself up.

I turned on a tap, taking a second to calm myself, and then I returned to my difficult task.

After another five or six attempts, the flight finally slotted into place. One done, one to go. I had three darts, but two would do. I hadn't got the time to get three ready for action.

The second dart proved to be just as difficult, and I began to panic. My breathing was now choppy and I wanted to cry.

I had to focus so intently and move so slowly to get the second flight to fit neatly onto the dart, but it finally slipped on.

I stood up, darts in hand, and I turned the tap off.

I took a couple of very deep breaths, told myself crying wasn't remotely helpful, and I stepped over to the bathroom door.

I quickly yanked it open. Nicholas was standing there, completely naked, looking very smug.

I lifted my arm. The chest was the obvious place to aim for. What if I struck his heart?

Without any time for consideration, I threw the dart right at him.

His hand swiftly moved up, knocking the dart away before it could slice him.

What?

'What the hell was that?' he said, angrily.

I lifted the second dart and threw it quickly, but again he knocked the speeding dart away, sending it shooting towards the carpet.

'You're trying to throw darts at me?' he said fiercely.

'How did you do that?'

'I have cat-like reflexes. As you well know. Are you an idiot?'

'No, I'm just desperate to get away from you!'

Fear crippled me as I sensed all my options vanish.

He picked me up, his blue eyes now electric with rage, and he threw me sharply onto the bed.

I didn't move. I knew I needed to fight back – to do something. But I was so scared now, I couldn't bring myself to do anything.

He stood over me and grabbed the hem of my dress, ready to yank it up.

He stopped and swiftly turned around.

There was a knock at the door.

Nicholas glared at me. He put his finger to his lips, warning me to be silent.

'Say a word and Jake dies,' he whispered in my ear, his breath freezing me to the spot. I had never believed anyone more.

The person knocked again. I couldn't think who it could be.

A third knock. This person was persistent. I prayed that

it would be my saving.

The knocking stopped and everything fell quiet. My erratic breathing was the only thing I could hear.

Was that it? Was that my chance of escape over with?

Should I scream?

All of a sudden the door lock clicked and the handle turned down. Someone was coming in. Someone was coming in!

Nicholas hid round the corner, his eyes still fixed on me, warning me not to say a word.

'It's me, Isobel,' a female voice said. 'Angela.'

Angela?

The moment of relief quickly diminished when Nicholas shot across the room and pinned her to the wall by her neck.

'You're Angela?' he said.

She nodded as best she could. Despite the fact that he seemed to have her firmly in his grip, she looked anything but scared.

'You're the Angela that...'

Nicholas suddenly recoiled, grabbing the right side of his stomach in agony.

'I'm the Angela that is ending the Felivires. Yes.' She turned to me. 'Quickly, Isobel. Help me. You have a bath?'

I didn't know what to do. What was going on?

'Help me push him into the bath!'

I didn't know what she was talking about, but I didn't ask. With my brain and body now working totally independently from one another, I found myself standing up and somehow pushing Nicholas towards the bathroom.

He tried to fight, and that's when I saw it. She stabbed him again deeply in his stomach with a large kitchen knife. Both it and her hand were now coated with blood.

I was the one to recoil this time. I was utterly horrified. By everything. It was too much. Far too much.

All I could do was watch as he yelled in pain and she pushed.

Every time it seemed as if he might fall to the carpet, she

pushed him up, somehow using his own strength against him and controlling him perfectly.

She got him right next to the bath, and with one more stab, she knocked him into it.

He fell awkwardly, hitting his head against the tiles, but he stayed conscious.

Before he could fathom any way out of the tub, she stabbed him again.

I turned away. I couldn't look. I could hear Nicholas's yells. He was in agony. Although he sounded more angry than scared.

Then in an instant everything went silent.

And everything remained eerily silent for a few moments.

'You can look now,' Angela said.

I shook my head. Images of Nichola's body hacked to pieces and dripping with blood came to mind.

'You need to look,' she ordered.

I couldn't.

'Trust me, Isobel. You need to look.' Her now softer voice convinced me to turn around. As the bath slowly came into view, I prepared myself for the sight of Nichola's corpse. But he wasn't there.

'What have you done with him?' I asked.

Angela beckoned me over, closer to her. 'Look.'

I stepped over and looked into the tub. There was so much blood. Tons of blood. It really was a blood bath. And there, right in the centre, was Smokey the cat. His grey fur was sticky and drenched, and it was clear he was dead.

'He's a cat,' I stated.

'When they die, they turn into their cat selves. It's one of the main reasons why I've been able to manage this so effectively.'

'You got him in the bath to limit the blood spreading about?' I asked.

'Yes. Baths are much easier to clean than a carpet.'

She really did know what she was doing. I would have

been impressed were I not so shocked.

'So... what now?' I stuttered. 'I... I don't have any cleaning products.'

'They're in my car.'

'You carry cleaning products around with you?'

'Only when a Felivire is involved.'

'How did you even know? How did you get in?'

'Jake gave me a key card when I saw you yesterday. After you stormed off. He said he was very worried and wanted someone else to be able to look after you, should the worst happen. I think he could sense that Nicholas was going to be splitting you up the first chance he got. He texted me a couple of hours ago from the hospital. I didn't hesitate. I got straight in my car and headed over here.'

'You guessed Nicholas would be here?'

'Of course he would be.'

'He was in my room. How would he have got in? Do you think he broke in?'

'He's a cat, not a cat burglar. Jake told me what happened to him. It wasn't just an attack to hurt Jake. He would have been looking for information too. I bet while the other cats were attacking him, he was emptying Jake's pockets.'

'With his paw?' I asked, dubiously.

'Stop thinking of him as a cat. He's a Felivire.'

'Shit!' I said in a panic. 'They're going to know it's me.' I couldn't breathe. I headed into the main room, having to move to stop myself from collapsing.

'What are you talking about?' Angela asked, following me.

'The police. Nicholas will be reported as missing. The first person they're going to suspect is me. Shit! Am I going to go to prison for murder?'

As the reality of that played out in my mind, I felt close to fainting.

THIRTY-FOUR

'You need to calm down!' Angela ordered as she led me to the bed. I sat down, barely able to breathe. 'First things first, you didn't kill him. I did. So you're not guilty of anything.'

'That doesn't matter!' I argued. 'They think I've been stalking him. They'll ask me. They'll come and ask me. I'll be all over the place. They'll know I'm guilty of something. I'll be prosecuted for murder. Isn't that life in prison?'

'Secondly, they will never find a body. They can't prosecute someone for murder if they don't know the person is dead. He'll just be missing. People go missing all the time.'

'It won't be that simple. Of course it won't.'

'You're forgetting that I have done this quite a few times and I've never been prosecuted for killing anyone.'

I stopped breathing. Stopped completely. All the panic and noise instantly halted and I looked at Angela.

'You've done that? Stabbed them all?'

Tears filled up in my eyes. It was horrific.

'I have never killed a human being. I have killed creatures - harmful creatures - that threatened to take away human life. Would you feel bad if I'd killed a shark or a bear that was trying to attack you? Of course you wouldn't. It's the same principle. He is not a man. You must remember that. He was an evil creature that had no consideration for you at all. He was going to end your free will and use you in order to continue his wicked species. In essence, if he hadn't died, you would have done. You must remember that.'

'He said if I didn't comply he'd kill Jake,' I whimpered.

'See! That's not right. He needed to be stopped. And we are the only people in the world who could stop him.'

I felt calmer as Angela's words soaked through. The guilt weighed heavy on me, but I also knew she'd just saved my life. And Jake's. It had come down to kill or be killed, and we'd made the only choice possible.

'What am I going to say when the police knock on my door?' I asked as I searched around for a tissue.

'Why are they going to knock on your door?' Angela said, soothingly. She headed into the bathroom and returned with a wad of toilet paper.

'Thank you,' I said blowing my nose. 'Nicholas will be missing. They're bound to ask questions.'

'How will they know?'

'When his employees can't get in touch with him, it's going to come out. He might live on his own, but he owns a massive company. Then there are his sisters. He must keep in touch with them. If what you said is true, then they'll be lined up ready to take care of the children he wanted me to have.'

'You're correct. The siblings don't tend to love one another in the way that human siblings do, but they protect one another. Their bond is tight.'

'Great! His sisters will point the finger at me straight away.'

'Of course they will. And we'll tell them directly what we did.'

'What?' I stood up in shock.

'And they'll do nothing about it.'

'Of course they will. We killed their brother.'

'No, *I* killed their brother. I've killed a lot of people's brothers. No one will report Nicholas missing, because if they do then I'll make sure that everyone knows about the existence of Felivires. They fear that more than anything. If anyone with power were ever to find out that an undiscovered species was living around us, those Felivires would be locked up and experimented on before you could say cat. You can't have human rights if you're not human.'

'Experimented on? You really think so?'

'It's proof of alien life. Imagine being told there's an alien living next door to you. Do you think that alien, as human as it might look, would ever get to live a normal life again? Of course it wouldn't. So I'll tell Nicholas's sisters - just as I've told every other sibling of my victims - that I'll keep their secret if they keep mine.'

I was lost for words. How could Angela be so calm and confident?

'It's up to them how they decide to explain Nicholas's disappearance,' she added. 'They will make it all seem very plausible, don't worry. Their lives will depend on it.'

'I can't believe you'd do that.'

'Kill or be killed. What choice do I have?'

I nodded.

'Right, so I'm going to get my cleaning products now,' Angela said. 'I know this is very hard, but I'm going to ask you to clean the bathroom. That's all you need to do. I will remove the body and take it away with me.'

'Where are you going to take it?'

Angela scanned the room. Her eyes stopped on Nichola's trousers that were neatly folded on the back of the chair by the desk.

She calmly walked over and felt through the pockets, then she turned around with a smile and presented a set of keys.

'I will take his car and drop it off at his house.' She hesitated. 'Does he have a security alarm?'

I shook my head. 'Not that I know of.'

'Good. Then I'll let myself in, put his clothes away and bury his cat form in the garden.'

'You're going to bury him in his own garden?'

'Who's going to question that? If your cat got run over and died, what would you do? The obvious thing is to bury the poor little creature in your garden. Agreed?'

I nodded. She really wasn't a novice at this.

'Then I'll leave everything as I found it and I'll come back here to collect my car.'

'How will you get back?'

'Taxi I suppose.'

'That will cost a fortune.'

'I'm sure you wouldn't mind giving me some money towards it.' It clearly wasn't a question, and I had no mind to argue with her.

'Of course. I can do a bank transfer. I'll be here anyway, so let me know when you get back.'

'That's kind of you.'

'You saved my life. It's the least I can do.'

'It's nice to have someone to share the work with for a change.'

This made me feel sick. Partners in crime.

'Right, I'll get the cleaning products.'

It took well over an hour before I was satisfied that the bathroom was free of blood. I was very grateful that we hadn't got the carpet to clean. I don't think we could have managed that.

I took off the marigolds she'd given me and I sat on the bed. Tears quickly came rushing to my eyes and I sobbed for a while.

I needed to get away. To get out of the room.

I checked myself in the mirror. I looked a right state. My hair was erratic, my cheeks puffy and my dress all askew. But at least I wasn't stained. I had scanned every inch of myself, but I couldn't see a single drop of blood.

I took a breath and headed out of the room. I made my

way to the bar and ordered a double vodka. Nothing else would do.

I didn't sleep well that night. Every time there was any chance of me dropping off, visions of Nicholas haunted me. The blood, his body, those piercing blue eyes. Whether it was Smokey or Nicholas, I didn't think I'd ever be able to forget those blue eyes.

I wondered if I'd ever sleep again.

I couldn't bring myself to step in the bath the next day to have a shower. I had to wash the night before off, but that bathroom was just too disturbing.

Instead I headed to the hotel spa. I did a length of the pool for effect, and then had a long leisurely shower in the spa facilities.

I went back to the room to smarten myself up and then I requested that the hotel order me a taxi. I needed to go back to the hospital. I couldn't face eating anything. I just had to get to Jake and I had to get through the day.

When I arrived Jake was sitting up in bed.

'Izzy,' he gasped as I approached. He seemed so relieved to see me. 'Are you okay? I've been worried sick about you. You haven't replied to any of my texts.' He looked at my expression. 'What happened?'

'Sorry,' I said, pulling the plastic chair over to the side of his bed. 'I haven't even looked at my phone. He was there last night.' I made sure to say it very quietly.

'What?'

'I think he'd stolen your key card when he attacked you.'

The rage across Jake's face was alarming.

'Angela turned up,' I added before Jake exploded.

Jake eagerly waited for me to say something more, but I couldn't. How could I explain?

'Izz?' he pushed.

I took a breath. 'Smokey the cat is now buried in his garden.'

It took Jake a few seconds to catch up. Then his eyes widened. 'She...?'

'Saved my life. Our lives.'
He grabbed my hand. 'It's over?' he asked.
I nodded.

THIRTY-FIVE

'Look at this!' I said, beckoning Jake to come over and look through the window. A "For Sale" sign was going up outside Nicholas's house.

'Wow. You've got to admire how they managed to sell a dead man's house when no one knows he's dead,' Jake said.

My stomach flipped.

It had been a month since Angela had ended Nicholas's life. We'd not heard a peep from her since she'd collected her cleaning products that night. She had driven back to Cambridgeshire and had completely disappeared.

I was glad.

'If Angela hadn't done what she'd done...' Jake said, repeating the same thing he always told me when he saw my face go pale. He knew I was feeling guilty again. We were getting to know each other very well. 'If she hadn't intervened then you'd be trapped in that house now, and you'd be nothing but a baby making machine for that twisted creature. And I might be dead. You must put things into perspective.'

A cool wave of relief calmed me as Jake's words settled in. I knew he was right. I dread to think what would have happened if Angela hadn't turned up that night. That notion was far worse than the guilt of ending Nicholas's life. He had backed us into a corner and there was no other way of escape.

But despite this respite from my guilt, something told me I'd never be free from the burden. In a few days those electric blue eyes would pop into my mind and once again they'd pin me to the spot. Whether it was Nicholas or Smokey, I knew I'd never forget those eyes. Eyes that were so beautiful, yet hid such evil.

It seemed whatever was going to happen, I was destined for a life tainted by Nicholas. But I was a bearer. That was just how it had to be.

'Are you ready?' Jake asked, picking up my suitcase.

Since Jake had come out of hospital, a couple of days after Nicholas's death, we had been pretty inseparable. He had healed quite well. There was still the odd mark across his skin, but thankfully there were no permanent scars. I was so pleased about that.

We'd checked out of the hotel that day and we'd headed back to his place while I arranged for a locksmith to give me access to my own. Then we spent the next week together at my house as we re-built my business.

I learnt very quickly just why Jake had so much money sitting idly in his bank account. He was a genius. Not only did he help me to recover half of my clients, but he also helped me to write an incredibly exciting business plan. He asked me what I wanted to achieve, and when I said I wanted to be the head of my own national company of Virtual Assistants, within a few hours we had a plan of action as to how I was going to make that happen. I was going to start a new franchise based on my very special way of working, and the ball was already rolling.

I knew that with Jake behind me, anything was possible. Not because he gave me all the answers, but because he made me believe in myself. He gave me a confidence I didn't know I had – and I had never lacked confidence. Working with him was exhilarating, and I was so excited about the future.

I'd also been helping Jake out as a Virtual Assistant. Despite his severe insistence against it, I owed him for all the clothes he'd bought me. Girlfriend or not, I was a woman of my word.

He'd hardly been giving me taxing jobs, but it had been great to get an insight into the world of Jake's work as well. He was a true inspiration.

'Ready,' I said to him as I grabbed my keys.

I locked the door and we got in his car. We were heading back to his mega house for another huge gathering. He hadn't seen his friends since the night we'd first kissed and I'd stormed out on him.

I had made the decision that as Jake was helping me rebuild my business, I would help him rebuild his friendships. He needed that. His friends thought the world of him, but he was letting them go because he was stupidly ashamed of his past. He needed to hold on tight to such special people, and I was going to make sure of that.

Jake had modified his home gym in the outside building to allow for a games room, with a pool table and a darts board. Well, he'd paid people to modify things for him, I should say. The night was kicking off with an all-out darts tournament and I couldn't wait. We felt it might be safer than revisiting the pub.

Before you ask, we'd binned the darts I'd thrown at Nicholas. Jake had bought me brand new ones with stunning ruby flights that went perfectly with my hair. I was much happier with them.

After I'd beaten everyone at darts (of course!), we were going to enjoy the last of the sun by the pool. It was now September and summer was inevitably fading away. But while there was still some warmth, we were going to make the most of it.

And, you may have guessed, as we were going to be out on the decking, Jake was going to treat everyone to one of his epic barbecues. He'd ordered a lot of meat, you might know.

It was an incredible night. His friends felt like my friends, and they all soaked up his story of the random cat attack. We laughed so much that I hardly thought about Nicholas and those staring blue eyes at all.

But do you know what the best part was? There was barely a second all night when Jake wasn't by my side. He was the most wonderfully doting and caring man who seemed so ridiculously proud to be with me. I had never felt more loved in my life.

Turns out he is the most excellent boyfriend after all.

ABOUT THE AUTHOR

Lindsay is a British author who lives in Warwickshire with her husband and cat. She's had a lifelong passion for writing, starting off as a child when she used to write stories about the Fraggles of Fraggle Rock.

Knowing there was nothing else she'd rather study, she did her degree in writing and has now turned her favourite hobby into a career.

Lindsay is also the author of:

- The *Bird* Series, a supernatural love story full of magical twists and turns.

- *Invisible*, her hugely popular romcom about a girl who's invisible but somehow ends up in a love triangle.

- *Emmett the Empathy Man*, a comic tale about a superhero who comes to life with disastrous results.

- *In the Blood*, a romance suspense about two people who could never have possibly met yet know everything about each other.

- *Shape the Future*, a science fiction love story about a girl who is told that her boyfriend is cheating on, only to realise that the truth is far more shocking.

All of her books are available on Amazon.

To find out more about Lindsay and her books, visit www.lindsay-woodward.com

LINDSAY WOODWARD